THE
LONG DARK

Other work by Ian S. Bott

Science fiction
Ghosts of Innocence

Master assassin Shayla Carver has killed many times. That's what assassins do, nothing to lose sleep over, but this mission is different ... she's never killed a whole planet before.

The Ashes of Home

Shayla Carver, master assassin (retired) and planetary governor, is exiled and tasked with rebuilding her home planet. But deadly ghosts from her past haunt her, and even her own survival is the least of Shayla's worries.

Tiamat's Nest

The virtual world comes alive and reaches out into the real world with deadly results. University professor and devout technophobe, Charles Hawthorne, confronts technology full on to end the hidden threat to humanity.

Non-fiction
The Critique Survival Guide

Even amongst friends a detailed critique can be hard to take, but blunt and honest critiques are a necessary growth pain for any writer. Venturing into the anonymous jungle of online critique groups in search of tough love is both terrifying and exponentially rewarding. *The Critique Survival Guide* shares practical tips for surviving - and thriving on - the harshest of critiquing experiences.

Breaking the Block

Writer's block fills writers with dread because it feels impassable, something we just have to accept and wait for inspiration to strike. But we needn't be passive victims of writer's block. We can strike back with a combination of self-awareness and a suitable kit of tools. *Breaking the Block* provides a collection of approaches to keep the words flowing.

THE LONG DARK

Ian S. Bott

Dark Sky Press

All rights reserved. No part of this publication may be reproduced, distributed, or transmitted in any form or by any means, or stored in a database or retrieval system, without the prior written permission of the publisher.

Published by Dark Sky Press,
an imprint of Ian S. Bott, Writer and Artist

Visit our website at www.iansbott.com

Book Design by Jim Bisakowski
Cover illustration by Ian S. Bott

ISBN 978-0-9937242-9-9

Printed in the United States of America
First Edition: November 2020
10 9 8 7 6 5 4 3 2 1

To anyone who struggles to understand the maddening, baffling, endlessly surprising quirk of nature that is humanity.

From the center seat in the crawler's drive cab, six meters above the ground, Anna 't Hooft studied the treacherous terrain ahead.

Ground radar painted a cross-section of the organic mass under her wheels. Labyrinthine chasms and crevices plunged hundreds of meters deep. Twisted columns and webs of plant tissue spread and interlocked to form a solid-looking surface.

On Sponge, looks could be fatally deceptive.

A tingle ran up Anna's back, and she blanked the radar screen. She could read the surface details well enough. She could tell what they concealed, and in her mind could reduce the plant mass to safe, clinical labels: soft, brittle, strong, source of water, building material, harvestable tubers. All the treasures Sponge had to offer could be divined from the colors, textures, and contours up here.

She preferred to not actually *see* what lay below.

Through the wraparound windows of the cab, Anna judged the distance to her goal. The marker beacon, standing two hundred meters away, had tilted at an angle, and the smooth olive ground nearby had a mottled look confirming the grim picture from the ground radar. Sponge's upper layers here had thinned dangerously.

Harvest crews relied on the beacons Anna and her colleagues planted to guide them safely to and from their work sites. The last few were being gathered in ahead of the northern hemisphere's long slide into winter. She couldn't risk the crawler any closer to retrieve that beacon, but the town needed to salvage all the working equipment it could for next season's harvesting operations.

Anna reached for the bank of controls alongside her seat, and the shortwave radio hissing and sputtering on top of the ground radar and inertial navigation screens.

"Serendipity Control, this is Charlie Tango seven niner, respond please."

She scrunched her face and hit the volume button at the blast of static from the radio. She fiddled with the decoding controls, tuning the software that struggled to pluck meaning from the waves of electromagnetic interference bathing the atmosphere.

"Serendipity Control, this is Charlie Tango seven niner. Anyone receiving?"

On the third try, a distorted voice answered. "Go ahead, Charlie Tango seven niner."

"Got eyes on my last beacon for this run. Nearest end of the southwest line, but approach is tricky. Will be off grid for an hour or so." She checked the chrono. Plenty of hours of daylight left. "See you for supper. Charlie Tango seven niner, out."

A quick scan of her surroundings. Glints in the distance reflected coppery sky from a network of catchpools. Beyond, grey shadows marked a series of ridges and a few clouds darkened the horizon, too far to be threatening just yet. To one side, the ground sloped up to merge with the bleached-bone swelling of a structural rib. Safe to travel on, but leading away in the wrong direction.

Anna pursed her lips. If she was going to stow that beacon, she'd have to fetch it the hard way.

———————

Jennifer Steel glared at the beige-green orb of Elysium with mixed feelings. She loved the Company's princely income from this soggy plant-covered rock, but as for the planet itself, it was hate at first sight.

"It's going to get bumpy in sixty seconds." The pilot's voice held just the right blend of deference and warning. He gave no sign of the resentment she knew she evoked. She was well aware of the rules about passengers in the cockpit, but she'd been curious to see first hand her reluctant home for the coming weeks. She also liked toying with underlings, a privilege that came with her executive rank.

Even Jennifer, however, knew better than to argue with physics. She turned from the cockpit window and drifted, weightless, back to the luxurious confines of the cabin. She took her seat and strapped in before they hit thick enough air to light the scramjet.

Jennifer glanced at the three other members of the Company's senior negotiating team before finally eyeing Simon Galloway coldly. He was no part of her team, and yet he'd invited himself onto her private shuttle, claiming to carry a message of vital importance from the President.

His green velvet jacket screamed extravagance. That, she could forgive, but worn over the top of a cream brocade waistcoat, silk cravat, with silk ruffs at the wrists it was ... over the top. Foppish.

Ice blue eyes regarded her patiently, destroying any illusion of whimsy.

"Well?" Better have this out in the open before her own simmering resentment got the better of her.

"I apologize for the unplanned intrusion." His voice held no trace of contrition. "My orders were to bring this to the senior team *only* once we were off the longship." He offered a slim white envelope, pinched delicately between thumb and forefinger, pinkie cocked like he was about to sup from a bone china teacup.

Wordlessly, Jennifer plucked the envelope from Galloway's limp grasp and turned it over in her fingers. The President's personal seal was intact, and the real deal, as she verified with a tap to her tablet. A physical missive in a pry-proof envelope, primed to destruct if anyone but her broke the seal. Guaranteed confidentiality. A shiver ran up her spine.

The seat's cream calfskin upholstery cradled her sudden weight as the craft lit its engines and began banking and maneuvering down through thickening air. As they banked, the skyward windows darkened against the sullen glare of the red giant star in the sky.

Tuned to her biometrics, the tablet confirmed her identity and disarmed the envelope's destruct. A hard and razor sharp thumbnail cracked the seal and slit the flap of the envelope. She read the contents, bringing all her negotiation-table training to the task of keeping her dismay from showing.

An exchange of puzzled glances between the other negotiators told Jennifer they at least had no knowledge of Galloway's message. The craft creaked and juddered in sudden turbulence, mirroring Jennifer's own turmoil. There were always hidden agendas at work, anywhere the Company's tentacles reached. That was a given. But Jennifer was used to being the architect, not the clay. How had Galloway slipped *this* past her?

As per its instructions, she passed the letter, already starting to degrade on contact with air, around the cabin. This handful of senior officials needed to know the score, to know how to steer the complex legal and financial discussions they were here to finalize.

"As you can see"–Jennifer fought to keep her voice steady and her tone matter-of-fact–"our mission has a new factor to take into account."

Galloway's expression couldn't be said to be smug, he was too experienced for that, but it held a quiet anticipation. He'd known exactly what the letter would say. "The President places a lot of faith in you."

Such precise wording. Outwardly a compliment, and nothing anyone would argue with. But 'places' rather than 'has'? That single word gave the barest and utterly deniable hint that faith might be misplaced.

"So," she said, "while we are busy renegotiating the Company's agreement with this colony, you have a mission of your own. Chasing a new drug."

"Confirming tantalizing reports of its existence." Galloway's eyes glittered. "And given the potential impact of this on the trade talks, this has to be of the utmost secrecy."

"Withholding inside information like that from the negotiations ..." Jasmine Golightly, Jennifer's legal expert, twisted her mouth. "Any whiff of it beyond this circle, and we all spend the rest of our lives in jail."

Jennifer pondered while the cabin windows shone with the plasma glow of their hypersonic passage across the sky. A faint tang of burnt flint hung in the air. "Are we to know the nature of this *potential* discovery?"

"The President chose not to commit that detail in writing." Galloway sniffed. "Just enough information to convince you of the gravity of this order."

Jennifer narrowed her eyes at him.

Galloway smirked. "Your job is to make sure the Company will have complete control of this discovery when it finally breaks. The colonists get *nothing*."

──────── ·•· ────────

Always patient when it came to safety, Anna reviewed the crawler's controls, checking the giant vehicle was safely immobilized. She grabbed her mask from a hook on the back of her seat, and pulled it over her head as she descended a narrow stairway to the cramped equipment bay beneath the drive deck. She paused to settle the mask properly in place and pull a strand of hair out from under the edge seal, then she hauled a pair of two-wheeled dollies and a tool belt from the neatly-stacked storage racks.

Through the crawler cab's lower airlock, Anna climbed down a ladder to the ground. Hints of over-ripe fruit in the air reminded her that the mask's filters would need cleaning when she reached home. Her unfastened jacket flapped around her thighs in fitful squalls. She ignored an icy chill working its way around her waist through gaps in her clothing, and lowered the dollies to the ground.

She knelt and pulled off a glove to test the plant's surface. Tight-knit matting and whorls of stringy fibers yielded to her touch. They felt dry, scratchy, but still held firm when she tugged on a handful. Seasonal changes were coming on fast, but maybe she'd arrived in time in this case. She suppressed a shiver of unease as she peered at the ground between her and the beacon. She had a job to do.

Up another hanging ladder, Anna mounted a slender catwalk suspended below the front of the cab. She selected a lightweight cable from the row of drums above her head and released the drum's clutch.

Once more on the ground, she fastened the dollies a few meters back from the end of the cable, then clipped herself on for safety. With the end of the line slung over one shoulder, and a sounding pole in her free hand, she tested the surface ahead as she trudged away, sinking ankle-deep with each step.

Despite the late season wind keening around her, sweat slicked the edge of her mask by the time Anna slogged her way to the beacon.

She slackened off the beacon's guy lines and carefully lowered the heavy three-meter pole to the ground, slipping the axle of a dolly beneath each end.

A sharp crack followed by a muted rumble startled her. She glanced instinctively back to the crawler, calming her heartbeat when she reassured herself it was okay. Five bright yellow boxes slung between silvery mesh wheels looked like a row of old-fashioned stagecoaches, except those ancient carriages were never built four decks tall. Home and safety. A crawler driver always looked to their rig first when danger threatened.

A faded echo rolled over her like distant thunder. Anna scanned the horizon. Her scalp crawled. There'd been no signs of a storm, and the landscape around her seemed placid, unmoving. Besides, that didn't sound like it came from the depths.

She squinted skywards. A vapor trail traced a fast-moving line across the coppery sky and cast an ethereal shadow on the skim of cirrus that muted Big Red's shine.

Anna puzzled for a moment, and released a pent-up breath. Dangerous time of year for craft to be chancing a landing. As if in answer to her thoughts, a powerful gust slammed into her. She steadied herself with the sounding pole and turned her attention back to the beacon. She had more important things to do than worry about *nutloos* offworlders dicing with the planet's turbulence.

S tairs!

Sweat streamed down Jennifer Steel's face and she gritted her teeth in effort.

Her contingent was housed near the center of Jorvick, the largest of Elysium's equatorial cities and the planet's de-facto capital. The locals had emptied out an entire dome to accommodate their visitors. A fragile-looking skin a hundred meters across kept the poisonous atmosphere out and admitted a sickly orange light. The skin sheltered an irregular pyramid of buildings ten floors high.

It seemed they hadn't mastered the art of elevators on this planet, so Jennifer toiled up flights of stairs on legs that had spent months in microgravity. Even though she'd always kept herself in good shape, and spent hours each day in the longship's well-equipped gym, the transition back to full gravity was tough. Tough but manageable. And if *she* could manage at the age of seventy-two, then so could everyone else.

She emerged on one side of a large common room on the third floor, and paused to catch her breath and compose herself. Intended for communal eating and socializing, the room had been turned into a makeshift dormitory for those still too weak to manage the climb to their rooms higher up the hive-like habitat.

Jennifer was gratified to see the dozen or so people still bunking here were on their feet, walking the perimeter, regaining lost strength and balance. Maybe some had heard her climbing the stairs and hastily risen from their cots. No matter. There was intense though unofficial competition to not be the last to acclimatize. Careers depended on it.

Jayne Kildare, Jennifer's head of security, appeared at her elbow. She must have followed Jennifer up.

"Any more casualties?" Jennifer asked. The return to gravity had taken its toll through a handful of minor injuries.

"I would have notified you."

"Of course." Jennifer let pass the implied rebuff. Jayne did know her job. "And Don Kozyr?"

"Unchanged."

Jennifer grimaced, though she'd known the answer to that question, too. Minor slips and sprains they could handle, but wormhole travel had claimed a precious sacrifice. Don Kozyr, Jennifer's elderly and obese senior financial analyst, had been a boor and a glutton. He could also break down a thousand-line financial statement at a glance and see opportunities for tax breaks and profit margins in the direst of balance sheets. More importantly, he could read the markets like a prophet. As a man, he would not be missed, but his obsessive love of all things pecuniary made him valuable to her.

Up until he'd emerged from that last wormhole transit a gibbering wreck.

Bleak thoughts crowded Jennifer's mind, but she pushed them roughly aside. "Make sure everyone takes note of Don Kozyr's misfortune. I've emphasized enough the need for prime health and fitness to guard against exactly this." Plus an unhealthy cocktail of drugs, of course. Human minds didn't react well to being squirted like toothpaste through non-space. They needed all the support they could get.

Jennifer scanned the room, looking for one individual in particular. Not finding him, she took a deep breath and started across to the next flight, up to her senior staff's quarters. *More stairs.* Her legs protested, but on the plus side it meant that Timothy Finch, her senior negotiation strategist, must be making a good recovery.

She found Timothy seated in a smaller dining area leading off the main hallway, hunched over a tablet and a steaming mug of … not coffee, judging by the bitter aroma wafting towards her. He looked up as she entered, and scrambled to his feet. She waved him to sit before he could injure himself with such sudden movements, and gratefully eased herself into a chair opposite.

"A local brew," he said. Jennifer realized she'd been staring at his mug and wrinkling her nose. His hand shook as he toyed with the handle of the mug. "They call it 'char'. Not sure what's in it. Some kind of tea, I think."

Timothy glanced over Jennifer's shoulder, and leaned across the table. "Simon Galloway's made a nonsense of all our strategic planning." His foot tapped the floor, and his gaze made nervous circuits of the room.

Jennifer had left Jayne Kildare guarding the hallway outside, and this suite looked empty. A few doors stood open, showing spartan living quarters.

"He needs us to sneak in one concession," she said. "To gain clear and sole title to any future new drug discoveries."

"The colonists will never agree to that. A share in Elysium's pharmaceuticals is their livelihood."

Jennifer's chair creaked as she sat back. Timothy had gone straight to the heart of the matter. She glanced around at the bare shell of a room. How private was this place, she wondered. "Nevertheless, we have to find a way. Make concessions elsewhere, maybe."

"Which would leave us seriously weak if Galloway's ... venture ... doesn't come through."

"That's the problem, isn't it?"

He swallowed and bobbed his head. "You're expecting us to pull off a miracle."

She allowed a shard of ice to enter her voice. "I'm *expecting* you to do your job. But this is not something we can either discuss or solve here. Galloway's mission remains private to our senior executive leads. Not a hint beyond that group. But the entire team needs to understand the goals we're after in the talks, and work on achieving them."

Timothy gestured to his tablet. "I knew you'd say that, but it's impossible to work properly with half the team still barely able to stand."

"Then the acclimatization period will need to be cut short. Everyone will be on their feet and ready for strategy meetings two days from now."

A flicker in Timothy's eyes was quickly masked. He nodded. "I'll pass the word."

Restless gusts rocked the crawler. Rain sluiced off the cab windows. Anna peered ahead through early afternoon gloom, seeking landmarks in the murk.

A mix of frustration and anxiety gnawed at her. Most of the town's twelve thousand inhabitants had already started on the grueling trek towards the equator. Anna was one of the last, facing another day cut short by gathering storms. Another delay in the autumn clean up before she and the remaining townspeople could join the great trek south.

Another day closer to the tipping point, where Sponge's fractious atmosphere would flip violently before settling into the next phase of its seasonal weather cycle. They all prayed they'd left themselves time to reach an equatorial city before *that* happened.

In her mind she worked back to when, under bright skies this morning, she'd last seen threads of yellow climbing the distant slopes of the southern ramparts. Today's convoy south had several hours head start on this weather front. They should reach the shelter of the first way station before it overtook them.

More worrying, what about the few crawlers like Anna's, still out in the field here? A glance out the corner of her eye at the radio beside her. Pointless. With the storm came swirling interference too deep to punch a signal through.

Anna pushed the unease aside and turned her attention back to her own run for shelter. At least, down here in the lowlands, a network of ridges broke the worst of the hurricane winds. All she had to contend with right now was sheeting rain and visibility measured in tens of meters.

Finally, the lights of a beacon glimmered, waxing and waning through gaps in the hard-driven downpour. Anna drew close enough to read the serial number glowing in her headlights on the side of the beacon, and gave a relieved cheer. This was a permanent pylon, marking the main route into Serendipity. She set a heading on the gyrocompass and angled the lumbering vehicle towards home.

An hour later, she nosed the crawler through an access tunnel into one of Serendipity's cavernous garages.

The place was eerily quiet, with so many vehicles already gone. A deck director in a bright orange jacket waved her down one side of a row of supporting columns, then guided her around in a wide U-turn to face the pair of access tunnels at the far end. Anna slowed to walking pace as she threaded the house-sized cars between the columns.

With a deep sigh, she acknowledged the director's hand signal to secure the rig. Before she began her long series of shutdown rituals, she gave in to her anxiety and contacted Control.

Chapter 1 – Just the Beginning

My name is Michael. I have a last name, but out of habit I'll say my last name is simply T. That's me; Michael T. I appreciate a small amount of security offered by obscurity. I never was one to stand in the spotlight, willingly, at least. Such an unusual precaution and keeping of secrets has granted me a degree of peace and normal living. Secrets have always been my business. Secrets are things that would be foolish to talk about openly. Secrets are foolish to talk about openly because those secrets would not be understood. When one person speaks to another, they speak to be understood. Anything that is not understood by the listener is naturally disregarded as foolishness by the listener, thereby making speaking of such things foolish to mention by the speaker, since such things will not be understood, even if such things are of great value and profound insight. Sometimes secrets are kept because no one is ready to understand, much less capable. There is a story I would like to share that is full of foolishness. Let me indulge in foolishness for a time and tell you all about it.

It all started on the evening of the end-of-the-semester social for the professors and their families. I looked in the mirror. I straightened my button-up shirt. I selected a few ties and held them up to my shirt. I narrowed down the selection to a couple of ties. Then I abandoned those as well and decided to go tieless. I undid the top button. I slipped on my suit coat and took another look in the mirror. I had only one suit. It was the same suit I had owned for the last twenty years. My physique hadn't changed much. Some would say that I had aged gracefully. My face, on the other hand, though still taut and chiseled around my clean-shaven jaw, betrayed the wear and tear of a life outside of the classroom. My cheeks were leathered from sun exposure. My hair was thick but short, with generous amounts of graying on the sides. My forehead between my eyes bore permanent wrinkles from the intense focus required in battle. My eyes peered back at me from under strong brows. I didn't like my eyes. They say the eyes are the window to the soul. It looked like my soul's windows were dark and barren, yet they seemed like the kind of windows that, if you peered hard enough, you would see someone in the darkness staring back at you. It could be a little unnerving, even for me. I felt like my eyes didn't reflect who I really was inside.

"Where are you going looking so sharp?" my father asked. "You couldn't possibly be going on a date, could you?" he grinned playfully, making the unshaven bristles on his heavy face stand straight out.

My parents had moved in with me after my wife had left me. They helped me through that challenging chapter in my life. But after I found my footing, they just stuck around. I didn't mind. I appreciated the company, and they seemed to be happy to leave their older, smaller home. It worked out for everyone. My father was getting too old to take care of the bigger challenges of maintaining a home and my parents never could afford to hire someone to fix their problems. So now I could help them in that regard. And then, when I needed to leave for extended periods of time on military business, they were there to watch the place and to make sure the few fruit trees I had were watered and the fruit was harvested. They were good about not asking questions I was not supposed to answer. They understood and accepted that a large part of my life was secretive and was required to remain that way.

"Not a date," I answered. "More like an appointment. It's the end of the semester, and, as usual, the staff members are invited to a social on campus."

"A party, eh?" My father's grin grew bigger. "Will there be girls?"

"Maybe," I said.

"Will you talk to any of them?"

"We'll see."

"Well, listen, if it turns into anything like that one party, remember, we aren't going to come down and pick you up from the police station again."

"Dad, that was almost twenty years ago. Besides, how can I get into that much trouble again with you there, watching?"

My father's smile vanished. "Eh? What do you mean?"

My mother entered the room. "Didn't I tell you, dear? We're going with him," she said in her trademarked cheerful demeanor. In contrast to my father, my mother was of a slender build. She was wearing a sparkly, black dress with shoes to match. Earrings resembling small crystal chandeliers swung from her lobes. Her silver hair was short and poufy. I don't know what they called that hair style back in her day (maybe bouffant), but I would have said it was borderline afro. In short, if someone had dumped glitter and smiles on the late '60s, she represented what it could have looked like.

"Oh. I guess I should go put on a clean shirt," my father said, looking down at his bulging stomach and examining the food stuck on his shirt. He left the room.

"We'll take a separate car," my mother told me, "just in case you meet a girl and start talking with her. We wouldn't want to interrupt you when Dad's indigestion kicks in and we need to hurry home."

I sighed. "Good idea," I said. My mother was always thoughtful like that, but even if I didn't meet someone interesting, I didn't want to be in the same car as my father when his indigestion kicked in, anyway.

In accordance with my mother's suggestion, we drove to the campus in separate cars, entered the designated building together, and found the event room.

I looked out across the many scattered tables that were set with satin table cloths, common china, and stainless utensils for the coming meal. It was a semi-casual setting, well-lit and inviting.

"Hey! Michael! Over here," a voice called to us.

I found the owner of the voice. It was one of my closest friends, Ronald McPhearson. We had known each other for the last decade, ever since we had both started working at the university, and we both happened to start on the same day. We didn't have much in common, but maybe that was why we got along so well. We knew each other's strengths and weaknesses, and we understood that we were nothing like each other, so jealousy and competition never found a way between us.

I raised a hand to let him know I saw him. He was wearing an avocado-green pair of pants, black shoes, and a sweater with large diamond shapes and hash lines of varying shades of brown that one would find on a ranch. Ronald never could grasp the concept of color-coordination. Long, hard hours in his office had left their mark on his physical state; soft around the middle, soft around the face, and content in a padded chair. His clean shaven face, pale complexion, and dark, unkempt hair were certainly befitting of a professor of his caliber. He smiled and waved a hand, beckoning us to join him. He had a good smile. It was a movie-star sort of smile. It fit well with his friendly eyes. I had often wondered if his wardrobe was the only thing keeping him from finding a nice woman and getting married. I led my mother by one hand and she led my father with her other hand, and together we wound through the tables to join Ronald.

"We saved a spot for you," Ronald said, still smiling. "Mr. T. and Mrs. T. Join us," he said with a hand stretched out toward the reserved seats.

"Thanks, Ron," I said as we took our seats with a few other professors and their families.

Introductions were made where necessary, and I thought the conversations around our table were pleasant and satisfying, up until the following events.

I sat at a table with some of the most brilliant minds of all my acquaintances, and yet we were all captivated by the words of one whose intellect could have been considered as the least at that table.

"Onnne. Twooo," said the speaker with such thoughtfulness and composure. "Three. Fourrr." We listened with attentive, raised brows and interested, pleased smiles. "Fiiive. Siiix." My attention slipped as I wondered how one with such a small voice and chubby little fingers could so easily captivate an intellectually esteemed circle as this. "Seveeen. Eighhht." Our brows creased upward ever more as our attention reached its pinnacle. "Niiine." The speaker hesitated for a moment, whether to check his calculations or to keep us in suspense, I do not know. "Ten!" he shouted, stretching his tiny arms high and extending all ten chubby fingers. We applauded and gave little cheers that matched the speaker's little shoes.

"Good job!" his mother praised him as she put an arm around and hugged him. "And how old are you going to be?" she asked.

6

He concentrated on raising the correct number of pudgy digits before announcing, "Three!"

"Three!" several attendees around our table repeated with amazement as we smiled at the toddler with admiration.

"Very good!" said his proud mother as she gave him another hug.

"Growing so old," Ron said. "It won't be long before he will be reasoning his way through one of Mr. T's philosophy classes, or elaborating on the laws of physics as explained by Newton or Einstein."

We all chuckled at the statement, as people do at parties, simply for the sake of being polite and keeping the mood light. In any other circumstance, I would not have considered it chuckle-worthy. I believe anyone would have considered it an obvious observation not worth mentioning. Such it is with idle small-talk.

"Yes," I said, picking up on the polite comment Ron had made and politely taking it further. "And there he will learn the art of counting in a more complicated manner," I said, with a smile.

Everyone stared at me with stern faces, as though I had spoken out of turn. Some things are only appropriate to say if the right person says it in the right way. Otherwise, shame and spite are the fruits of such idle speech.

"When he studies mathematics," I explained awkwardly. "Because mathematics is like counting, but more complicated." My face felt uncomfortably warm.

Slowly, so slowly, everyone's attention turned back to the child, and the unbearable spotlight with them.

"And what do you want to be when you grow up?" another professor asked the child.

"Ice-cream man!" was his enthusiastic reply with a chubby smile.

Everyone laughed heartily. Even I smiled at the innocent ambitions of that little one. But then my mood became sober again as haunting memories surfaced from the pools of darkness within my mind, and I hoped, for the child's sake, that selling ice-cream would still be an occupational option for him during his adult years. I hoped he would never need to bear scars like mine.

Chapter 2 – The Punch Bowl

The social went on as socials do, everyone eating and talking, sometimes rudely doing both at the same time, until people gradually left for home, all saturated with punch and satiated with casual conversation. My parents had gone home on account of my father's indigestion. The other people with whom I had been earlier were all gone, except for my friend, Ronald McPhearson. And, as usual, our conversations wound through thought-provoking territory; this time more so than usual.

"Mike," Ron began tentatively, "you know me to be a reasonable man, yes?"

"Indeed," I answered.

"My views and opinions sometimes vary from the general consensus of others from time to time, do they not?"

"They do," I replied with a bit of a chuckle.

"And yet, I explain my reasoning in a satisfactory manner."

My head bobbed side to side as I searched my memory. "Most of the time."

"Then, please, humor me on this matter," he said soberly.

"On what matter?" I asked, my attention now undivided.

"I have a theory... Well, I guess it's more than a theory now, but let me start from the beginning. Einstein's theories of relativity have always bothered me because they are based on old, incorrect theories, and so they go wrong right from the start. It began with the idea of space being filled with a substance, or a medium, through which light travels, which light rides upon, kind of like a boat needs water to carry it from one shore to another. This medium was called the 'ether'."

"And this 'ether' is what was supposed to carry light through space?" I asked, checking my bearings in unfamiliar territory.

"That's right. There were many calculations made to discover the mass of this supposed ether, and many more experiments were conducted to observe the 'flow' of the ether."

"That's right. I remember this one," I said. "The Michelson-Morley experiment had something to say about it."

"Yes, and Einstein never confirmed nor denied the existence of the ether –"

"How politically correct," I mumbled.

"- but his theory suggests the experiment failed to reveal the ether because, he claimed, light travels at the same speed regardless of the speed of anything involved!" Ron declared irately.

"I believe the postulate was a little more specific and sophisticated if I remember correctly," I said apprehensively because I could see my colleague was becoming agitated rather quickly.

"My point is, it's not true."

I involuntarily raised an eyebrow. "Go on."

"We say a wave is made of water. We say sound travels through air. We say light travels through space. We say this because we think of waves and matter as two different things. That's why scientists can't decide if light is a wave or a particle. This is all wrong. We should say that the wave IS *water*. Sound IS *air*. And light - *it's everywhere!* Light *fills* space!"

"Uh…," fell the dull sound from my hanging mouth.

"Stay with me," Ron pleaded. "I believe space is full of light, just as an ocean is full of water. The wave in the water formed because some form of energy pushed it; a boat, a fish, a thrown rock. Sound waves are formed because something pushed the air; a speaker, lightning, a clap. Light waves are formed because some force *pushed* the light! And so waves lap up on the shore, sound fills our ears, and light enters our eyes because energy has forced itself into the water, the air, and the light."

He paused and stared at me, looking for some indication of understanding. I let this idea sink into my mind, but, frankly, I had no idea what he was talking about.

"The universe is full of light," he said, hinting at the building frustration from not being able to express his thoughts adequately. Ron was never good at patience. "Light we perceive as being *produced* by something - the sun, a flashlight, a flame - is actually being *pushed* away from that thing by the *energy* it *is* producing. Light is *not* produced by the sun any more than water is produced by the wind. The sun and the wind push energy into something that already exists and it causes a wave, more specifically, a wave of matter. Light exists everywhere, just as the ocean is filled with water, just as the atmosphere is full of air, but we only notice light when it is pushed into a wave that our eyes can detect *and* when that wave is pushed towards us."

"Wait," I said, holding up a hand. "So what you are saying is that light is sitting stagnant in space until something pushes it? Is light self-existent?"

"For the time being, let's say that it is," he replied.

"Then why don't we see a blinding light all the time in all directions?" I asked.

"Because of how we perceive and discern things around us. We notice a wave because of the peaks and valleys in the water. We hear sound because we perceive the pulsations in the air. We notice light because of the frequencies that excite the cones and rods in our eyes. As you know, we illustrate light waves as having peaks and valleys, and based on the size of the peaks and valleys as well as the frequency of the peaks our eyes perceive different colors. In fact, that's how most of our senses work. We sense opposites. In the cases of sight and sound, the high and the low parts of the waves is what makes the light and sound detectable. We don't recognize anything exists unless there is an opposite to compare it to."

My mind was still hung up on the idea of light being everywhere and yet not visible. "And the harmful light we don't see, like UV rays; why aren't we cooked to a crisp right now?"

His shoulders slumped, and he looked at me as though it should be obvious. "A bullet isn't lethal unless it is moving," he simply stated. "Those rays are harmless until they are forced into motion by the sun or some other adequate energy source."

I thought for a moment. "So if I understand you correctly, I could infer that the sun, that great, big, glowing thing in the sky, isn't really *making* light?"

"Yes!" He said excitedly. "Actually, you can forego inferring it, because I have already explicitly stated it! The sun merely *pushes* the light towards us."

"Then," I closed my eyes and chose my words carefully, "where does all the light come from? If all this light is being pushed at us, wouldn't the sun have run out of light to push?"

He walked over to a bowl of punch. He put the ladle in the punch bowl and swirled it around. "This ladle is pushing punch ahead of it. But what is happening behind it?" he asked.

I looked and said, "More punch is following the ladle to fill the vacancy."

"Exactly!" Ron exclaimed. "Just as water fills all the holes; just like air fills a vacuum; *light* fills the void. More light cycles in to take the place of the light that was pushed away, and eventually gets pushed away itself. Light is fluid. I don't mean light *is* a fluid. What I mean is that light flows. And I can guess your next question. You're thinking, 'I can see the water filling in the space, so why can't we see light filling a void?' The answer again is in how we see light, or how we perceive light. We only see light that is *coming* at us and not the light going *away* from us. Point at your eye, and that is the direction light must travel for *you* to see it. However, have you ever wondered why the sun's corona is so much hotter than the surface of the sun?" He pointed at me and raised his eyebrows, as though he were suggesting the answer was somewhere in the question.

13

"I wasn't aware that it was. What is the corona?" I asked, feeling rather ignorant. In my defense, I am merely a humble philosopher.

"The corona is that glow or that halo you see around the sun when the actual sun is blocked out, like during an eclipse. It has been a long-time mystery as to why the area around the sun is hotter than the surface of the sun. Consider a flame. The air gets cooler as you get further away from a flame and hotter as you get closer. The corona is further from the sun than the surface, obviously, and it stands to reason that the corona should be cooler. But, on the contrary, it is not. So why is the corona so hot?"

"I assume you are going to tell me."

He swirled the ladle in the punch bowl again. "Do you see the little swirls behind the ladle where the water is following to fill the void? I believe that is what the corona is for light. It is where the light that is rushing in to fill the void is being pushed into a u-turn and forced away from the sun. It's where most of the light is being infused with energy. It's much like the beginning of a wave; it is the place where the wind is having an effect on the water. In this case it is where the power of the sun is having an effect on the flow of the light, or, perhaps more likely, it is where the energy is made evident. From there, it disperses into what we perceive as ordinary light."

"Interesting," I mused. "But how does the sun push the light?"

"One lesson at a time," Ron said with a laugh.

"Ron," I said, ponderously. "I see a problem with your idea already."

He looked worried for a moment. "What's that?"

"How does the light filling the void get past the light that is being pushed away? Wouldn't the two 'flows of light' crash into each other and cancel out?"

"Excellent question," he said, pointing to me as though I were a student in his class. "The answer is in frequencies. Consider radio waves. We send hundreds of signals across the same air space and yet the signals do not interrupt each other because they are on different frequencies. The closest visible comparison I can think of are, again, ocean waves. One wave rolls onto the beach, and then, with its energy diffused onto the shore, it retreats back into the ocean while another wave that is still carrying the energy the wind has forced into it crashes over the top of the first wave. It's a similar situation with light. The light approaches the sun in one set of wave frequencies and, being infused with energy, races away from the sun as a different set of wave frequencies. So the coming-rays and the going-rays do not substantially interfere with each other."

"If you're right," I said, "most fields of science are going to have a lot to change."

"Well, they didn't seem to have too much trouble with that when Einstein presented his idea," he said obstinately.

"But you are not Einstein," I countered with a smile.

"Don't get me wrong," Ron said, holding up a warning finger. "Einstein's work was brilliant. I do not believe we could have advanced into this modern age as far as we have without him. But there's more. His theory explains things as they appear, but not always as they are. So it was with the people of Christopher Columbus's day. The entire world believed the earth was flat, and when Columbus suggested otherwise, they ignored him, even mocked him. They stood on the shore, pointing to the horizon, and said to old Christopher, 'You're mad! The world is flat! Look! You can see it!'" Ronald pointed out to an imaginary horizon. "They believed only as far as what their eyes could reveal, and their eyes told them that the world was flat. Flat!" he shouted in disbelief and frustration. "Like a pancake! Can you imagine how embarrassed they were when Columbus sailed over the edge of their flat world and *continued* sailing? Yeah. That was not a good day in the science department, I can assure you."

"So what horizon are you planning to sail over?" I asked, amused by his animated behavior.

"That's going to take some more explaining. You see, after this realization about light and the important role of wave frequencies, I wondered if the same idea of frequencies could be applied to molecules and atoms at a particular level, or what I mean is at the level of particles. And I wondered: what if...?"

I waited for him to continue, but he didn't. I saw that he had retreated deep within his mind to ponder the topic anew. This was clearly a pet-topic, one he could easily lose himself in.

"Please, do share," I encouraged.

His mind returned to this world and he began. "Atoms are some of the smallest building blocks we know of, and yet atoms are made of even smaller bits and pieces, such as protons, neutrons, and electrons. And those are made of smaller bits still. In the atom, the protons and neutrons huddle together in the middle in what we call the nucleus, and the electrons circle the nucleus in an orbit, kind of like the moon going around the earth. And just like the moon and the earth, there is a lot of seemingly empty space between the nucleus and the electrons. A lot of empty space where something could be..."

He wandered off again down the winding paths of his brain.

"Could be what?" I asked.

He looked back at me. "Just that. Where something could *be*."

"Like what?"

"Let me begin by illustrating. Newton said that no two objects could occupy the same space at the same time. Well, I think he was wrong."

"You are going to attack Newton now?!" I exclaimed in disbelief. "Is anyone correct in their perception of how the world works?" I asked, being rather alarmed by what I saw as growing arrogance.

"Hold on. Let me explain," he said calmly. "Let's assume there is a two-story building made entirely of transparent glass. The walls are glass, the floors are glass, the ceiling is glass - even the toilet is glass."

"That's very disturbing," I said, looking disgusted.

He bowed his head and held up a finger to pause further objections. "There are two people in this imaginary, glass building. One is standing on the first floor, and the other is standing on the second floor. There is a third person flying overhead who has absolutely no depth perception. Effectively, this flying person sees only two dimensions. This flying, third person looks down at the building and sees the two people in the glass building. Then the person on the first floor walks under the person on the second floor and stands directly under the second-floor person. That's perfectly normal. Neither person is bothered by that action. However, to the third person flying overhead with no depth perception, it appears that the two people are occupying the same space. This would be rather alarming.

"To illustrate the same idea with a different example, let's look at how the universe is set up. Newton says no two things can occupy the same space at the same time. Very well. So it appears. But what about this? In the universe is our galaxy. In our galaxy is our solar system. In our solar system is our planet Earth. On our planet Earth are people. People are made of cells. Cells are made of atoms. Atoms have neutrons. Neutrons are made of quarks. And *all* of these things – the universe, the galaxy, the solar system, Earth, you, your cells, the atoms, the neutrons, the quarks - are in the *same* space at the *same* time. And this thought raised a question. At what point does one body interact with another?"

"Well," I said, feeling like my head was about to spin off, "that does put the whole picture into perspective, doesn't it?"

"I believe," began Ronald, "that quantum mechanics -"

"Whoa! No! Just stop," I pleaded, holding up my hand. "My head is already hurting. I don't have any more brain cells to spare."

"Fine. I will skip to the point. I believe there is or are different states of existence, different frequencies that matter can pass into that would allow an entire world, or maybe even universe, to exist in the same space as we do."

"What? Like another dimension?" I asked.

"No," was his short reply.

"Like an alternate reality? A parallel universe?"

"No."

"Another world existing in the same space as we do?" I repeated, making sure I heard correctly. "Are we talking about a very tiny planet?"

"No."

"A very big planet?" I spread my arms wide, as though the idea needed to be illustrated.

"No," he repeated. "What I mean is within the same three-dimensional space that we understand there are worlds without number existing right here on the same scale as us, but on a *different* energy frequency. Atoms are made mostly of empty space. I believe other atoms, the building blocks of life and galaxies, could pass *through* that empty space without interrupting or interacting with that atom, the same way radio waves pass through each other. And I believe it could be done by the frequency or energy levels of those atoms, namely, the electrons."

"So, are we talking about matter phasing?"

"No."

"Matter altering?"

"No."

"Transitioning matter?"

"I should hope not," he replied with a chuckle. "We are talking about changing the matter-energy frequencies of an atom, which, theoretically, would change the entire energy frequency of a body, and then that body would still exist in its same form, but on a different frequency of energy."

"Ah," I said, raising a finger, "that is the fallacy of composition, believing that the state of the whole is equal to the state of the parts; a major hiccup in logical reasoning."

"We will see," he said calmly. A confident smile smeared across his face.

I stared at him, bewildered. "You need a hobby, my friend."

"I'm sorry," he said, genuinely apologetic. "You tire of this. It is a lot to take in all at once."

"No, no," I objected. "But I am concerned about you. I understand you are a physicist, and so you would talk about actions and reactions all day long. But most physicists talk about what *other* physicists have worked on and how they can apply that knowledge to their own work. They normally don't go out to rewrite the books."

"But what if the books are wrong?"

"Ron," I said, placing a caring hand on his shoulder, "you are talking about over a hundred years of theories, experiments, equations, papers, and people's entire life's work. You can't just change all that."

"Columbus did," he stated, undeterred.

"But you aren't Columbus!" I said in frustration while trying to keep my voice down.

"Okay then, philosopher," he said in a challenging voice. "Answer this: one man has the opportunity to teach and educate an otherwise ignorant people, and what he has to teach could improve their lives as well as their understanding, but the people don't want to change. Should he share what he knows?"

"Let me ask you this," I countered. "Do 'Socrates' and 'hemlock' mean anything to you? Do you remember those two ever mixing together? Do you remember *why* those two got mixed together? People aren't afraid to express themselves when they don't like what they hear, and sometimes those expressions are very – let's say - *forceful*."

Ron's eyes grew big, and his mouth scrunched together. "Yes. Yes, I see what you mean," he replied. "But surely anyone with a basic knowledge and understanding of the modern theories I mentioned can see the problems with them. I've read papers by other respected experts, and they ask the same thing: Why does the general scientific community believe and teach it?"

"Before I answer that, I have another question. Are any of those 'respected experts' still respected? Actually, forget I asked. But to answer your question; they believe because they want to believe. These theories help them explain so much and in a manner that they *want* to explain it that they otherwise could not."

"But they cause so much confusion in the process."

I sighed. "Ron, scientists are like lawyers; if they can cause more confusion, then they can make more money trying to clear up that confusion."

"But wouldn't it be easier to just get it right the first time? Isn't it more difficult to go right if you start off wrong, rather than just starting off right from the beginning?"

"Now you are talking like a philosopher," I said with a smile. "Scientists are in it for the truth, but sometimes the truth doesn't pay very well. We may be enlightening humankind, but at the end of the day, we are paid to tell people what they want to hear. And people want to hear surprising and shocking things. So if you tell the world that you have an equation that predicts time travel and black holes that consume entire galaxies, then you will find ten more years of employment." I sighed a heavy and weary sigh. "People prefer to be entertained; not educated."

"Well!" exclaimed Ron, with a renewed zeal that appeared from nowhere. But he was like that. Once something got into his head that he believed in, he could not be dissuaded. "Regardless of what others may think or say, I want the truth, and I intend to find it."

"Very good," I said, feeling a little concerned for my friend's mental state. "Let me know when you find the answer."

I was only trying to be supportive, as a good friend should be. I had no idea how much I would come to regret those words, nor what an adventure and revelation they would produce.

Chapter 3 – The Jump

Gunfire rattled all around. Smoke and dust hung heavy in the air. Sand had fallen into my boot, but there was no time to fix that. A mortar shell landed nearby, releasing a deafening boom and a shower of more sand. The heat beat down on my already sweaty brow. My scalp itched under my helmet. I clutched my gun tightly. I lay against the sandy berm and waited for a lull in the firing. I ventured a peek over the top of the berm and got a bearing on the enemy's position. I ducked back down and turned to my squad.

"They are two hundred yards northeast," I shouted to my squad over the din of battle. "We're going to go west along this berm and drop into the dried riverbed. Then we'll go north and fire down on them from their flank. Understood?"

"Yes, sir!" my squad replied.

"Let's go!"

We moved quickly and entered the riverbed. We ran, with our heads down. Suddenly, I heard the dreaded click of a landmine. Then there was a terrible explosion. I instinctively hit the dirt and kept my head down until the debris settled.

"Fall back!" I ordered and started crawling back the way I had come, with my head down.

When I reached our entry point, I rose up to a crouch and looked around. Where was my squad?

"Jefferson!" I called. "Adams!" No reply. They were gone. They were all gone.

The phone rang, and my eyes opened. The afternoon sun gently poured through the window and had lulled me into a pleasant slumber and an uneasy dream. The phone rang again. Then it waited for a response. It rang again. I rubbed the sleep from my eyes and picked up the phone. My eyes may have been open, but I was still waking up, mentally, and I forgot to say "hello" after picking up.

"Michael?" called out Ron's voice through the earpiece.

"Yes," I answered.

"Mike! I've done it! I've done it, Mike!" Ron's voice was nearly frantic. "I've been able to isolate a frequency bandwidth of matter and locate a planet within our solar system that is on a direct and perfect collision course with Earth!"

I froze, as all my energy and effort was involuntarily diverted to my mind in an inadequate attempt to make sense of what I was hearing. My biggest hang-up was with the words "perfect" and "collision". I didn't like those two words in the same room, much less sitting next to each other in the same sentence.

I slowly stood up, took a deep breath, thereby refueling my groggy brain, and I spoke. "And your first thought was to call *me*?"

There was no answer, but I could imagine him nodding.

"What do you expect *me* to do about it?!" I asked in a fit of hysteria that is unbecoming of me, except for in the few moments after being woken up. Then the fit is quite normal. "Shouldn't you tell NASA or someone else?"

"Mike, I need your help," Ron pleaded. "I'm asking as a friend, Mike. Help me."

Those were the magic words. I couldn't refuse. So I sat down, calmed down, and asked, "Okay, what do you need?"

"I need you to meet me on the eightieth floor of the Empire State Building tonight at 1:37 am," came his swift reply, "and not a moment later! Repeat it back to me."

"Empire State Building, tonight, 1:37 am," I repeated.

"And not a moment later! I'll see you there!" And he hung up.

I sat for a moment, with the phone dangling in my hands as I processed what had just happened.

"Empire State Building…" I mumbled in confusion. "Eightieth floor… Not a moment later?" Then a lightning bolt of horror struck me and the phone dropped to the floor. I jumped to my feet. "Oh no! He's gonna jump!"

I quickly booked the earliest flight to New York, ordered a ticket to the observation deck of the Empire State Building (just to get me to the eightieth floor), put on my coat, left a note on the fridge to let my parents know I would be gone for an undetermined amount of time (they were accustomed to such notes), locked the front door of my house, jumped into my car, and raced to the airport. The lines at the airport were long, as usual, but the wait was even longer; nearly unbearable. I looked at some of the smaller private planes parked near the distant hangers and wondered if it wouldn't be faster to hire a private pilot. But then the lines began to slowly move, and eventually I was on a plane and in the air heading for New York. I spent the flight checking my watch frequently and staring out at the moonlit cloud tops of a cold winter's night.

The plane landed and I was out of the airport in record time. I cut in front of someone who was about to get into a taxi.

"To the Empire State Building, and, please, hurry!" I urgently said as I locked the door to keep out the shouting person I had taken the cab from. I handed the driver a large bill to cover "expediting fees". The driver sped away with a generous amount of wheel chirp and wound his way skillfully through the traffic while not sparing the horn. Snow whirled around the windshield and lightly frosted the streets.

We came to a sliding stop in front of the Empire State Building. The stone structure reached proudly toward the city-light illuminated clouds. I paid the driver, leaped from the cab, and scrambled across the slippery sidewalks to the doors of the building. I slid across the polished floors to the attendant who checked my ticket. He was dark, had excellent posture, and wore a sharp uniform.

"Is this your first time visiting us?" the attendant asked slowly and clearly through a neatly trimmed, graying goatee as he examined the ticket and handed it back.

"Yes," I replied hastily. "And hopefully it will be my last," I added as I snatched my ticket and ran up the escalators. I seemed to be the only visitor that night, but the queuing ropes were still arranged for a large crowd. I started running the winding path through the empty queuing ropes until I came to a good straight where I built up some speed and then dropped to a hip and slid under the remaining ropes.

Another well-groomed and attractive attendant stood at the elevators. "Whoa! It's okay. You've made it," she laughed as she pointed to the open elevator doors.

"How fast are these elevators?" I asked between breaths as I rushed into the elevator.

"It will take less than a minute to reach the eightieth floor," she answered.

I didn't think that was fast enough. The elevator doors closed, and I endured the longest elevator ride I had ever taken. I stared at the floor-counter as it ticked away the moments.

I reached the eightieth floor and was prying my way through the elevator doors before they could open all the way. And there I was, on the eightieth floor, alone. I looked to the left, and I looked to the right. There was no sign of Ron, nor did I have any idea where to go looking for him. So I picked a direction and walked that way. Then I changed my mind and walked the other way down the hall.

I moved at a brisk pace until I heard a knocking sound from one of the doors I passed. I stopped, because up to that point I hadn't found the slightest indication that there was anyone else on that floor. I walked back to the door. It was the custodian's closet. I heard the knock again, and then a cat hiss. I put my hand on the doorknob and slowly turned it. When the doorknob wouldn't turn any further, I began opening the door. Suddenly, the door snapped open, just wide enough for me to pass through, and I was forcefully pulled in. The door shut and locked behind me. Aside from being the size of a small bedroom, it was a typical custodian's closet. There were mops, brooms, shelves full of cleaners and hand soaps, towels, paper towels, toilet paper, spare light bulbs, brushes, buckets, a couple of carts, and one fluorescent tube light that filled the small room with an eerie, blue light. And there was Ron.

He threw some kind of jumpsuit at me. "Put this on," he ordered.

"What?" I said in confusion. "Wait! No! What is going on?" I demanded. "What is this planet you mentioned? And why are you going to jump off this building?"

"How did you know about the jump?" Ron asked with an intense, inquisitive look.

"Because we are here!"

"Does everyone who comes to the Empire State Building in the middle of the night jump from it?"

"Only if they want to die!" I exclaimed. "Ron, you have so much to live for. You have a great career, and good friends, and… and… a great career. And your scooter! You love riding your scooter around campus, and waving to all the students! Listen, you didn't need to go and make up a story about a planet colliding with Earth to get me here. We're friends, Ron, and if you are having trouble or need -"

Ron started laughing. I was taken aback. I would have thought he had lost his mind for sure, but it was an honest, full-hearted, merry laugh.

"You think I am going to jump *off* this building, don't you?" he asked.

"Uh… I did. But now I'm not sure what you are up to," I replied hesitantly. Then I finally noticed he was wearing a jumpsuit with circuit boards and wires scattered across it. I looked in my hand at the suit he had tossed at me and saw that it was similar to the one he was wearing. I held the suit up before me with both hands and studied it closer. The back was heavy and shaped like a large battery back. The chest piece had a large, flat square mounted to it with a small fan whirring away, suggesting that this thing had already been powered up and was ready to go. Wires stretched from the square on the chest to the limbs where they entered the fabric. Strange patterns were woven through the fabric, almost like a circuit board had been woven into the suit itself. "So, what's really going on?" I asked.

"Like I told you," Ron began, "I have isolated a condition of matter with its own spectrum of interacting energy frequencies separate from our own."

"Huh?" I uttered, utterly bewildered.

"Do you remember the conversation we had about light?" he asked.

"Yes."

"Do you remember how we applied those ideas to tangible matter?"

"Yes."

"Do you remember the analogy of the glass building and the two people on different floors?"

"Yes," I replied.

"Do you understand where this is going, then?"

"No! Not a clue!" I shouted, frustrated.

"Michael, we are like one of those people in that glass building I told you about, except we can't see through the floor. But I have found a way, and I've seen the other person."

I stared at him, befuddled. "You still aren't making any sense. Maybe you should just tell me what you are trying to say and skip the analogy," I suggested.

His shoulders slumped and he rolled his head back with mild frustration. "I've been saying what I've been trying to say! There is a planet that is about to pass *through* Earth and no one would have known it, except I discovered it when I found a way to detect atoms with electron orbits that are not compatible with matter as we know it, so they have gone unnoticed, until now."

31

"You mean that other dimension?"

"It's not another dimension!" Ron protested.

"Well, if it looks like a duck and sounds like a duck…"

"Listen," he interrupted, "the atoms of *that* world will be passing through the *same* three dimensional space as the atoms of *this* world, but we won't notice because those atoms of that world will be passing *through* the space *between* these atoms of this world. The condition that the matter of *that* world is in is not interactionably compatible with the condition of the matter of *this* world," he explained.

I stared at him. "I think you are making up words," I stated.

"That's trivial!" he shouted. "And, yes, I am making up words, because there are no words that mean what I want to explain! I'm no language expert, but I understand that words are expressions of ideas, and if an idea isn't common enough among people then it won't have a word, because no one will be trying to express that idea! A hundred and fifty years ago, if you had said 'time-space continuum', *everyone* would have thought you were speaking nonsense. Even today, a lot of people have no idea what idea those words are referring to!" He took a deep breath because it had been a while since his last one.

I ventured to show that I had some understanding of what he was talking about because I was feeling rather ignorant at this point and needed something to redeem my self-respect. "You mentioned electrons and something about their orbits. Is this how, uh, *that* planet is going to, um, pass *through* ours without causing any… damage?"

"Yes," he stated emphatically and with a hint of relief.

"Could you elaborate?"

He was too eager to oblige. "Electrons, as we understand them, orbit the nucleus of an atom at certain energy levels, or distances from the nucleus. The electrons can change orbits, or their distance from the nucleus, when they receive enough energy to make the jump. But a distinct energy threshold must be obtained for the electron to make the jump, because electrons, as we understand them, have very specific orbits that they will follow. So they won't change orbits until the energy threshold is exceeded so they can jump to the next specific orbit. The amount of energy required to make the jump is called a 'quantum', and the jump itself is called a 'quantum leap'. And the electrons don't, as we understand them, *pass* through other orbit possibilities, but jump, in an instant, to the next orbit. It would be like Earth leaving its current orbit around the sun and suddenly jumping to the same orbit as Mars without really going through the space in-between. Electrons can also jump to orbits of lower energy levels, but they need to expel a specific amount of energy - a quantum - to drop down to the next viable orbit. I have discovered that these specific orbits are what makes matter tangible to us. It is what forces them or allows them to interact with each other in the way that we currently understand. But I have found a way to track atoms that have electrons with orbits that are *between* the orbits of the electrons of the atoms that we currently interact with. This allows a whole range of elements to exist in what we consider to be the same place, but they do not interact with each other because the orbits of the electrons are a lot like radio frequencies. If you want to listen to a radio station, then you need to tune to that frequency. If we want to interact with those other atoms, then we need to get the electrons of our atoms to match the energy levels of the electrons in the atoms of the realm we wish to interact with."

My mind lagged for a moment as I tried to keep up with his explanation. "Is that difficult?" I asked.

"Yes," Ron replied. "The electrons of our realm want to follow orbits that we could label as orbits one, two, three, and so on. That is our current set of energy frequencies, or our radio station - to continue with the analogy. But if we want to go to another realm, then we need to get our electrons to tune to the orbits or energy frequencies of one half, one and a half, two and a half, and so on, or some other set of discrete energy frequencies depending on what realm we are trying to enter."

There was something in Ron's language, something in the tense he was using, something about the pronouns that was really bothering me. I looked down again at the suit he had tossed to me, and the pieces slowly came together. I looked back at Ron.

I tried to speak. "You have… There is… A, uh…" I struggled to get my mouth to voice my concerns. "You have discovered a way to detect atoms of another realm?" I asked, seeking clarification.

Ron smiled and nodded. He could already see where this was going and that I just needed time to let the idea solidify.

"And you have discovered a planet in another realm?"

He nodded again.

"And that planet is on a 'perfect collision course' with us?" I asked, using his words.

He nodded yet again, and his smile grew a little wider.

I lifted the suit in my hand. "And you plan on going there?"

This time he shook his head. "*We,*" he emphasized. "*We* are going there."

"Why *we*?" I asked, feeling very anxious all of a sudden.

"This was too exciting for me to keep to myself," he explained. "I needed to tell someone about my discovery. You are the only one whom I believed would believe me, but I knew that once you had found out, then your adventurous spirit would want to come, too. So I prepared another suit." He pointed at the suit I held.

"No!" I exclaimed. "No. I…" I hesitated.
"I…I…Ieee…" Then I paused before I asked, "How do you know this is safe?"

Ron laughed triumphantly. "Haha! I thought so," he said as he gave my shoulder a playful punch. "We're going to let Mr. Whiskers tell us how safe it is." He pointed an outstretched hand and presented the testifier.

Mr. Whiskers stood stiff and rigid, and he stared up at us with wide eyes. He wore one of Ron's suits, but his suit was smaller and accommodated his physical structure. Mr. Whiskers uttered an annoyed meow.

"You are going to send a cat first?" I asked. "How is he going to tell us if he made it or not?"

"He really can't," replied Ron. "I don't have a way of tracking him. But there are only a few ways this suit can go. Either the suit won't do anything, or it will work." Ron turned to attend to the cat, but then he looked back at me. "Or Mr. Whiskers will turn into a pile of ashes," he added.

"Are those the only options?" I asked.

"The only ones I can foresee, as far as the suit is concerned," he replied while he made some last adjustments to Mr. Whiskers' suit. "But there are plenty of other things that could go wrong."

"Like what?"

Ron ignored my question and looked at his watch. "The planet will be passing through in two and a half minutes. Put your suit on."

I jumped into action, kicked off my shoes, slipped into the jumpsuit, and put my shoes back on.

"Okay," said Ron, "Mr. Whiskers is ready. Standby." Ron studied his watch and waited for the right time.

I remembered what Ron had said about Mr. Whiskers becoming a pile of ashes and I grabbed a nearby fire extinguisher. My uneasiness grew. Ron appeared to remain calm and observant. Mr. Whiskers looked as annoyed as ever about wearing the suit.

"In ten…," Ron finally said. The next few seconds quietly ticked by until - "Three, two, one. Engage."

Ron pressed a red button on Mr. Whiskers' suit and stepped back. We heard a faint electrical humming that steadily grew louder. Mr. Whiskers looked around with even bigger eyes. We looked at Mr. Whiskers with eyes equally as big until there was a sudden flash of red light, and Mr. Whiskers was gone. There wasn't even a pile of ashes. I put down the fire extinguisher.

"Well," Ron said in a satisfied tone. "I'd say that was a success. Now it's our turn. We have only three minutes to make the jump ourselves."

"Alright," I said, now full of enthusiasm. "How does this work?"

"We'll be taking the elevator," Ron answered as he exited the custodian closet and walked to the elevators.

I followed him. "The elevator?" I asked, puzzled.

"Yes. I have - how should I put this? - *arranged* for an elevator to be reserved for us." He pointed to a set of elevator doors with an "out of service" sign on them.

"Why are we taking the elevator?"

"Because we need to match our relative speed with the relative speed of the planet we are jumping to, otherwise we will hit that planet like a bug on a windshield," Ron replied.

I suddenly felt sick as I watched Ron wheel an elevator door jack into position and pump the jack until the elevator doors were wide open, revealing an empty shaft.

"The suit will automatically engage when you reach the bottom of the elevator shaft, but this red button," he pointed to a large, red button with a clear cover over it on my chest, "will manually engage the suit and adjust your electron energy frequency to make the jump." And with that, he walked to the elevator doors and looked down the shaft. He looked back at me and said, "I'll see you on the other side." Then he jumped.

I ran to the elevator doors and looked down the very deep shaft just in time to watch Ron fall to the size of a pinpoint and vanish in a red flash of light.

"Ooohh boy," I said nervously. I made a few false starts for the jump and then groaned in mental and emotional turmoil.

Suddenly, a sultry, female voice broke my frustration. "Jump window expiring. Jump. Jump. Jump," the voice repeated. I spun around, but no one was there. I quickly realized it was the suit talking to me. "Jump. Jump. Jump," it continued.

I went for the jump, fully committed. Then another voice, shrill and gruff, shouted, "No! Don't do it!"

I spun around in mid-run, lost my balance, and tripped over the elevator door jack. It was the janitor, with a large bundle of keys on his belt loop and a rag hanging out of his overalls pocket. His frightened eyes stood out in sharp contrast to his dirt-smudged face. My arms swung about wildly as I teetered on the edge. And then I fell.

"Blast it!" I heard the janitor exclaim. "Not again!"

I careened through the air and down the elevator shaft, spinning and tumbling. Somehow, despite the dizzying somersaults, I heard the distinct noise of an elevator motor and saw, to my great horror, that the elevator car below me was coming up. I immediately knew this meant the computer in the suit would not make the jump before I splattered on the roof of the elevator. I cried out in terror and struggled to get the cover off the red button on my chest. I threw the cover clear and thumped the red button. I felt a tingling sensation through my whole body and saw a flash of red just before I would have crashed into the elevator beneath me.

When my vision cleared away the red, I was still falling and tumbling. I saw white, and then black, and then white again as I spun through the air. I cried out. And then I abruptly stopped, face first, in something soft, cold, and wet. It was snow.

I rolled over and struggled to catch my breath. Ron ran to my side and hovered over me.

"Are you alright?" he asked. "You fell a lot further than you should have."

"The elevator started coming up," I gasped. "I hit the button."

"Oh," he said casually. "I was worried it may have been a miscalculation on my part. I put a great deal of work into figuring out the precise time of the jump window based on the trajectory and speeds of the two planets, as well as their rotations in relation to our vertical motion. The only real unknown was where the ground was on this planet. We could have come in underground or in outer space, but I made my estimate based on the detectable mass of this planet and scaled it to the average distance of the surface from the core of our own planet to -"

"Forget it," I groaned. "I'm fine." I got my feet underneath me and slowly stood up. I looked around, and for as far as I could see, there was snow. The terrain was flat, barren, and cold.

Ron walked a little ways, then stopped abruptly and looked at the ground. "Oh! Oh my," he exclaimed.

"What is it?" I asked.

"I found the cat," he replied.

"How is he?"

"He's, um," Ron hesitated. "Well, I'm glad we took the elevator. I'll say that."

"I'm sorry."

"Sorry for what?"

"Your cat. I'm sorry he didn't make it."

"Oh. He wasn't my cat. I'm not sure he belonged to anyone, actually. He was just sitting on my doorstep when I needed him," he said nonchalantly and walked away.

I shook my head at Ron's indifference. Then I looked around. "Where are we?" I asked as I continued searching for some kind of landmark.

"In relation to what?" Ron asked. "I can tell you we're not on Earth. But as for this planet," he threw his arms up and let them fall, "I don't know."

I looked up at the clear night sky. "Are you sure we aren't still on Earth? The constellations look the same."

"And they would," Ron said. "The stars put out a light that spans all spectrums of matter-energy frequencies. But notice the color. You will notice some stars appear to be bluer than they did on Earth. Take Betelgeuse in Orion's armpit for example." He pointed to the constellation. "It looks red from Earth, but it looks

41

pure white here. That reminds me; one of Einstein's thought experiments explored the idea of what someone's surroundings would look like if they were to travel near the speed of light. He believed time would appear to be standing still since the observer would be traveling very near the same speed as the light that reflected off the objects observed. That presumably would hold true, if the speed of light were really the same for every observer regardless of relative speed. However, light behaves quite similarly to sound, since it is a wave of matter, after all. You know how a race car sounds louder and higher pitched when it is coming toward you than when it is going away from you? That's called the Doppler Effect. When the car is coming towards you, each pulse of a sound wave is a little closer than the previous one and a little further away when the car is going away from you, effectively causing the sound waves to be scrunched together and then spread out, respectively, and making the sound of the car higher pitched and then lower pitched. The same is true with stars. When a star is moving towards us, the color shifts more toward blue, because you are getting each subsequent lightwave a little closer than the one before. And you get a redshift when the star is moving away. That is how astronomers determined that the universe is expanding. But everyone seems to ignore that when it comes to the theory of relativity. Actually, if you were to travel near the speed of light, this realm would become invisible to you because the spectrum of visible light would shift, and the 'new' spectrum of visible light would reveal something different. We do something similar with telescopes and x-ray machines. We are either slowing down or speeding up the light we are trying to observe to bring it into our visible spectrum. Actually, I shouldn't say 'speeding up' or 'slowing down' because it's the light wave frequency that is being altered, and not the speed."

I stared at him blankly. These long explanations were starting to get old. "Huh," I barked. Then I looked back up at the stars. "I guess we should at least find Polaris to navigate by, just so we don't waste our time going in circles."

"Um, that won't work," Ron said. "The rotation of this planet is different than Earth's rotation, so its northern pole doesn't line up with the same star. In fact, I'm not even sure which hemisphere we are in. I suppose we could wait through the night and watch the movement of the stars. That would give us an idea of which way the planet is spinning."

I shivered. "We could freeze to death by then. We don't have time. We need to find shelter."

"You're right," Ron agreed. "Besides, watching the stars could be a waste of time. For all we know, this planet could be tidally locked with the sun, and the night may never end."

"What is 'tidally locked'?" I asked.

"Oh. Uh, the same side of the planet always faces the point it is orbiting. In this case, it would be the sun. In the case of Earth's moon, it would be Earth. That's why we always see the same side of the moon."

I was only half listening to the explanation. "There's a slight rise over there," I said, pointing out into the distant landscape. "We can get a better idea of our surroundings from there."

We started trudging through the snow toward the small crest. The crest was quite a ways out and the walk through the snow was slow-going.

"So," I said, as a more serious question crossed my mind, "how do we get back?"

Ron didn't reply but kept walking. I stopped.

"Ron," I said sternly. "How do we get back to Earth?"

Ron also stopped and looked at me with a grim face. Then he looked away. "I don't know," he said quietly.

I was silent for a moment before I asked, "Did you have a plan for getting back before you decided to bring both of us here?"

"I tried to, but… but the excitement was blinding. And I...," he sighed. "I couldn't find a way."

My first feeling was anger; crude, vicious anger. But I took a deep breath and thought, because we were in no situation for either of us to be losing our wits.

"Why can't we just jump back to Earth before it gets too far away?" I asked.

"Earth is already too far away. We would end up in empty space."

"Okay," I said, just barely keeping myself together. "How about next year? We survive, prepare the suits for another jump, and next year, when the planets have another 'perfect collision', then we jump back to Earth. We can even build some scaffolding tall enough to match our relative speed with Earth's." I felt a little better, believing for a moment that we had a half-hatched plan; even just some basic course of action.

Ron slowly shook his head. "This planet's orbit is nearly perpendicular with Earth's orbit, and its years are shorter."

"Sooo…" I didn't like where this was going.

"So," Ron picked up where I left off, "that 'perfect collision' only happens once every thousand years or so."

"Or so?" I repeated. My anger was slowly winning, but I held it together. "Okay." I started pacing in circles around Ron. My feet quickly and steadily crunched the snow beneath me. "What if we could discover and track other planets in other realms that all have paths with 'perfect collisions', planets whose orbits cross each other, and we will chart a course through our solar system by jumping from planet to planet until we can make it back to Earth? No problem. It's just like changing planes in the middle of a trip with long, boring layovers," I said hopefully. "We can do this."

"Mike," Ron said, "the equipment I need to do that is large and complicated. I don't think we can build that here."

I lost it, and in an instant, I was bearing down on him. "We're not quitting like that, Ron! Not on my watch! If you need big, complicated machines, then we will build them on every planet we visit! We are not going to be stuck here exploring some unknown world for the rest of our lives!" I yelled as I flailed a wild arm about at our surroundings. "You keep seeing yourself as a 'Christopher Columbus', but Columbus had a plan for getting back! He did not abandon himself and the crews of his ships to die in some foreign new world! We are jumping planets across every realm until we make it home! That's the plan!" I yelled, pointing an imposing finger at Ron's face. I took a deep breath and stepped away. "But if you come up with a better plan," I said calmly, "you let me know, and I will help you get us home."

Ron stared at me pitifully. Then he nodded and looked away. I patted his shoulder and said, "Come on. Let's get to the top of that crest."

We walked in silence for a few minutes. My anger began to slowly wear off, but I could see that Ron's guilt was not. I tried to ease the mood with conversation.

"How many realms are there?" I asked.

"Hm?"

"How many different frequencies of matter are there?" I reiterated.

"Oh. There are nearly infinite possibilities because the finest movement of an electron from its orbit alters its ability to interact with other matter," he replied.

"Nearly infinite?" I raised my eyebrows. "How can it be '*nearly* infinite'?"

"What I mean is," Ron explained, "there are a lot."

"Now you're speaking my language," I said with a grin. "So that means there are nearly infinite ways to get home, right?"

Ron gave a half agreeable nod. "Theoretically, yes."

"I like the sound of that. We can do this," I said heartily.

A gruff humming sound in the distance caught our attention. It sounded like it was coming our way. I realized it was an engine, maybe two. My suspicions were confirmed when two lights crested the hill and sped towards us. I raised a hand to block the blinding light. The lights stopped directly in front of us, but we could not see the machines or riders who were veiled by the glaring lights.

Chapter 4 - Reception

Ron raised his hands with his palms out. "Greetings!" he hailed. "We come from the blue and green planet that we call Earth! With peaceful feelings, we arrive!"

I looked at Ron strangely. He was always awkward with first impressions. However, he had a knack for making friends quickly. I intended to let Ron do his thing, but a loud voice from behind the lights interrupted him.

"Both of you, put your hands up! Now!" the voice ordered.

"They already are," replied Ron, "because I just finished saying something like 'we come in peace'."

"They speak English," I said in amazement. "Ron! We're still on Earth!" I said excitedly.

Ron's arms fell, and he looked at me. He was both confused and disappointed. "Huh? But... but how?"

"Put your hands up now or we will shoot!!" the voice urgently commanded.

Our hands shot up into the air and we froze, wide-eyed. I heard the snow crunching behind the lights. It sounded like four pairs of feet. The sounds moved towards both sides of the lights and rushed forward. I briefly made out four shadows before they were upon us and we were cuffed. Now we were captives. They dragged us closer to the lights. Our captors appeared to be human in shape and form, but their faces were covered with masks and goggles, so I could not be sure what they really were.

They dragged us around the lights, and I got a brief look at the large vehicle they pushed us around. The vehicle had snow tracks on the front, set at a wide stance, and there was a much larger, longer, centered track in the rear. It was set up much like a snowmobile, but with tracks in the front instead of skids. The body of the machine was low, wide, and dome-shaped, like a turtle's shell. It was painted with an arctic camouflage pattern. We were pushed into the vehicle through a rear hatch that also doubled as a ramp when it was opened. The interior was all too familiar. It was an assault transport vehicle.

We were forced into seats where they fastened our four-point seatbelts and chained our cuffs to the floor. The chains were just short enough that we couldn't quite lean against the backrests of our seats. Then the vehicle made a whirring noise that wound up louder and louder until the vehicle started moving. It was a strange sound. I assumed it was the engine, or engines. Whatever the vehicle was powered by, it moved us across the frozen landscape at an alarming speed. I watched the outside scenery race by for a moment through a small viewport in the opposite side of the vehicle.

I looked around at our captors. They were clothed like humans. They wore what I recognized as shirts, pants, sturdy boots, gloves with four fingers plus an opposing thumb, and their headwear suggested their facial features were also human. Their goggles were where their eyes should be. A small lump in the middle of their masks suggested their nose was in the correct place. And flat plateaus on their thin helmets indicated they may even have ears on the sides of their head.

Everything suggested they were not aliens, but very human.

The weapons they carried, however, were a little different. They didn't look like phasers or plasma blasters or death-ray guns. The weapons appeared to be ballistic, but I didn't recognize the model. I told myself that we must have been captured by some elite task force with the latest weaponry.

"What planet are we on?" Ron asked, taking a more direct approach to learning about our captors, but they did not reply. "Where are you taking us?" Ron asked. Again, he was answered with silence, but Ron persisted. "Are you human? Are we still on Earth? My friend and I were conducting an experiment, and I fear something may have gone wrong."

One of our captors stood up and approached Ron with a bottle that had a breathing mask on top of it.

"What's this?" Ron asked. "Are we going into orbit? Are you taking us to the mothership?"

The figure with the bottle put the mask to Ron's face and squeezed the bottle. There was a quiet hissing noise. Ron's eyes rolled back in his head and he went limp. The captor with the bottle looked at him and cocked his head to one side. I couldn't tell if it was curiously observing or confused, but it returned to its seat and put the bottle away.

"Ron," I whispered worriedly.

Ron gave a slight groan. I assumed he was well enough and withheld any questions I had for fear of receiving the same treatment. I prefer to have all my senses about me.

We rode on for what felt like hours, but the darkness outside never faltered, and the frozen landscape never changed. The sound of the vehicle droned on. Then we abruptly stopped. Our captors stood up and released us from our seats but still kept us cuffed. Ron slumped to the floor as soon as his seatbelt was released. Two of our captors picked him up and a third put another mask-and-bottle to his face. Ron started with a sudden spasm.

"Whoa! Hello!" He looked around in confusion. "What did I miss?"

"Apparently we have arrived," I explained.

"Where? The mothership?"

"We never left the surface." I pointed outside the little window with my cuffed hands.

Then the rear hatch opened with a mechanical whirring noise and artificial light poured into the vehicle. Once the ramp was fully deployed, our captors herded us out into the open. I quickly looked around and gathered as much information as I could. Tall, stadium-like lights flooded the area in a warm light - and when I say "warm light" I'm not talking about just the color. The light felt warm. There were other machines moving about just like the one we had arrived in. Hard-shelled shelters were laid out in rows and columns, much like a small town. The construction of the shelters appeared to be modular, suggesting they were built quickly and designed to be moved easily. Other beings like our captors marched with weapons in hand in small formations around and between the structures. Everyone I saw was covered head to toe in the same attire as our captors. I concluded this was a military base of some kind.

We were pulled along, guided by our captors, until we came to a concrete structure with heavy steel doors. The structure was small and sloped at the back. Two guards at these heavy doors stopped our captors.

"Who are they?" one of the guards asked.

"We don't know," replied our foremost captor. "We are taking them to interrogation."

"Carry on," ordered the guard.

The large steel doors swung open, spewing an orange light across the snow and revealing a staircase that dove underground. We descended down a few flights of stairs and entered a large room that slightly resembled a subway station. A large tube lay before us, the ends of which plunged into the walls on either side through a tunnel that fit so snugly around the tube that I could not see even a few inches beyond its mouth. Hatches in the sides of the tube swung up to reveal several rows of seats within. We were ordered to enter the tube and sit. Again, our cuffs were chained to the floor, but this time the chain was long enough for us to lean back in the chairs. Our captors took their seats and the hatches closed, locking us inside the tube.

One of our captors looked back at us and said, "Lean back, put your head against the headrest, and take a deep breath when the countdown begins. Otherwise, you won't be able to stand when we get there."

We leaned against our chairs and pressed our heads into the headrest. Ron looked over at me.

"Was it threatening us?" he asked in a hushed voice.

"No," replied our captor, unbidden. "I was warning you."

"They have *good* hearing!" Ron silently lipped.

A voice suddenly chimed from unseen speakers. "Transport departing in three, two, one."

Instantly, we were pushed against our chairs by an invisible force. It felt like we were falling forward, like cresting the first plunge on a rollercoaster, except we were being pushed into the fall. I felt the flabbier parts of my face squishing around my skull to the sides of my head. Just when I thought my body would succumb to the extreme pressure, we stopped.

I gasped for breath while our captors stood and unchained our cuffs. Ron slumped to the floor, unconscious, again. They put the mask-and-bottle to his face and he awoke with a jolt.

"What happened?" he asked. "Are we on the mothership yet?"

"You didn't hold your breath," replied a captor. "At least you had your head against the seat. You could have been paralyzed."

We exited the tube, and I thought we hadn't gone anywhere. The room looked exactly the same as when we had entered the tube. We even walked back up the same stairs in the same orange light. But when the doors opened, blinding daylight bombarded us, and warm air wafted around us. My eyes slowly adjusted to the light, and I saw pleasant sidewalks lined with full, green trees and shrubs. Towering, glass skyscrapers loomed over us and people - plain, ordinary people – walked around us. The style of clothing they wore varied little from one person to the next. The men wore gray jackets with sleeves that came just short of the wrists, and most wore their jacket opened with a gray, pullover shirt beneath that was tucked into their gray pants. They wore a simple black belt around their waist and gray footwear that I considered to be casual dress shoes. Their hair was short and neat. Most had clean shaven faces and any facial hair was also short and neat. The women wore similar gray jackets, but with more rounded shoulders and longer in the back. They wore long, gray skirts that came down to just above their shoes. Their hair was long and their styles were simple. I would have thought we had walked into some kind of neo-Amish settlement, but a small vehicle rushed over our heads and glided through the air.

I didn't have much time to study my surroundings before we were rushed into the back of a large, armored truck. The truck was not as unusual as the snow vehicle that we were first loaded into, but it did have its oddities. It was built like a half-track except it had only one very wide track at the back that appeared to be made of rubber. The driver was seated in the center of the cab, rather than off to one side, and armed soldiers sat on either side of the driver, constantly looking out their side windows. The outside of the vehicle was more angular and much wider near the bottom than at the top. The inside of the vehicle, where we were once again chained to a loop in the floor, looked very similar to the snow vehicle. I wondered if these vehicles were not all modular, sharing as many similar parts as possible.

I had only a little time to wonder before our transport charged through the streets with a rushing rumble. This ride took only a few minutes. We stopped, and we were unloaded. I looked up after jumping out of the armored truck and saw a clean and elegant structure wrapping around us in a large half-circle. We were the only people in sight. We were taken into the building through its sliding glass doors at the center of its sweeping curve. The inside of the building was clean, spacious, and felt very empty. The ceiling rose about two stories above us, and there was a balcony on the second floor overlooking the entrance. There were other doors that looked like they went to offices. Hallways divided from the main foyer and led to unknown rooms. And there was not another living being in sight. As far as I could tell, Ron, I, and our captors were the only people in the entire structure.

I had to ask, "Where are we?"

"Normally, you would be blindfolded before being brought here," explained one of our captors through their mask and goggles. "But we have no idea who you are, so we don't know whether we should treat you as friends or as enemies. Therefore, you get a little bit of both. You are cuffed, but you are permitted to see where we are going."

"For the record," said Ron, "we consider you guys to be very good friends, and we thank you for your hospitality."

Our captors silently stared at him through their unblinking masks with large, dark lensed goggles, like confused bugs. I, too, stared at him, but my expressions were very transparent and unreserved.

"I don't think your butt-kissing is going to help us here, Ron," I said, feeling slightly embarrassed to be associated with him at that moment.

All of our captors' goggled eyes now turned towards me, and I suddenly felt embarrassed about myself.

"Butt-kissing…?" mumbled our foremost captor. "Disgusting barbarians."

I blushed. "It's a figure of speech."

They didn't reply. They just stared at me from behind their expressionless masks.

"So," I ventured again, "where are we?"

"This is where we treat you as an enemy, and you don't get an answer," was the reply.

They all stared in silence a little longer. Finally, to my relief, we were marched down one of the many hallways. We came to a blank wall at the end of the hall. Our foremost captor reached out a hand and tapped out a signal on the wall. The wall issued a loud clunking sound and slowly slid to one side, exposing a hidden passageway. We walked in, and the wall closed behind us. The passageway opened up into a large room with maps, screens, computers, and people rushing about and talking in short bursts to each other as they passed.

As I watched all the hustle and bustle, our captors must have taken Ron and me in different directions, because Ron was nowhere to be found.

"What did you do with my friend?" I asked, looking around frantically.

"The same thing we are going to do to you," one of my captors answered. "This is also where we treat you as an enemy."

A mask-and-bottle was placed over my face, and I blacked out.

Chapter 5 – Many Matters

I opened my eyes. My vision was fuzzy. I could make out vague shapes of doors, windows, chairs, and bedsheets. I heard several voices in casual conversation outside the room, spiked by the occasional announcement over an intercom or the official tone of a receptionist. The air was a little stuffy and coated in strange smells, but I recognized the smells of cafeteria food and a few different disinfectants. I was in a hospital.

"Hey," I heard a familiar voice. "How are you feeling?" It was Ron.

"Like I got hit by a bomb," I said. It wasn't too far from the truth.

"We almost lost you," Ron said. "They flew you in from a different hospital. They didn't tell me which one. You had lost a lot of blood, and you are a rare breed. They couldn't find any of your blood type to refill you with. I guess we have more in common than we thought. We have the same blood type, lucky for you."

I smiled. "I guess our friendship has gone to a new level."

"That's right. We're blood-brothers now."

We both laughed, and I winced in pain.

"There's something else you need to know," Ron said. He stood up. A bottle with a breathing mask was in his hand. He walked towards me. "This isn't real," he said as he raised the bottle in front of me. "This is just a dream of a memory. We need to get you back into reality." He pressed the mask against my face.

I awoke with a jolt. "Get that away from me!" I shouted. I looked around. I was alone in a room, and sitting in a chair with my hands chained to the back of the backrest. There were no doors and no windows. The walls were made of concrete and painted a ghastly shade of green.

I looked around for any sign of a crack in the wall that may be a door, or a hole that may be a camera or speaker, but it was only me, the chair, and smooth, concrete walls.

"Hello?" I called out.

"Hello." a gentle, female voice replied. "What is your name?" she asked.

"My... my name is Michael T.,"

"Who are you working for?" she asked.

"I work at the university. I'm a teacher," I answered.

"What is taught at the university?"

"Just the usual. Math, English, history, art."

"What do you teach?"

"I teach philosophy."

The voice was silent for a moment. "Explain," she ordered.

"Um, I give lectures about the theoretical nature of moral reasoning and deductive understanding. Occasionally, I'll teach a class on the structure of logical arguments, just to shake things up a bit," I said with a light chuckle.

"What are you wearing?"

I looked down at the jumpsuit with its circuit boards and blinking lights. "It's the latest in fashion-design wear. All the cool kids are wearing these." I smiled at the walls. "Actually, it's a bit of a story. We were trying to jump to a different planet by changing..." I scrunched up my face as I tried to remember. There was something else happening in my head. I couldn't tell what it was. I just knew something was wrong.

"…something in our atoms. I'm still a little shaky on that," I said.

"Did it work?" she asked.

I laughed. "Well, it was quite a ride, but I think all it did was get us lost. Where are we, by the way?"

There was no reply.

"Hello?" I called out.

"What planet are you from, Michael?"

I raised an eyebrow. "Pardon?"

"What do you call your planet?"

"Um, okay. I'll play along," I snorted. "My planet is called Earth. I've never understood why it's called Earth because there's a whole lot more water than earth. But no one asked me when they were naming it." I waited for another question or a response. "Hello?" I called out. "Are you there?" There was no answer.

I shifted in my chair and studied the walls again. My vision was still a little blurry, and I tried to get my eyes to focus. I started by staring at one upper corner and I followed the joint between the wall and the ceiling to the other upper corner. Then I followed the vertical joint between the walls to the floor, then along the floor, and then I noticed something at my feet. I looked down, and I realized that the floor was not concrete, but green, tinted glass; or maybe it was reflecting the green from the walls. I bent over as far as I could to get a closer look. I squinted to see if I could see through it. That was when I noticed something looking back at me. I gasped when I realized it was some*one*. And there were other faces, too, all looking up at me through the floor with distorted features.

"WHAYEEeeyaAA!! HAAA!!!" I shrieked in a panic, and I vigorously stomped my feet about at the staring faces. Then a noise overhead caught my attention and I looked up. There was a bright light, with another face staring down at me from the center of the light. Their features were blurred by the glare. "AAAHHH!!" I started anew. I felt the floor move. I looked down, then back up, then at the walls. I was being lifted up toward the light, or the light was coming down toward me; I couldn't tell. Either way, the faces in the floor were getting larger, and the face above was getting nearer. It was all very disorienting and strangely frightening. "Whoa!! WHAT IS WRONG WITH YOU PEOPLE?" I yelled.

"Calm yourself, Mr. T. You are going to trigger my migraines, and we don't want that now, do we? What with all the work there is to do," said a clear, carefully spoken, male voice from above.

"The faces! What are these faces?!" I shouted.

"Those are called 'reflections', Mr. T. They happen to be reflections of me, thank you very much. Are there reflections on your planet?"

"Not in the floor!" I panted as I tried to calm down.

"We built these holding chambers like that so the prisoner and the interrogator could see each other when they spoke. We did notice you prefer talking to the walls. Such odd behavior. I'm starting to believe that maybe you *are* from a different planet, like your friend claims."

As the floor raised me through a hole in the ceiling, the light gathered itself together, and I could see the speaker clearly now. He was an older gentleman, with a silver, wooly mustache and a fading hairline. He was a bit soft under the chin and around the belly. His shoulders were narrow and his shoes were very long, even for his towering height. He wore a long lab coat that barely gave his large shoes any breathing room. I looked around. Now I was in a white room with a visible, ordinary door in front of me.

"I thought there was a woman asking me questions," I stated, a little perplexed.

"You thought correctly. That was Professor Litona. But she is done with questions for now. She may have some more later on. But for the time being," he stood a little taller, suggesting he was quite proud of his height, "I am Doctor Dalmour, and I'll be taking blood samples for testing to see if you are, um… as alien as your associate suggests."

He rolled a small table next to me and picked up something that looked like an otoscope. He put it to my arm and pressed a button. I felt a small pinch, and he removed the tool to look at a small screen on its side.

"Well," said Doctor Dalmour, as he studied the screen, "I can tell you, I have never seen this blood signature before, except for when I took a sample from your associate."

"It's called 'AB negative'. Ron has the same blood type. He donated his blood one time when I was in an… In a really bad accident," I explained. That was only partly true, but even Ron didn't know the whole story. "Wait a minute." I paused. "How can you be a doctor and not know about blood types?" I looked up at him accusingly.

He just looked back at me. Then he turned away and walked out of the room with his cart. That was when the questions I should have been wondering this whole time came flooding to my head. Were they playing mind games with me? What did they want to learn? What were they going to do with us? Where was Ron?

My head felt clearer. "I must have been drugged," I said to myself. I looked at the door. It was an ordinary door with an ordinary lock and ordinary hinges. "We're still on Earth, but clearly we went somewhere. This may be a secret research base." I quietly reasoned with myself as I tried to put all the pieces together. My head still felt a little fuzzy.

The wall to my right moved and retracted into the ceiling to reveal an adjacent room, similar to the one I was in, and a chair similar to the one I was sitting in, but the striking difference was that Ron was in that chair, also chained in a similar manner.

63

"Mike!" Ron said excitedly. "Are you okay?"

"Yeah," I replied. "It was weird. They asked a bunch of questions and I gave all the answers without really thinking about it. How about you?"

"Same story. I think they gave us some kind of truth serum. I don't know why," he said, puzzled. "We don't have anything to hide. We're from a different planet. What good would it do?" Then he gasped. "How do they know the serum won't kill us?! They can't possibly know enough about our physiology to take that kind of risk!"

"Ron," I said wearily. "Take a look at the door. It's like nearly every door on Earth. It was built by humans, just like us. That's how they knew the serum wouldn't hurt us. They are humans, just like us. I'm sorry, Ron, but we're still on Earth."

I watched the cogs turn inside his head as he studied the door in front of him. Then his shoulders slumped as disappointment set in. "Then where are we?" he asked, with a hint of frustration in his tone. "We aren't in New York. So where are we?"

"I don't know," I answered. "Your suits did something. They may have teleported us to the other side of the world. We're going to need to figure that out so we can make a plan for getting home." I looked around. "Do you think these suits can get us out of here?"

Ron looked down and studied the lights on his suit. "No. There isn't enough power left for a jump. We will need to recharge them somehow."

64

"Okay," I said. "We get free, recharge the suits, find a cliff or tower, jump from it, and go home."

"It won't be that simple," Ron said, bobbing his head side to side, agitated. "We'll need to figure out what *actually* happened and try to reverse it. I'll need to make the correct calculations to make sure we don't pop up somewhere we don't want to be, like buried under a mountain or falling from the sky. We'll figure that out later, I guess. How do we get free?"

"Turn your cuffs towards me so I can see how they have us locked up," I told Ron.

Just then, both doors of our rooms opened. Doctor Dalmour entered through my door, and a woman, with brown hair neatly tucked into a bun and wearing a navy-blue business suit, entered through Ron's door. The doctor and the woman looked at each other, then at Ron and me.

"You two have put us into a bit of a quandary," the woman stated.

"Professor Litona, I presume?" I inquired.

She stared sternly at me.

I stared back and smiled. "Quandary," I said slowly, seeing how the word felt in my mouth. "Good word."

"I would have introduced myself if who I am was not so obvious," she snapped as she turned her piercing, light-brown eyes on me.

I was smitten into silence. I prefer to be a gentleman, and I'd rather assume every woman would prefer to be a lady. However, when a woman acts with less refinement than what is befitting of a lady, the gentleman part of me slips into hibernation, and I tend to quickly lose respect for the uncouth female. But this one was a little different. For some reason, I was willing to tolerate her curt mannerism.

She began to explain. "We are currently at war, and we found you in our territory, without identification and without any record in our databases. Protocol dictates that you are to be treated as spies."

"Which results in what, exactly?" Ron asked, apprehensively.

"It usually results in Doctor Dalmour administering a lethal injection, after which your bodies will be incinerated to guarantee you are not revived," she replied

Ron's eyes grew wide, and he was about to protest. Professor Litona raised a hand to stop him.

"But," she sighed, "we are willing to give you the benefit of the doubt, after considering the circumstances."

"How generous," I said with a grin.

She narrowed her eyes at me. I thought it was a pretty look for her, and it made me smile more.

She continued. "You both say you are from somewhere called 'Earth'."

Ron and I looked at each other, surprised. Were they mocking us, or were we actually on a different planet?

"You suddenly appeared on our sensors, far behind the battlefront and well within our sensors' range," Professor Litona explained. "We have diagnosed the sensors and found them to be faultless. So we need to know, how did you do it?"

"To answer that," Ron said, as he struggled to contain his excitement, "we need you to answer a question first. In all seriousness, what do you call this planet?"

She stared at him for a moment before answering. "Very well. Our planet is called 'Edengone'."

Ron became even more elated. "May we see a map of your planet?"

"Professor," Doctor Dalmour said sternly as he shook his head, "it is against protocol."

"If my suspicions are correct," she said, "then protocol does not apply to them." She pulled a device from her pocket that looked like a cellphone, and she pointed it at the wall. An image projected from the device and showed a map that I did not recognize. She pressed a button and the image changed to something that looked like a live feed from a satellite, but the view was very far from the planet and seemed to be orbiting so fast that it only took a few seconds to see the entire planet. The side facing the sun was one, giant desert. The side away from the sun was a giant icecap. But there was a thin, green ring wrapping around the planet between the desert and the ice.

"We did it!!" Ron shouted as he rattled his cuffs in jubilance.

I was stunned. "But, Ron, that means we're back to square one. How are we going to get home?"

"I don't know!" he laughed hysterically. "We did it! Yes! We did it!"

"So then," Professor Litona said, "you *are* from a different planet. That brings us back to *my* question. How did you do it?"

I shrugged my shoulders. "You'll have to ask him." I nodded my head toward Ron, who was flailing about as much as a bound man could while repeating "We did it! We did it! We did IT!!"

"This may take a while," I said soberly.

"Mr. McPhearson, please," she said sternly.

Ron took a deep breath and looked up at her. "Our planet and your planet exist on different frequencies of energy," Ron explained, "and they just recently passed through each other. We jumped from our planet to yours by –"

"By altering your structural energy frequency at the atomic level," she finished for him.

"Yes!" Ron exclaimed happily. Then he looked at her with a puzzled expression. "How did you know?" he asked.

Litona pressed another button on the device in her hand and a star system appeared on the wall. "This is our solar system within this realm," she explained. "You may not recognize it because these planets are not tangible to the energy frequency you are from." She pressed the button again, and I recognized our solar system. I looked longingly at the sphere that represented Earth. "This is the solar system as you probably recognize it, based on your information and our data on inter-passing planets. And these," she pressed the button again, "are *all* the planets orbiting our star in *all* the frequencies that we are aware of." One by one, layer by layer, planets were added around the sun until it was one giant, glob of planets and other celestial bodies.

"How many are there?" I asked in wonder.

"We aren't sure," she replied. "We only know that they are there. We regularly discover more as our sensor technology advances and we are able to detect ever higher and ever lower frequencies of light. Light is the great revealer. By it, we see what is in the room, and by it, we see what is out in the cosmos." She stared intently at the image of twirling spheres on the wall.

"How many have your people visited?" Ron asked.

"None," she answered curtly. She turned off the projector.

"Why?" Ron pried.

"Because it's a stupid idea." She turned toward Ron. "Clearly you have no idea what could have gone wrong, other than your highly-probable deaths."

What she said must have hit Ron to the core, because I saw his battle face emerge.

"What is the point of living," he said, "if you don't take risks to learn something new, to improve yourself and everyone around you? This is what learning is about; to take a challenge, confront its difficulties, and to triumph over them."

I was surprised, and a little proud. Ron normally wasn't at all philosophical.

"You shouldn't go meddling with things you don't understand," she said irately, "especially when you barely understand your own planet. This is our planet. This is where we belong. Why would we go visit other worlds while we still have so much to learn here?"

"Because there is something to be learned in the journey," I stated. "I still have plenty to learn back at my office, even at my house, but here we are because what we needed to learn could not be found by staying where it is comfortable."

"Watch yourself, Mr. T., because that line of thinking, if taken to an extreme, can lead to catastrophic consequences."

"Such as what?" I challenged.

"Such as what brought on this war," she promptly replied. "There is a faction bent on inflicting their radical ideas on everyone. They aren't just zealous about their philosophies. They are fanatical."

"What have they done?" Ron asked.

"They are insistent on pushing the limits of science to the point of altering everything they can lay their hands on. They pervert the structure of organic life.

They corrupt the ideals and order of humanity. They claim they are improving life, but the destruction and havoc they leave in their wake suggest otherwise. They call themselves 'Advansynergists'."

"Can you give any specific examples?" Ron asked.

Professor Litona glared at him. "You ask a lot of questions," she said in an annoyed tone.

Doctor Dalmour stepped forward. "However, that does bring us to the next step of confirming that you are not spies. The Advansynergists have developed implants for their soldiers that enable them to sustain serious injuries and still survive. It's like an implanted life support. It allows them to live long enough to get medical treatment, heal, and then reenter the battlefield. It is a great boon to them, and a bane to us. Our soldiers are dying while theirs are sustaining the same injuries and simply walking away. In some cases, we thought they were dead, but their implant revived them, gave them a surge of energy, and they escaped."

"That's why you wanted to incinerate us," I deduced.

He gave me a disgusted look. "I don't *want* to incinerate anyone. But, yes, that is why we burn their dead. We had an instance, long ago, when our soldiers had gathered the dead and were about to give them a respectful burial. Then many of the Advansynergists suddenly got up, killed the burial detail, and returned to

71

their own people, just to come back and fight again at a later day."

"They sound like zombies," Ron said, his eyes wide with terror. "I hate zombies."

"Do you have a similar problem with people coming back to life and killing others back on your planet?" Dalmour asked. "Back on Earth?"

"Not really," Ron answered. "We just have a lot of movies about it. People seem to... enjoy... the idea." Ron looked away awkwardly.

Doctor Dalmour raised an eyebrow at Ron. "Savages," he whispered. Then he continued. "Enemy soldiers with this implant are called 'the undying'."

"That doesn't bring any comfort," I cringed.

"No. It doesn't. We need to scan both of you for implants, modifications, or other corruptions before we can finally remove your bonds." He walked back to the door and leaned out into the hall. "We're ready," he said.

A few guards entered the room and freed us from our chairs. We were escorted out of the room, down the barren hall, and into a room with a large machine that looked like a full-length MRI scanner.

"Right," said the doctor, with a pleased smile. "Who wants to go first?"

Ron and I looked at the machine.

"Don't we need to change into some scrubs or a gown or something?" Ron asked.

The doctor laughed. "You aren't going to a party and you aren't a woman... Are you?" Doctor Dalmour looked worried. Ron shook his head. "No. I thought not. So why do you need a gown? You are just going to lie on the table and the table will roll into the machine."

"But all the equipment on our jumpsuits, shouldn't we at least change into some scrubs?"

Doctor Dalmour continued smiling and looked back and forth between the two of us while he rocked his weight from one foot to the other and back again, clearly very excited to use his machine but absolutely clueless as to what we were talking about. "What is 'scrubs'?" he finally asked, still smiling.

"They are clothes they wear in hospitals back on Earth," I answered.

"Oh. We have some *scrapes*," he said cheerily. He pointed to some clothes neatly folded on a nearby shelf.

Ron leaned toward me and quietly said out of the corner of his mouth, "Those look like scrubs to me."

"Mm-hm," I affirmatively replied.

The doctor's head twitched about as though he were watching a fly hover around his head. "Well, no matter. Your suits are fine. The machine knows the difference," he said. "How about you go first?" He pointed at Ron.

"Okay," Ron replied apprehensively. He walked over to the table in front of the machine and, with his hands still cuffed behind his back, he did his best to maintain his dignity while he climbed onto the table.

"This is the fun part," Doctor Dalmour said with a smile. He pushed a button, and the table Ron laid on slowly slid into the machine.

"I've always wanted to do this on the baggage scanners at the airport," Ron casually said.

Once Ron was in the machine, Dalmour rubbed his hands together and said, "Now for the exciting part!" His smile grew wider as he walked to the computer at the control board and, with a dramatic flick of his hand, he pushed a button.

A few lights on the machine softly glowed into life and it made a soft whirring sound. Doctor Dalmour gazed into the large computer screen built into the wall opposite from the control panel, and his smile grew wider as his eyebrows slowly crawled up his forehead. The blue light from the screen cast its hue across his face, giving him a maniacal appearance. The computer played a short jingle and displayed a message that simply read, "Image captured".

"Yes!" The doctor threw his arms up in the air. "That never gets old!" he laughed.

Litona sighed, rolled her eyes, and folded her arms.

The machine slowly spat out the table Ron was on, and Ron rolled off onto his feet and walked over to the large screen everyone else was standing around.

"Now for the messy part," said the doctor.

"Do you have an adjective for every 'part' of this?" I asked, wondering about the doctor's credibility.

"Um, I believe so," he answered, after thinking for a moment. "Now, let's see what you're made of, Mr. McPhearson." He tapped an icon on the screen. A skeleton appeared. "There you are," he said to Ron as he pointed.

"We have machines like this on Earth," Ron explained. "Our machines use x-rays."

Doctor Dalmour didn't seem impressed. "Now let's give you some organs," he said, as he tapped another icon and the skeleton was filled with entrails. "This is where we look for anything unusual."

"Whoa!" Ron exclaimed. "We don't have machines like this on Earth."

Doctor Dalmour began tapping various organs on the screen. Then he slid his fingers across sections he wanted to investigate, as though his fingers were a scalpel, and the image would remove a layer, revealing what lay within.

"Let's see what you had for breakfast, shall we?" the doctor asked as he swept a finger across the stomach and opened it up.

"I really didn't want to see that," I said, as I turned away from the gruesome image.

"How did it do that?" Ron asked in amazement. "It's like performing an autopsy on a living person."

"It's been my pet project for years," Doctor Dalmour said with pride. "I take the same technology that found the planets Professor Litona showed you earlier, I dial it back a bit, and with so many more light frequencies at my disposal, I can focus on different densities of matter. And that is how we can see everything in you without cutting you up, just by focusing on specific frequencies of light that interact with different parts of your body in different ways. I call it 'the Dalmour-inator'," he said dramatically. Then he sighed. "But no one else calls it that," he said, disappointed. "They just call it 'Dalmour's scanning machine'," he said in a mocking tone, and he made a ridiculous face.

"We have similar machines on Earth, but nothing to this extent. They use x-rays and magnetic, um, field...something...imaging." Ron stammered.

"Yes, you said that," the doctor said, uninterested. "But if you think that is amazing, then I'm sure you've never seen this." The doctor tapped an icon and an image of Ron, as we saw him in person, appeared on the screen. "Now, if we remove everything we would see as though we were to slice you and dice you in an autopsy," he made several slashing motions, which made Ron cringe and wince at each swipe, and at each swipe more of Ron's image disappeared until the image was back to the bare skeleton, "then we are back to the bare bones structure. And this is where it ends, right? Have we seen all the matter that makes you?"

We both nodded. He zoomed in on the skull and slashed at it. The skeleton vanished, and the giant screen was blank and white, devoid of any body parts. Then he pulled up a dial on the screen and swirled his finger around it several times. Slowly, a faint, blue image began to appear.

"You will need to step across the room to see it. All the pieces need to be blurred together a little for the brain to make sense of it," said the doctor.

We crossed the room and looked at the screen from a distance. Ron and I were surprised to see a light-blue image of Ron's face staring back at us.

"What is it?" asked Ron. "Is that me?"

"It is," said Doctor Dalmour, "at an extraordinarily high frequency of light. We call it 'the blueprint'." He chuckled. "Just a little play on words there. But *this*, this is what makes you *you*. For ages, we thought it was the DNA, but then we asked, 'If every cell has the full DNA code to make another complete *you*, then how does each new cell you grow know what to become?' And that is when we delved deeper. We have discovered that *this* is what tells the cells what they are to become. This is the blueprint that the cells follow to know what part of the DNA to use. It's like giving a bunch of builders the same building supplies and telling all of them to build the same house. Unless each builder knows what part of the house they are working on and how it should look in the end, you are likely to end up with a deformed and dilapidated house. We found that to be the case with cells. Whenever the cells diverged from the design of the blueprint, we have found that is where cancer and innate diseases occur. With this knowledge, we have developed cures to help the cells realign to the form of the blueprint and eliminate the afflicting disease or cancer. We can even heal scars and, in less extreme cases, help someone grow back parts of an appendage."

"We kind of have something like that back on Earth," Ron said. "We call it chemotherapy."

"Actually, chemotherapy is nothing like this," I said. Then I quickly changed the topic. "You know," I said, intrigued by the image, "there are a lot of religions back on Earth who would call that the 'immortal part of the soul', or the 'spirit of man'. They would say this is what gives a person life."

"We try to keep things less superstitious around here," Litona sneered.

"It's funny that you should mention that," Doctor Dalmour said, as he faced me, "because we have performed scans on the deceased, and we could not find the blueprint."

"Do you know what it is or what it is made of? Where does it come from? What keeps it together?" I asked.

The doctor and professor looked at each other, and then back at me. "We don't know," the doctor answered.

"You said you could alter the cells to conform to the blueprint," Ron recalled. "Can you encourage the cells to perform their tasks more efficiently by creating a stronger adhesion with the blueprint?"

Doctor Dalmour stood taller and a severe look shot from his eyes. "You are talking about enhancing a person's abilities through manipulation," the doctor stated in a suddenly aggressive tone. "The practice is not only forbidden but highly unethical and dangerous. A person's skills and abilities come to them through development, training, discipline, and will. To intentionally amplify those traits, genetically or otherwise, would grant a person power and abilities they are neither prepared for nor capable of controlling. And *that*," he took an aggressive step forward and pointed at Ron, "is exactly what an Advansynergist would suggest doing!"

"I was just curious," Ron said timidly. "So... How do you cure people? Do you use that machine or a different one?"

"That's the beauty of my invention," said the doctor. His tone immediately softened as he explained, "This machine can diagnose *and* cure. It is very efficient and effective. It uses light to scan the patient, and it uses light to heal the patient. It uses alternating light frequencies focused at different intensities on a targeted, afflicted area to encourage the cells to comply with the blueprint. It also imbues the cells with the energy they need to perform the healing, much like how a plant photosynthesizes sunlight. But back to the primary reason that brought all of us here; your scan is clean. You are not spies, we don't need to kill you, and we can remove those cuffs."

"Great," I said dryly.

A couple of guards stepped forward and removed the cuffs from our wrists. Then we all stood there for a moment, unsure of what to do next.

Doctor Dalmour looked around at everyone and said, "I'm hungry. Is anyone else hungry?"

Chapter 6 – A Matter Of Truth

We were given some "scrapes" to change into. Then Ron and I followed Litona and Dalmour to the cafeteria. We walked to the serving counter and I surveyed the options.

"Mashed potatoes, green beans, steak, and cherry pie, am I right?" I asked. "I expected food on a different planet to be… different."

"That's because you clearly do not understand there is an order to all things," Litona stated impatiently. "There are natural and irrevocable governing laws of the universe that establish order, and when those laws are broken or disregarded, there are dire consequences. So it would make sense that if you found a planet that could support your life, then there should be others like you. And if there are others like you, then they would eat food that is similar to what you eat."

"Governing laws?" Ron snorted. "I know there are laws that science discovers, but you make it sound like there is a law for everything. Is there a law that dictates how I should live?" he asked defiantly.

"There is," she replied.

"Yeah? Well, where we come from, people are free to believe what they want to believe, and they can act how they want to act," Ron said obstinately.

"We are free to do the same here," Litona retorted. "But to disregard the truth simply because you choose to believe something else makes you as ignorant and as foolish as an ostrich with its head in the sand; oblivious of and unprepared for the dangers prowling about us. On this planet, within our faction, we are free to believe what we want, and we *want* to believe the *truth*."

"And what is the truth?" Ron was sounding a little heated.

"Careful, Ron," I cautioned. "You know your reasoning gets a little shaky when you get philosophical... and when you're hungry... and when someone tells you what to do... and when you're angry... and when you speak to women. Come to think of it, you should sit down for this conversation before you fall down." They both ignored me.

"The truth," Litona began, "is how things were, how they are, and how they will be. It is a grasp on reality. It is the vaccine to insanity. It is the guardian of freedom and the bane to oppression."

I tried to come to Ron's rescue. "There was this wise guy back on Earth who argued that reality is what our senses make of it. So a rose may not actually be a rose, or Ron may not perceive a rose the same way I do."

"What a moron," Litona huffed. "Are there many morons on your planet?"

I chuckled. "Unfortunately, there are."

"Is that why you left Earth and came here?" she asked harshly.

I decided to let this one go and make a hasty retreat. I looked at the pie. "You know, that pie looks really good. And I think it's calling my name. Excuse me." I walked over to the pie and finished loading my tray with food.

Ron walked with Doctor Dalmour, and they began talking together as they went to sit down, but Litona went to a different table where she sat down alone and began to aggressively stab at the green beans on her tray.

I stood across the table from her. "Do you mind if I join you?" I asked.

"Yes," she snapped.

I sat down anyway, and she glared at me.

I put on a shocked, innocent face and said, "Oh, I'm sorry. On my planet 'yes' means, 'yes, it's okay for you to sit there'." I smiled.

She stared at me and then went back to stabbing the unfortunate green beans on her tray.

"I guess it's safe to ask now," I ventured, "where we are?"

"We are at our military's primary base of operations," Litona answered.

"Base of operations," I repeated. "Sounds big. Do you have wars often?"

"Yes."

"How many wars have you had on this planet?"

"Four."

"Four?! That's it? How long do these wars last?"

"Two or three hundred years."

"Wow. So when you guys go at it, it must be over something pretty big."

"The fate of the planet and all the people on it *is* big."

"On Earth, it seems like we have a war every time someone sneezes in the wrong direction. So who is involved in your current war?"

"Us and them."

I looked at her. "Just the two of you? Are there any other countries or factions involved who this may affect?"

"What other factions?" she asked back.

"Do you mean there are only two nations on this planet?"

"Why would there be more? How many nations are on your planet?"

I thought for a second and shrugged. "I don't really know; maybe a couple hundred."

"Why are there so many?"

"I guess we all have our own way of thinking and our own opinions on how something should be done."

"How could there be so many nations, so many... opinions, when there are only two ways to do anything; either it is done correctly or incorrectly."

"I suppose we see things a little differently, not so black and white. We see things as 'good, better, best', but we can't seem to agree on what 'best' is."

"Here, we *do* see things differently. If it isn't 'best', then it isn't 'correct'."

"You are perfectionists," I said.

"We are improvers," she corrected. "When we find a 'better' way, it becomes the 'best' and 'correct' way."

"And who decides what is 'best'?"

"Usually it is obvious, but if the question is more complicated or impacts a sufficient number of people, then the question is put to a vote. A paper arguing all current points of view is drafted and distributed to the population to educate them on the matter before the vote is taken."

"What if the people don't read the paper?"

"Then they clearly do not care if the matter goes one way or the other, and clearly they don't care about the fate of our people. Those who ignore such influencing matters are fools, and the opinion of a fool is of no matter anyway. Their vote won't be missed."

"How do you know what the people voted for is actually 'best'?"

"People are generally rational. If our people ever became irrational, then we, as a people, would be doomed to fall. And it would serve us right."

I nodded. Then I asked, "Why are your wars so long?"

"It takes a long time to deplete a faction of its resources."

"So you fight until the other guy runs out of punches. Who normally wins?"

"The faction that can produce faster than the other is always victorious. Each war has nearly destroyed this planet by its end. How are wars fought on your planet?"

"Well, resources do play a large part in it, but normally there is an objective, a weakness, somewhere or something about the enemy where we can put a chokehold on them and force them to surrender without needing to kill their entire army or deplete their resources."

"How do you get to these objectives?" she asked.

"Sometimes by punching right through the enemy, but if our enemy is just as strong as us or even stronger then we rely more on strategy and tactics. Then we can sometimes get around the main force and press on to the objective."

"How would you go around?"

I thought that was an oddly simple question for her to be asking, especially after considering her attitude up to that point. "What do you mean?"

"How do you get around your enemy?"

"You go around their flank," I said, fearing she was asking a trick question, but the confusion on her face convinced me that she was sincere. "Show me a map of the battlefront," I said when it occurred to me that I didn't have all of the pertinent information.

She slid both of our trays to one side, pulled out the device that looked like a phone, and pressed a button. "There are two battlefronts on this planet, due to our geography. Here is one of them," she said. A map was cast on the table top, and I studied it.

"This is all strangely linear," I observed, "almost like trench warfare during World War I back on Earth." I touched the map and discovered I could move it about. "This battlefront is huge. It looks like it spans from this dessert all the way to this arctic region. But look," I said, pointing to the ends of the battlefront line. "The line stops far into the desert and equally as far into the snowy regions with no real geographical barriers to keep you from sending a force out and around the line to attack your enemy from the sides, or even from behind. It would cause confusion in their ranks, and your forces could potentially cut off their supply line to the battlefront. That would give your main force the opportunity to press the attack, to push through the enemy lines. The main force could then unite with the flanking forces and continue their push together into enemy territory before the enemy could regroup. It's a simple pincer movement."

She studied the map for a moment. "That could work," she said. "We have always fought our wars in this manner because of the geography of our planet. It's been this way for as long as the history books can remember. We've never fought battles in any way other than head-on. The desert gets too hot in this direction and the arctic gets too cold in this direction. We can only sweep out so far before temperatures exceed the limits of our machines and soldiers"

"The desert is too hot and the arctic is too cold? How could that be?"

She grabbed the map and changed the scale so that we viewed the entire planet. "Our planet is tidally locked," she explained. "The same side is always facing the sun. So it is always day on that side and always hot. It is one giant desert covering nearly half of Edengone. The other side is just the opposite; always night, always cold, and all covered in ice and snow. Then there is this narrow track of green between the two extremes, where fire and ice meet. This is the habitable zone, where we are now, and it wraps all the way around the planet. This is the only place on this planet where life can survive. Because of this, our wars have always been fought in lines on two fronts, since all we needed to do to keep the enemy from overrunning our land is to build a wall and fight head on. The heat and the cold protected our flanks.

But now," she said with a smile, "we have technology capable of pushing the limits."

"Pushing the limits," I repeated with a smile. "You are starting to sound like an Advansynergist."

"We will beat them at their own game," she said enthusiastically.

Just then, Doctor Dalmour walked up to our table. "Have either of you seen Ron? It seems he has wandered off," he said, as though he had lost a dog.

Then a voice sounded over the intercom. "Doctor Dalmour to scanning. Doctor Dalmour to scanning."

A sick knot formed in my stomach. "Doctor, please tell me you keep the scanning room locked."

I could tell he got my meaning. His eyes widened and his mouth opened as though he was going to say something. He didn't say anything. He just turned quickly and put his large shoes into action. Litona and I got up and chased after him. We ran down the hall past the cells where Ron and I were questioned and hurried on to the scanning room where Dalmour had checked Ron for implants.

Two guards stood outside the doors to the scanning room.

"He's locked himself in," one of the guards said, pointing through the window in the door.

Ron was on the table and sliding into the scanning machine. Dalmour quickly withdrew a key from his pocket and thrust it into the lock. He firmly pushed the door.

"He's barricaded the door!" the doctor shouted.

"Stand clear!" I ordered.

Dalmour stepped aside, and I gave the door a solid kick near the latches. The chairs Ron had used to barricade the door tumbled across the floor as the doors burst open. The scanning machine began to whirr. Doctor Dalmour ran to the control panel.

"It's too late," he said in distress. "Whatever he was trying to do is done!" He ran to the machine as Ron slid out on the table. "Ron! Ron, what are you doing? Are you alright? How do you feel?"

Ron bounded from the scanner table to his feet with a smile. "Never better. In fact, I feel…" His face suddenly paled, his smile faded, and his eyes rolled back into his head. "Uh-oh," he muttered.

"Ron, lie down, now," Doctor Dalmour ordered as he helped Ron to the floor. Suddenly, Ron violently convulsed, causing him to involuntarily throw the doctor aside. The doctor got back to his feet. "He's having a seizu-," he started but was abruptly stopped when a powerful shock wave, centered on Ron, burst through the room, throwing everyone to the floor and launching anything lighter than a person against the walls.

Papers slowly fluttered to the floor in the wake of the blast. I carefully raised my head while I remained on the floor and exclaimed, "What the halibut was *that*?" Then I noticed Ron's still form on the floor. "Ron."

Doctor Dalmour scrambled to Ron's side and began examining him. "He has a pulse. He's breathing. Help me get him back on the table."

I helped lift Ron back onto the scanner table and followed the doctor back to the control panel. He brushed some scattered papers and other debris off the panel and went to work. The bed Ron was on slid back into the machine and his scan appeared on the screen. Dalmour made a few gentle swipes on the screen around Ron's head, revealing his brain.

"There it is," said the doctor, pointing at a spot where the brain folds seemed to be more frequent. "It appears he was trying to make himself smarter by increasing his mind's energy capacity and endurance."

"How?" I asked.

"The brain is like a muscle, Mike. Just like a muscle," was all he said while he started to rapidly select icons and make occasional swipes at the screen.

"Is he going to be alright?" I asked.

"It appears so. He was smart enough to strengthen the proper regions before applying the enhancements. Now, please, I need to work," he said.

I stared at the machine Ron was in as Litona lead me out of the scanning room. The guards closed the doors behind us and stood in front of them. Litona left, and I remained as close to the doors as the guards permitted. I took up the tasks of waiting and watching through the windows.

The minutes ticked by, but anxiety and concern exaggerated them to feel like days. I paced, I stood, I stared, I shook my head, I walked away, I returned. Doctor Dalmour emerged and closed the door behind him.

"He will wake up in a few minutes," he said.

"Is he back to normal?" I asked.

Doctor Dalmour got a sly look in his eye as he said, "Let's just say that I left well enough alone."

"What was that explosion?"

"Energy," was the doctor's short reply.

"From where?"

"From him. We are capable of extraordinary feats, but understanding and prudence equal to our abilities must accompany those abilities to be properly controlled. Ron has an amazing ability to learn and apply."

"But sometimes he knows too much for his own good," I observed.

Doctor Dalmour chuckled. "I'm glad *you* said it. He needs to be balanced with more understanding before he acts."

"How did he learn to do that?"

"The explosion was an accident. He doesn't have the discipline to control that much power. But I'm afraid he learned how to alter himself from me. We were talking while we were eating, and I was running my mouth about my machine, my creation. It is my gift to my people. It is my pride and my weak spot."

We heard the door open behind us, and Ron staggered out.

Doctor Dalmour raised his eyebrows. "That didn't take long. How are you feeling?" he asked.

"I have a splitting headache," Ron replied, with a palm pressing against his drooping head.

"Thanks for your help, doctor," I said. "I'm sorry about your operating room. Ron is curious and compulsive, but he is a good friend. Is there some way I can make this right?"

A booming voice from down the hall answered the question. "There most certainly is!"

I looked toward the corner from where the voice had come, and I saw high, brown hiking boots; yellow khakis; a thick, leather belt; a yellow uniform jacket adorned with medals; a white handkerchief, crisp and puffy, pluming from between the lapels and beneath the collar; thick, white mutton chops; a head full of snowy hair; and a stern, ruddy face all came marching around the corner and toward the doctor and me. Litona followed in his wake. They abruptly stopped in front of us.

Ron threw a salute, suddenly forgetting about his headache, and said, "Colonel Mustard, sir, I have always been a fan of yours, but in the hallway with the rope? Really?"

He stared at Ron strangely and said nothing.

I broke the awkward silence. "Ron, stop embarrassing me. This isn't Earth. They don't have…"

"They don't have a clue?" Ron finished for me.

"Right," I answered.

"Sorry," Ron said to the stern man dressed in yellow. "It has meaning back on Earth."

"Hmph!" the yellow-clad man barked.

"Mike," Litona said, "this is General Kulek. I have briefed him on your strategy and he is impressed."

I looked at her. "My what, now?"

"Pincer movement," General Kulek spat out. "I don't know why our strategists hadn't seen it before."

"Because we didn't have the technology before, sir," Litona explained. "It wasn't an option before. But now everything seems to be coming together."

"Well, if they weren't so busy propping up their small, lazy heads on a needlepoint, they would have seen it," General Kulek countered gruffly. "I understand you are a long way from home," he said to me.

"Yes, sir. In a manner of speaking," I answered.

"In a manner of speaking?!" he shouted. "Your planet is on a different frequency of existence, hundreds of thousands of miles away by now, and several thousand years away from crossing our world again. Any way you look at it, son, you are a LONG way from home!"

"Yes, sir. You are right, sir," I quickly agreed.

"So I have a proposition." He looked at Litona and then back at me. "If you help us, we will help you."

"Sounds fair enough," I observed.

"Indeed!" he said with a smile as he stood a little straighter, which before that moment I hadn't thought was possible. "Fall in and follow me," he ordered.

We followed General Kulek into a conference room where a large circular table sat at its center. The table appeared to be made from a dark hardwood, but I didn't recognize the species. An obsidian dome rested in the middle of the table. The general tapped the table's edge. A hologram of the planet appeared and slowly spun over the black dome.

"As you know," General Kulek started, "The Advansynergists have placed implants in their soldiers that give them unnatural resistance to pain and incredible durability against injury. We know them as 'the undying'. As you can understand, this gives our enemy a nearly endless supply of trained troops. It effectively makes our forces outnumbered. We have learned that when one of their soldiers is injured beyond the normal human's capacity to cope, the implant takes over and keeps them alive until they can return behind their own lines. From there, we've tracked them by satellite to see where they are taken. They are collected and brought to a facility where they are mended, rested, and then deployed again. This facility houses all the specialized equipment, knowledge, and trained skill to maintain this…," his upper lip curled and his mustache quivered with repugnance, "abomination," he growled.

I raised my eyebrows, and the general saw my expression.

"I couldn't think of another word to describe it," he said, almost apologetically.

"Regardless of what you call it," I said, "it sounds like a nightmare of a life; to nearly die and recover just to be sent to nearly die again," I felt disgusted at the thought of the torment the soldiers must endure.

"That is one of the minor side effects of the implants," the general explained, "and a self-inflicted one at that. The implants also slowly and permanently reduce the host's sensitivity in every sense. Their hearing, sight, smell, touch, and even taste go to garbage after too long. Eventually, they become… senseless; literally senseless."

"I guess it's better than losing your life," Ron reasoned. "They trade their senses for time."

"What is life if you can't experience it?" I challenged. "It wouldn't be life. It would be a living death." I said, thoroughly terrified at the thought.

"You two can argue that out later," General Kulek interrupted. "But that is what we are up against. They are fanatics, practically torturing themselves to inflict and enforce their shady ideas of what ideal is. Seems ironic to me, really, when I think too hard about it." His bushy eyebrows scrunched together.

Litona stepped to the table. "The facility these 'undying' are taken to is on the exact opposite side of the planet from us, in the heart of their territory," Litona explained. The hologram focused on a point within the habitable zone. "They call this place 'Death's Grave'."

Litona and General Kulek abruptly turned toward me and stared.

I looked back at them. "What?" I asked.

"We are ready to proceed to the next part of the negotiations," Litona said in an annoyed tone.

"The next step... I, um... What is the next step?" I stammered. Then I explained, "On Earth, one party asks the other party to do something and offers something in return, and if the other party doesn't like it, then they make a counteroffer. So... what do you want me to do?"

General Kulek squared his shoulders, took a deep breath, and said, "We are not on Earth. Here, on Edengone, we tell you our problem. You tell us how you are going to help us. Then you tell us your problem, and we will tell you how we can help you. Keep in mind that your generosity in helping us will play a large part in how we hold up our part of the deal."

"Oh," I said, as I carefully thought about how I was going to make my play. "If it's okay with you, could you show me a map of the city around Death's Grave, as well as a layout of Death's Grave itself?"

Without hesitating, General Kulek tapped the table, and the hologram focused on the city. The hologram systematically highlighted the roads, military movements, civilian concentrations, and air traffic. Then the facility was highlighted before the image zoomed in to focus on it. It showed a layout of the buildings. Then it dissected each building and revealed what was inside to an alarming amount of detail.

"I need structural details," I said, as I studied the hologram.

The image highlighted steel support beams, foundation structures, reinforced concrete, power lines, and routing for pipelines.

"This is amazing," I said. "How did you get all of this?"

"It was a joint effort on a satellite project between Doctor Dalmour and Professor Litona. The satellite uses some key components from Doctor Dalmour's scanning machine."

I nodded as I continued studying the maps. "What is in this giant room here, the one with the huge pillar?" I asked, pointing to the room in question, which was littered with blurry dots, each about the size of a phone booth.

"We don't know. We couldn't get a clear scan. Based on the power draw, heat output, and activity levels, we suspect it is a large, super-computer facility or data bank."

"I need to know the enemies capabilities in that region, their response times, and the facility's security systems," I requested.

General Kulek tapped the table again and the map highlighted troop movements with mini holograms next to them showing what weapons and vehicles were available to that unit as well as vehicle specifications. Then it went through the facility's systems, controls, and connections. It showed hypothetical scenarios of security breaches and how the automated systems would respond. I reviewed the information again and thought carefully. I made a rough plan in my head and some approximate calculations for the amount of force we would need. Then I had my answer.

"With the right equipment and team, I can destroy that facility," I looked down as I said the next part. My memory flashed terrifying images of fire and destruction before my mind's eye. "And everyone in it," I said in a quieter, regretful tone. Then I looked back at Litona and General Kulek. They looked at me with raised, wrinkled foreheads and unblinking eyes.

"Well," the general finally said. "That was more than what we were hoping for, but we will gladly accept it. How many men will you need?"

"This is a very large facility," I said. I looked back at the map, double checked my calculations, and said, "Thirty."

"Only thirty?" Litona asked in disbelief.

"And at least a hundred pounds of demolition high-explosives, or some C-4, if you've got it," I added, hoping she was impressed.

"I will put your team together," General Kulek said with a pleased look, "and Litona will provide you with the means of getting there."

"Hold on just a moment!" Ron exclaimed. "Mike, you can't just make promises like that! You're a teacher, not a soldier."

I pulled Ron aside, with my arm over his shoulder and said, not too quietly, "Do you remember that 'accident' I was in, the one where you had to donate blood to save my life?"

"Of course," he answered. "I won't let you forget it."

"That 'accident'," I explained, "was caused by shrapnel through an artery." I watched his puzzled face for a moment before I said, "I *was* a soldier. Now I'm, um, an undercover operative."

Ron covered his eyes. Then he looked curiously at me. "And you became a philosophy teacher?"

I shrugged. "It's how I made my peace," I said. "War leaves scars; not just on the body, but on the mind and... elsewhere." I was about to say "soul", but I didn't want to give Doctor Dalmour, who I could tell was listening intently, the idea of putting me in the scanning machine to be examined.

"Indeed," General Kulek solemnly agreed. "Now, let's get to our tasks. We will meet back here at thirty-six hundred hours."

Ron and I looked at each other, then at the general, confused. We hadn't considered that a tidally locked planet may count it's time differently.

"Is there a clock somewhere? Our watches are not set to that time system." Ron asked.

"A what?" the general asked, now looking as confused as we were.

"Where can we see a timepiece?" Ron rephrased the question.

Litona pointed up to a hexagon on the wall with strange symbols around its border.

"Which one is thirty-six?" I asked as I studied the symbols.

"The top one," Litona replied.

"Ah," I said, "We call that 'high noon' back on Earth."

"We are not on your Earth," General Kulek reminded me, annoyed. Then he turned and marched out of the room with Professor Litona and Doctor Dalmour in tow, leaving Ron and me alone in the room.

"Do I really look like Colonel Mustard?" I overheard General Kulek ask Doctor Dalmour as they walked away.

"No, sir," Dalmour replied. "You look nothing like that maniacal tyrant."

We watched the door for a moment to see if anyone would ask us to follow them, but no one came.

"They seem trusting," I observed.

"Do you think this is a test?" Ron asked.

"I don't know. Do you think we could recharge the suits and get home?"

Ron shook his head. "Earth is thousands of miles away by now. The suits only alter energy frequencies. They don't travel through space."

"So we couldn't even use them to get to Death's Grave?"

Ron shook his head. "What do we do now?"

"We plan our operation," I answered, as I turned my attention to the hologram and gave the table a few experimental swipes. I examined each new image and diagram as they appeared, and I felt a part of my mind that I had not used in a long time suddenly awaken and quicken. I started seeing weaknesses and blind spots, advantages and threats. I felt anticipation and a little anxiety, even some excitement. I foresaw obstacles and losses. I plotted counters and considered contingencies. I had almost forgotten Ron was still there.

"What are you thinking about," he asked.

"Do you see how the building has one main pillar in the center and all of the other support beams are dependent on that one pillar?" I asked as I pointed at the hologram. "If we take out that pillar, then everything else falls with it."

"Why don't they just launch a missile at it and be done?"

"I'm sure they've tried that. But even on Earth, defense systems make missiles nearly obsolete. Sometimes old fashioned soldiers are the only way to get something done. Everything else is too predictable. Projectiles follow a predetermined path and can be intercepted. Machines are too specialized with mobility restrictions and limitations. Even artificial intelligence can be systematically countered. Only people on their

101

own two feet possess the ability and creativity to be completely unpredictable and adaptable. That makes us the all-time ultimate weapon. A soldier will always have employment."

"Before we get carried away here, I need to ask: How do we know we are fighting for the right side?" Ron asked. "How do we know these people are telling us the truth and that *they* aren't the monsters? Or worse still, how do we know that not everyone is a monster?"

"I guess we'll find out when we get to Death's Grave," I calmly replied. "There will be plenty of time to observe these Advansynergists on their own turf to see if they are really all that bad."

"And if they aren't?"

I shrugged. "Then we defect or desert. We'll play it by ear."

"You say that rather casually. Should that make me nervous?"

"You asked a good question, Ron. These people are still strangers to us. We still don't know who to really trust. We don't know if they will even make good on their part of the deal. I haven't sworn any allegiance to anyone on this planet, so I don't have any qualms about switching sides or abandoning the entire thing if new information prompts that course of action. We only have each other to rely on, Ron. That's how it was with me and my team. We would be dropped into hostile territory, and from there on out, we only had each other."

"I may not be much good in a fight, Mike, but you can depend on me, whatever you need."

"Don't be getting mushy," I said, as I went back to the holograms. Then I smiled. "But thanks. And I'm here for you, too. I'm here." Then I groaned with frustration.

"What?" Ron asked. "What is it?"

"The deal," I said angrily. "They didn't complete the deal! What is their part of the deal? We told them how we can help them, but they never said how they are going to help *us*!"

Chapter 7 – The Mission!

A few hours later, Ron and I were changed into tan, combat uniforms and joined again by Professor Litona, Doctor Dalmour, and General Kulek. A small band of soldiers followed behind them, also wearing tan uniforms.

General Kulek spoke. "As you have been told, we are here to infiltrate and destroy Death's Grave. The operation and your squad have been code-named 'Death's End'."

I promptly interrupted. "General, I need to address one concern before we proceed."

He studied me for a moment and said, "The deal. We didn't give you our half of the deal."

"Yes," I said, a little surprised that he so readily brought it up.

"I sincerely apologize. In our excitement, we overlooked that one detail," General Kulek said. "I will admit we only expected you to offer advice or instruction on how to accomplish our goals. But since you were gracious enough to go and solve our entire problem for us, we have decided to solve your entire problem for you. Litona, present our offer."

Litona stepped forward. "As you know, your suits cannot get you back home, because they do not transport you across space. They only alter matter."

A revelation dawned on me. "They were listening to our conversation," I whispered to Ron. "We weren't as alone as we thought."

Litona continued. "But I have had a theory, and it will soon be ready for testing. I have been developing a machine that operates much like your suits but is capable of accessing energy frequencies much, much greater than what your suits could ever achieve. This higher frequency should enable you to travel through space and get you back to Earth."

"Sounds good," I said. "What's the catch?"

"What do you mean?" Litona asked innocently.

"There's always a catch," I chuckled.

"I don't understand what a 'catch' is."

"Oh," I said, mildly embarrassed and at a loss for a definition to give her. "Um, help me out here, Ron."

Ron was happy to do so. "Is there a complication or an unusually high chance of failure?" Ron asked.

"Oh. It is a new technology, and it's never been tested." She hesitated. "And, yes, it could kill you, but it's your only chance of getting home."

"That's what I was talking about," I said, as I folded my arms, disgruntled.

"It's nothing we haven't faced before," said Ron.

"Touché," I nodded, as I thought about the elevator in the Empire State Building. "So, this machine you're going to build will change our matter enough to get us to the correct energy frequency and get us across space at the same time?" I recapped.

"That's the theory, anyway. I will have details by the time you return," she said.

"That's what you have to offer?" I asked snidely, "a fatally, half-baked theory?"

"Your idea is only 'half-baked' as well, soldier," the general growled, "until we proceed with this briefing and get the operation underway."

I backed off and clasped my hands behind my back. "Yes, sir," I said.

"Now, let's get on with the briefing," General Kulek said, in an all-business tone. "Your mission is to destroy Death's Grave, completely and entirely. That includes all buildings, machinery, information, and personnel associated with the creation and production of the undying. To get there, you will be traveling across uncharted terrain through one of the harshest extremes this planet has to offer. You will be traveling across the entire Demog Desert."

A hint of worry crossed the soldiers' faces.

"Professor Litona will now tell you how you will avoid becoming a fried fritter."

Litona stepped forward and lifted a helmeted suit that appeared to be entirely gold plated. "This is the culmination of many years of research, development, and good old trial and error. This is a cherub-suit."

"It looks like a golden space suit," Ron interrupted.

Everyone stared at him.

"It looks just like the suits the astronauts wore when they landed on the moon, except that one is covered in gold," he reiterated.

"You're people have been to the moon?" one of the soldiers asked.

"Impossible," Litona snorted. "There's no air in space and the moon is too far away. There's no way you could carry enough air with you to survive the journey."

"I guess our moon is closer," Ron reasoned, "because they packed air with them. They also recycled the air they breathed." Everyone continued staring at him. "And they made it to the moon," Ron added with a shrug. "And they made it back to Earth… several times."

"Can we get back to the mission, now?" General Kulek growled.

Litona resumed her presentation. "These suits will protect you from the intense heat and sand-blasting winds of the desert if you find it necessary to exit your vehicles. Your vehicles have been outfitted with similar protection and an airlock for exiting the vehicle without exposing the cabin to the elements. They have also been converted to run on water."

"How are we going to carry enough water for both us and the vehicles?" a soldier asked.

Litona explained. "There will be enough water for only the crews. The vehicles will be fueled before departure and will be refilled by you," she indicated to the squad with outstretched hands, "with *your* water; your wastewater, to be exact."

Ron wrinkled his nose. "I suppose that's efficient. How is the water turned into power?"

"The water will be superheated into high-pressure steam by the ambient temperatures of the desert and passed through oscillating, double-action pistons," she answered.

"Oh. Like a steam engine."

"The mission!" General Kulek grumbled. He leaned on the table with both hands and his head drooped forward wearily, as though his patience was a heavy burden to bear.

Litona continued again. "The engine has been designed to recycle the water as much as possible by passing the exhausted steam through condensers and pumping it back as water into the heating tanks. The vehicles will need to be stopped from time to time to allow the condenser to catch up, so keep this in mind while you are traveling. You will want to take advantage of safe zones."

"What are 'safe zones'?" I asked, seeing how no one else seemed confused by the term.

General Kulek spoke. "Safe zones are areas where wind currents are the calmest, like eddies in a river. Once you enter the desert, the winds become savage and move the sand around constantly. You will be buried alive in the moving sand if you aren't careful about where you stop. The 'safe zones' are the only places you can stay for any considerable amount of time without being buried. That is one reason the battlefront does not extend very far into the arid or even arctic regions."

"Do you have a map of the safe zones?" I asked.

"We have given maps of all known safe zones to the drivers and navigators, but there are regions we are not sure about," Litona said

"Can't you send a satellite to scout out a path?"

"We have, but it's not that simple. Some safe zones are short term, and we don't know when the winds will blow through those areas again. There are also dust-clouds stirred up by the winds that hover in the atmosphere. Cold air constantly flows from the arctic region and across the desert where it is heated and rapidly rises, carrying dust and sand with it. Those dust clouds obscure the vision of our satellites."

General Kulek took over explaining, "The clouds are particularly thick around the center of the Demog Desert; the Bull's Eye is what we call it," he said, looking at me. "The opposite side of the planet is called the Bull's Tail, just in case you were wondering. The Bull's Eye is the region that constantly takes the direct heat-force from the sun. We don't know what is in the Bull's Eye region. It could be a giant, bottomless pit for all we know."

"General, don't be absurd," Litona said in an agitated tone. "If there is a pit there, then it can't be bottomless."

"I think it could be!" General Kulek fired back. "No one has been to the Bull's Tail to see what's there, either. It could be the other side of a bottomless pit! The pit could go right through the entire planet; making this world one, giant, flying donut!"

"Then it would be a tunnel, General. Not a pit."

"You wouldn't know that unless you tried jumping to the bottom of it and find yourself flying out the other side! You would fall into the Bull's Eye just to find yourself flying out from beneath the Bull's Tail! Until then, it would look like a pit!"

"But what something looks like and what something is, is not always the same."

Doctor Dalmour, who had been silent and motionless up to this point, leaned toward Ron and me as General Kulek and Professor Litona continued arguing and said, "This is a favorite topic here. No one knows what is at the center of the two extreme regions, and everyone loves to speculate about what is there or what isn't there." His mustache curled up in a patient smile as he turned his attention back to the debate.

"Either way!" the general roared when it was clear the debate would need to be continued elsewhere, and he looked back at the squad. "That is your secondary mission: To carry out recognizance in the unknown regions and record what you find. Map as much as you can. Bring back what you can. And above all!" he looked directly at Litona with grating teeth as he growled, "Don't fall into the bottomless pit!"

Litona rolled her eyes.

"This mission," the general continued, "relies on secrecy. Therefore, there is to be no communication between your squad and the rest of the world. You will be entirely on your own. There will be no backup. There will be no rescue. There will be no last words home. Your squad will be all you have. You will be traveling alone, cut off from the rest of the world. No one else knows you will be out there. If you fail, you fail alone, and we don't want to hear about it. Are there any questions?"

"How will you know if we succeeded?" Ron asked.

"We will know," Kulek growled, "when the enemies we shoot down stay down."

"General," one of the soldiers raised his hand, "what vehicle type will we be using?" he asked.

"You will be taking four half-tracks of the colossal class."

The soldiers smiled amidst murmurs of excitement and approval.

"What is a colossal class half-track?" I had to ask, after seeing and hearing the enthusiasm of the squad.

The general just looked at me and said, with the closest thing he had to a grin, "You'll like it." He patted me on the back as he walked out of the room.

A few moments later, we were outside and looking up at a huge, steel-clad machine. It was a half-track. And it was colossal. The sides and tracks were made of heavy plated steel. Even the front tires had been replaced with large steel rollers that were hinged to act much like tank tracks, but they held their round shape by using torsion springs in place of where the spokes would have been on a wheel. There were three turreted gun emplacements on the roof, accessible from inside; one large caliber cannon toward the front, another toward the rear, and a flak gun between the two. I recognized targeting cameras on the bubbles that the large guns protruded from, so that the gunners could see their targets without exposing themselves, or, in our case, without exposing the cab to the elements. The cannons also sported smaller round machine guns parallel to the large barrels. The only windows were those around the driver's cab. Thick, angled armor protected the vehicle. The two large tracks at the rear promised the traction we

111

would need to travel across the desert sands. In short, the vehicle was all business.

"I like it," I said, with a look of approval.

Litona walked around to the back of one of the half-tracks and pulled a lever. A hatch swiftly opened with a hydraulic hissing sound and folded down to become a ramp. There was another door. She walked up the ramp to the door and turned a lever. The door opened with a small whooshing sound, like when a refrigerator door is opened. There was a small room with enough space for only one person, but there was yet another door. This one also opened with a whoosh. Then she entered the vehicle and the rest of us followed. It was a tight fit trying to get the entire squad inside, but I imagined there would be sufficient space once the squad had divided into crews and entered their own half-tracks.

"Some of the inner armor and defenses have been removed to accommodate living space," Litona said, as she renewed her presentation. "Hammocks have been attached to the walls for sleeping, and they zip shut so you won't fall out when you encounter rough terrain. They are located above the seats. Both the driver and navigator have fully functional controls for the vehicle so that they can seamlessly alternate driving, and the seats are designed to recline into a cot, so there should be little reason for them to leave their positions. It is important that the vehicles keep moving for as long as possible. The vehicle's interior refueling funnel, which doubles as the water closet, is located here." She opened a small door, revealing the lavatory. She closed the door. "Light weapons are stored overhead…" I smiled as she pointed with both hands to the overhead compartments. It reminded me of a flight attendant. "…and heavy ordnance is stored in the floor compartments. Food stores are in the side panels toward the back, along with the cherub-suits."

"It's like an armored motorhome," Ron said. "How long will the journey be?"

"We expect the vehicles to travel around the clock and at least a thousand miles per day. You should arrive at Death's Grave in at least two weeks."

"Wait. Is a mile on this planet the same as a mile on Earth? And how long is a week?" Ron asked.

"We'll figure that out by experience," I said to him. I patted his shoulder.

"Alright. When are we leaving?" Ron asked.

"Now," was her short reply.

"Now? Don't we need to get things ready?" Ron asked.

"We've been preparing all day. Now everything is ready to go, and *now* is when you all go. Good luck."

Everyone filed out of the vehicle and crews were formed from the squad.

"Hey," I said to Ron. I could tell he was distraught about the rapid course of events. He was normally the one in charge and was accustomed to knowing exactly what was happening. Now he was on the receiving end of the orders. "Try to not think too much. Just go for the ride and relax. We've got two weeks to figure things out."

"Michael! Ronald!" a voice called. We turned around to see one of the soldiers waving us over to a different half-track. "You're riding with us!"

General Kulek approached us as we made our way to the half-track. Professor Litona was with him.

"Michael," General Kulek said as he stopped directly in front of us, effectively halting our march, "we expect you to take charge when the squad has reached Death's Grave. We are hoping your unique tactical experience will provide our soldiers with the advantage they will need to successfully complete the mission."

"Yes, sir," I replied.

Then he turned to Ron. "We hope you don't get killed," was all he said. Then he turned to leave, but Ron spoke up.

"About that, sir; I'm not sure what I have to offer on this mission. Would it be better to send someone who is more familiar with this planet, such as Professor Litona, if I may be so bold as to suggest?"

"Nonsense," the general retorted. "Litona's expertise is required here. She is irreplaceable. Besides, your inclusion in this mission comes at the recommendations of Professor Litona and Doctor Dalmour. They are both impressed with your recent exploits, namely arriving on our planet and quickly learning how to use Doctor Dalmour's scanning machine," Then he mumbled, "And I think the doctor recommended you to keep you away from his scanning machine." Then in a normal tone, he added, "And I think it's best to keep you two together. Where you are going, you will need friends you can rely on."

I chimed in because I saw an opportunity to get the answer I had been wondering about. I was about to discover the answer came at the cost of some embarrassment. "So it's not because you and Litona are... you know... a thing?"

"I don't understand your question," General Kulek said plainly.

So I tried again. "You two aren't...um," I coughed awkwardly. "You aren't dating each other?"

He squinted his eyes and cocked his head to one side. His eyes looked at Ron, then back at me, as though he was still waiting for an explanation. He didn't understand.

"Are you and Professor Litona courting?" I said more directly.

He stood taller, squared his shoulders, and narrowed his eyes at me. "Absolutely not!" he growled. "I'm married," he said, holding his left ring finger upright for me to see. He wore a ring on that finger.

"And I'm not," Litona said irately, also holding her bare ring finger upright.

"So you are," I said, embarrassed. "Is that what that means?" They both glared at me, each with their ring fingers up – just their ring fingers. "And that closely resembles a gesture of disapproval back on Earth," I said timidly.

"A miscommunication, I'm sure," Ron said with a smirk.

General Kulek lowered his hand and said, "I believe you have a mission waiting for you."

I saluted, and we quickly marched away to our half-track.

"Try not to think too much, Mike," Ron said with a big smile. "Just go for the ride and relax. You've got two weeks to figure things out; four, actually, if you count the return trip."

"Yeah, yeah, yeah," I said, somewhat bitterly.

"Did you see the look on her face?" Ron jabbed.

"Yeah. I thought I was going to die," I answered grimly.

"I thought *I* was going to die," Ron said with a chuckle, "from laughing!"

I chuckled as well. "You punk."

"Seriously, though," Ron said as he gave me a playful shove, "I think she likes you."

"Huh. I was getting the opposite impression."

"Why do you think she made it a point to let you know she's single?"

I smiled. "You may be right."

Chapter 8 – The Crew

Ron and I boarded our assigned colossal half-track and sat down in the nearest empty bucket seats. The seats were mounted to the walls of the half-track and faced the center of the vehicle. We fastened our four-point seatbelts and looked around at the other crew members. They stared back at us.

I raised my hand to them and spread my fingers between my middle finger and ring finger with my thumb sticking out as I said, "Wud up, Edengonelings?"

A few of them tried to raise their hands in a similar manner, some with more success than others.

"Is that how you greet people on your planet?" asked a soldier of average build, buzzed light-brown hair, dark eyes, and a square jaw.

"Only among certain social circles," I answered with a smile.

"My name is Tinear," said the soldier. "I'm the squad leader and head commander of this operation until we get to Death's Grave."

"Yes, sir," I replied.

"Once we get to Death's Grave, you will be in command." Then he looked sternly at me and a fierce glint shot from his eye as he said, "I will hold you personally responsible for what happens to my squad."

"Understood," I said, equally as stern.

Then Tinear smiled and struck out a hand. "Welcome aboard," he said. Ron and I shook his hand. "Now that we've got that item of business over with, let me introduce you to the finest crew you will be spending the next two weeks with. In the driver's seat, we have Numigh. He's a dune racing champion on the weekends."

All I saw of Numigh from around the back of the driver's seat was a couple of large ears sticking out from a head of short, dirty-blonde hair and a hand that he raised and flicked in a jaunty manner.

Tinear continued, "Next to him is our navigator, Murlem. He is one of the best kite flyers on this side of the Demog Desert."

"What's a kite?" I asked, assuming it wasn't the same as a kite back on Earth.

"It's a high altitude recognizance drone used on the battlefront," Murlem explained. He had bright, vibrant eyes and black hair.

"He knows how the desert works," Tinear said. "He's familiar with wind patterns, sand movements, and how to find safe zones in a pinch. Numigh and Murlem will be cycling as drivers and taking turns sleeping in their seats. They will always be up in the front of the cab." Tinear turned around and pointed. "Then we have Colem. He's one of our cannon gunners."

Colem stood up from his seat and stepped forward with an outstretched hand. "Pleasure to meet you," he said, baring a fine set of teeth over a double-decker chin. He had a large, barrel-shaped torso, a face that was soft around the edges, light hair, and hazel eyes. I shook his outstretched hand.

"And our other cannon gunner is Saeui," Tinear said.

A shadow rose up to my right. I looked up at the tall, muscular figure beside me and found small eyes on either side of a large nose, all beneath a bald crown.

"Good guppy!" I exclaimed. "You're huge!"

Everyone laughed.

"And he's the runt in his family," Tinear chortled. "You should see his sisters. He's almost too big to fit in the gunner's seat."

"What did you say your name was?" I asked.

"Saeui," he said in a deep, clear voice and with a crooked grin.

"Say what?" I asked.

"Saeui," he repeated.

"Oo ee," I said.

"No. That's not it."

"Say your name," I requested.

"No, that's not it either. It's Saeui. It's pronounced 'say-oo-ee'," Saeui said with an amused smile.

"Oh. Got it. Saeui," I repeated.

Tinear pointed to another soldier sitting in the corner. "And that's John."

"There's a name I recognize," I said. "What do you do, John?"

John just stared at me like a statue with cold, close-set, light blue eyes and thin, tight lips. His dark brown hair was covered with a military cap.

"John doesn't say much," Tinear explained. "But he's an ace flak-gunner. We're lucky to have him."

"All of this was organized quickly; a little too quickly. You guys didn't just do this in the spur of the moment, did you?" I asked suspiciously.

"I don't understand your question or what a spur is, but this took years of planning and preparation," Tinear explained.

I raised my eyebrows. "But General Kulek said they hadn't thought of this until we showed up."

"That was just a smoke screen. They still weren't sure if you could be trusted. But now that we are about to be cut off from the rest of civilization, I can tell you the truth. We've been planning to destroy Death's Grave for a while, but destroying a structure, much less an entire facility, with a few soldiers is unprecedented on this planet. We have always fought wars in lines and only attacked soldiers. We've never attacked a building. Top-Command has been playing with a few ideas, but when you showed up and came up with the pincer attack, the general knew you were the man for the job. Top-Command spent months coming up with that maneuver, and these vehicles and cherub-suits were the prototypes for that attack, and you just casually suggested that like it was a walk to the convenience store. That's what got you here and got the gundon running. This was all a part of the plan. We just didn't have the know how to figure out details."

I nodded. Then I asked, "What's a gundon?"

A haunted expression clouded Tinear's countenance as he said, "They're difficult to describe, and they come in different shapes and sizes. You need to see one to know what it is. All I can say is that it's big, ugly, rare, and dangerous. Few people ever see one. Murlem claims to have seen one."

"I saw it out in the distance with my kite," Murlem explained. "It wasn't close enough for a good look. It was just a moving black dot on my screen; very big for how far away it was."

"I think it was just a fly on the camera lens," Tinear said with a knowing smile.

"I've been flying kites for years. I know when there's a fly on the camera," Murlem said in an annoyed tone. Clearly, that wasn't the first time he had been teased about that, and he expected to be teased again many times after.

"How far away is the desert?" Ron asked.

"About two hundred and fifty kililes," Murlem answered.

"How far is a kilile?" Ron asked.

I smiled. Not knowing how time, distances, and even mass are counted is difficult for a physicist. Time and distance were critical parts of Ron's life.

"It's about three thousands of these," John said as he stomped the floor.

"What?" Ron asked, confused by John's meaning. "Three thousand colossal half-tracks?"

John lifted his foot and pointed at it.

"Oh." Ron did some quick calculations in his head. "Assuming your foot is twelve inches, the Demog Desert is about one hundred and forty-two miles away, according to Earth measurements."

"But we aren't on Earth," Tinear pointed out.

"It's something he needs to figure out," I explained. "It was his job back home."

Ron had another scaling issue to figure out. "How long will it take us to get there?"

"We'll be using the hyper transport. So it will only be about an hour."

"How many hours are in a day?"

"Thirty-six," Tinear replied.

"I shouldn't have asked that. The planet is tidally locked. You wouldn't measure time by its rotation. Okay, how long is an hour?"

"Two hundred elioms."

"Then how long is an eliom?"

Tinear thought for a moment. "If you count ten kabahabuchillichubahabaks, that's an eliom."

Numigh started coughing and Murlem patted his back. I noticed a flick of a grin on Murlem's face and I suspected some kind of joke was in the making.

"Count a what?" Ron asked.

"Kabahabuchillichubahabak," Tinear repeated with a straight face.

"Oh. So, like counting Mississippi to find a second. Okay. One kabahabuchillichubahabak," Ron started. "Two kabahabuchillichubahabak."

122

There were several stifled snickers.

Ron kept going. "Three kabahabuchillichubahabak. Four kabahabuchillichubahabak."

Everyone was openly smiling by now.

"Five kabahabuchillichubahabak. Six kabahabuchillichubahabak."

There was audible laughter from everyone, including me. He sounded ridiculous.

Ron paused and looked around, confused, at all the laughing faces before he said, "Seven kabahabuchillichubahabak. Wait. What's a kabahabuchillichubahabak?"

The entire vehicle erupted with riotous laughter. Colem fell out of his seat and rolled on the floor. Ron looked at me, and I shrugged my shoulders. I was laughing, too; not as vigorously as the others, but purely because of the ridiculous spectacle they made. Eventually, their laughter began to slowly subside.

Then Ron repeated, "Really though, what's a kabahabuchillichubahabak?"

But this threw them into another fit of hysterical laughter.

After a few more rounds of laughter, Ron was no longer worrying about the time, and our small convoy of massive half-tracks began to move. We drove onto something that resembled a flat railcar. Then the entire platform our vehicles rested on, with us inside, slid sideways into the opening of a large tube, similar to the one that brought Ron and me from the arctic region to the city. Then a door rolled shut, and I began to feel the invisible force pushing me sideways in my seat, though it was not as violent as the first time, and Ron actually managed to stay conscious for the entire trip.

"This is the end of the line!" Tinear shouted as I felt the invisible force release me.

I felt tremors through the floor of the half-track. A door rolled open on the side of the tube, and the platform slid out. The only windows in the cab of the half-track were the windshield and the side windows next to Numigh and Murlem. I watched curiously through those small windows as we left the tube. The sight we saw surpassed any battle I had seen on Earth.

"Is that the battlefront?" I asked.

I saw vehicles and aircraft of the strangest varieties and sizes. Some of the war machines were mountainous, in a very literal sense. But beyond them, I could only imagine the horrors we would have seen if we were closer.

"It is," Tinear replied solemnly. "It may be the death of us all."

Fiery explosion after billowing, fiery explosion left a constant wall of smoke and flame at the frontline. Dirt, parts of machines, and who knows what else were flung into the air at a steady rate by the blasts. Aircraft plummeted, vehicles toppled, but more rushed in to take their places.

"Litona said these wars go on for hundreds of years. Has there ever been a temporary ceasefire?" I asked.

"A what?" Tinear asked, confused.

"I guess that answers my question," I said gravely.

"Do we have to go through that?" Ron asked, terrified.

"No," Murlem responded. "In fact, we will be going the opposite direction until we are out of range of their kites so that we aren't seen. Then we will turn sharp sunny-side."

"Sharp sunny-side?" I asked.

"We will turn into the desert," Murlem reiterated.

"That makes sense," Ron said. "They wouldn't use magnetic poles or the rising and setting sun to navigate by compass directions, because their planet always faces the same way and they live in a circumferential ring. They use the sun's steady position in the sky to navigate. The sun is their 'north star'."

"What's he going on about?" Colem asked me.

"Ron is discovering how you navigate," I answered with a bored, glazed look.

"It's a little more complicated navigating on the dark side," Murlem explained, happy to expound upon what Ron had said. "We have a sophisticated system of using the stars and correlating charts for finding our way around, depending on the time of the year." Then he paused. "And we still use the magnetic poles to navigate, as well."

Numigh started the engine, and our half-track rumbled as we drove off the loading platform. Our convoy was stopped at a gate where Murlem handed the attending guard some papers, and then we continued on our way. I wish I had a better view of our surroundings, the front windows were the only way of seeing the outside world. We drove on a path that resembled a highway held up on tall pillars. Vegetation was sparse and small. Windblown piles of sand were scattered about the landscape below.

After some time, Numigh took a ramp off the highway, and we entered a small town. The buildings we passed were clean, neat, and made of a material that almost looked like polished aluminum, but it had a sort of glassy shine to it. The architecture of the buildings was not simply square or rectangular or circular. It was more like rounded pillars staggered symmetrically next to each other.

People stood by and watched the colossal half-tracks growl past them. We eventually came to the edge of the town and pulled over at some sort of station. Lying before us was nothing but sand.

"There it is," Murlem said, "our wonderful home for the next few weeks."

I heard a gurgling sound from the floor and one of the rear side compartments.

"It sounds like they are filling us up," I noted.

"Yep. Everyone, canteens," Tinear ordered. "Fill them up. Drink them up. Fill them again. We need to take on as much water as we can in every way we can. I want you drinking so much right now that we should be fighting for our turn at the lavatory in ten minutes."

Numigh and Murlem passed their canteens back.

"Where do I refill my canteen?" Ron asked.

"Right there at the spigot," Tinear said. He pointed to a receptacle in one of the rear compartments. "Just press your canteen against the lever and it will refill."

Ron did so and noted, "Just like the soda fountains back home."

Saeui also refilled his canteen and took a drink. He raised his eyebrows. "They gave us the good stuff," he said. "This has been enriched."

"How so?" Ron asked.

"Vitamins and such to help us stay in top shape since we'll be cramped up in here for a while."

"How is that supposed to help?"

"You've heard of cabin fever, haven't you?" I asked. "People aren't meant to be cooped for too long. We start to go stir crazy. Staying healthy helps prevent that."

"Then I hope there will be something between here and there to shake things up," Ron said.

The gurgling sound stopped and we were on the move again, this time right into the sands of the desert.

As we hit the sand, the others gave each other a slap on the back of the head.

Colem slapped me on the back of the head and said, "It's for good luck."

I looked at Ron and gave him a good slap. "You're gonna need it," I said with a grin.

"Thanks," he said as he rubbed the back of his skull. That seemed to jog Ron's memory and curiosity. "Litona said these half-tracks are steam-powered."

"That's right," Tinear answered.

"She said they were heated by the ambient temperature. It isn't hot enough here to build up enough steam pressure. How are we moving?" Ron asked.

"You're right," Numigh stated. "We've been running on electric motors and will be until we get deeper into the desert."

"Why aren't these set up with solar panels so they could run on the electric motors for the entire distance?"

"Most of our desert machines are designed to run like that, but where we're going, the sun won't always be shining," Murlem explained. "When we get closer to the center of the desert, the sun will be blocked by dust clouds. There won't be enough light to power the electric motors, and the distance is too far for any other means of propulsion that we know of. This steam system lets us carry the same fluid that will power us and the machines."

"That makes sense," Ron said. "That would cut down on weight and improve your range. But why don't the steam engines just recharge the batteries for the motors?"

"Some efficiency is lost in the power transfer from the engine to the generator," Numigh explained, "and again from the generator to the batteries, and yet again from the batteries to the motors, still yet again from the motors through the drivetrain."

"You could have used a smaller steam engine," Ron argued. "That would have lightened the vehicle and reduced the power requirements."

"That system would work fine for a get-around-town car, but you are forgetting," Numigh countered, "this is a military vehicle. When we get into a situation where I need to put my foot down and get us moving, you'll be grateful for the larger engine. Trust me."

"I'm going to get some sleep," Murlem told Numigh. "You know where to go from here. Just keep the sun in front of us."

"Got it," Numigh replied.

Murlem reclined his seat and closed his eyes. The others settled in as well. John pulled out a book and began reading. Saeui released one of the hammocks from the wall, climbed in, and zipped it shut. Colem and Tinear rummaged through the provisions. I got comfortable, and I let my mind roam. I thought about the facility we were going to destroy, and I reviewed the maps and schematics in my head, as well as the plan of execution. Then I thought better. There would be plenty of time for that later. So I reviewed the events of the last few days. I thought of home, of my office, of the campus, the students, the call I got from Ron, New York, the fall down the elevator shaft, and this planet. This planet…this completely different sphere of life that we had never before considered, that Ron had discovered by the revelation of light floating around the same star as us, basking in the same light. Light… what is it? I understand that we only see such a very small part of it, but how far does it go? If we could see in all the colors of the entire light spectrum, from gamma rays to radio waves and beyond in both directions, what would we see?

Chapter 9 – Working Out The Bugs

It had been several days, by Earth's reckoning according to my wristwatch, since we had entered the Demog Desert, and still, we scooted through gentle waves of golden sand under an unfailing sun. The temperature had risen dangerously high, and Numigh had engaged the steam engine. Our great, iron behemoth trundled along with a steady purr issuing from its giant throat. Tinear and John were playing some sort of strategic game involving pegs placed into holes on a wooden board. Saeui was doing pushups in the middle of the cabin. Numigh slept while Murlem drove. I, too, was beginning to doze off in my seat.

Suddenly, the vehicle began to shake side to side. I held onto the grab bars mounted to the sides of my seat. The shaking steadily grew and became vicious. Colem was in a hammock, and the hammock began to swing wildly.

"Oof! Oof! Oof!" Colem barked each time his hammock swung against the wall.

Numigh woke up and took the wheel.

"Hey! Slow it down up there!" Tinear ordered.

"It isn't me, sir! The path is flat, and we are barely moving!" Numigh reported.

"Is it the wind?"

"Negative. We're in an eddy," Murlem replied.

"Ground tremors?"

"No, sir."

Everyone looked around, as though the answer or cause was somewhere on the walls and ceiling.

"Colossal one, come in, colossal one," the radio buzzed.

Murlem picked up the radio. "This is colossal one. We read you. Over."

"Colossal one, your half-track is shaking pretty bad. None of the other vehicles are experiencing that issue. You may have a problem with your vehicle. We suggest halting the convoy and examining your vehicle. Over."

Tinear nodded his approval.

"Copy that. Halting convoy. Over."

Numigh stopped the half-track, but the shaking persisted. "That's not good," he said. "That makes me think it's an engine problem." He turned off the engine, but the shaking still persisted.

I looked at Ron, who was sitting next to me. His current expression was familiar. Ron had a trick where he would hold a pencil sideways in his mouth and whistle like a bird. No one would suspect it was him because he had a pencil in his mouth, and everyone would look around for the bird. The expression on his face at that moment matched the same expression when he would make bird calls around a pencil. Then I remembered the incident with Dalmour's scanning machine and the explosion. I also remembered Dalmour saying that he "left well enough alone."

I discreetly jabbed Ron in the side. "Stop it!" I hissed.

The truck stopped shaking. I glared at Ron, and he looked back at me like a deer in the headlights.

"Are you two okay?" Tinear asked.

"Yes," I replied. "Ron just gets a little weird sometimes," I said in a censuring tone and with an accusing eye.

"Everything is going to be fine," Tinear reassured us. "We'll see if this isn't something we can't fix, and even in the worst case scenario, we'll transfer the water, munitions, and provisions from this vehicle to the others and divide us among the other half-tracks. I'll go outside and discuss our situation with the squad mechanic in colossal three." And with that, he slipped into a cherub-suit and entered the airlock.

"How long have you been able to do that?" I asked Ron in a hushed whisper.

"A few days now," Ron replied. "Edengone days, I mean. It gets really boring sitting in a truck for days on end. It's what has kept me from going crazy. I first noticed it with a fork I was holding, and I've been slowly working up to bigger things. Today was the first time I shook the half-track."

"You should probably keep that to yourself for the rest of the trip. We don't want anyone blaming you for something you didn't do," I cautioned.

"Would they do that?" he asked nervously.

"I've seen people do a lot of crazy things when situations get tense," I replied seriously.

"Alright," he answered. "By the way, have you noticed your hammock swaying more than usual?"

"Yes," I growled, annoyed. "I just thought I had the bad luck of taking my turn to sleep when we hit rough terrain."

"Sorry," Ron said apologetically.

"How do you do it?" I asked.

"I'm not sure. It's like moving a limb, I guess. When you move a finger or an arm, you focus on that limb and… and move. To move something else, I focus on it and," he shrugged, "it moves. I don't really understand it."

Tinear and the mechanic had raised the hood and kneeled on the giant fenders as they leaned over the engine compartment. Now our only view of the outside world was blocked by another great chunk of steel. Ron was not the only one bored of sitting in a giant breadbox. I could feel it beginning to wear on me, too. We quietly waited until the hood was lowered back down and Tinear and the mechanic walked back around the half-track.

Tinear came back through the airlock and climbed out of this cherub-suit. "The mechanic says everything checks out," he reported cheerily. "He figures it's just a really bad air pocket in the system that needs to be worked loose. Go ahead and fire her up, Numigh."

Numigh started the engine and everything was normal again. Tinear shrugged his shoulders. "Let's get going," he said.

We started moving and climbed up to the crest of a small dune.

"Whoa. Stop. Stop!" Murlem said urgently.

The vehicle came to an abrupt stop.

"Colossal one, is everything alright? Over," the radio asked.

Murlem answered the radio. "Affirmative. We are re-charting our course. Standby." He hung up the radio and pointed to a dune in front of us. "There's something wrong with that dune. Do you see how all of the other dunes have the steep side blown away from us? Why is that one smooth? Both dunes right next to it on either side are normal, but that one spot… I suspect it may be a sinkhole. Veer far left and we will cross over at that saddle." He pointed to a different pair of dunes in the distance and picked up the radio. "This is colossal one. Be aware, there is a sinkhole straight ahead. We are taking a different route. Follow our lead. Over."

We began to pick up speed across the soft sands. All seemed well and fine, but as we passed the questionable dune, the vehicle began to shake again. I gave Ron a sharp jab.

"That isn't me!" he hissed at me.

"Crabapples and sea cucumbers! This isn't what we need," Tinear growled as he reached for the radio. "This is colossal one. We're experiencing mechanical issues again. Colossal three, please advise. Should we halt for repairs? Over."

"Negative, colossal one," the radio replied. "Our vehicles are shaking, too. It's not mechanical."

Murlem studied several sensor readings on the dashboard. "It's ground tremors, sir," he said, "but they are right on the surface. It's not like an earthquake. It's more like a bomb exploding…for a really long time."

"Which direction is it coming from?" Tinear asked.

Murlem studied the readings again before he said, "That way." He pointed at the smooth dune.

The vehicle bucked and rocked suddenly. Then the sand around the smooth dune bounced and spew up into the air in fast bursts that grew higher and higher and threw more and more sand with each eruption. Two tall, slender, black pillars sprouted from the tossing sand, followed by two more. The pillars toppled over and braced against the ground. Then the smooth dune heaved and an enormous set of black jaws rose from the ground. The creature that belonged to those jaws emerged and lifted its great hulk from the ground. It looked at us. Sand rolled off its huge shell and around its giant, unblinking eyes. It was like a black, streamlined, camping trailer the size of a motel standing on stilts, with enormous jaws.

"That is a BIG Hercules beetle!" Ron exclaimed, evidently seeing a resemblance to something on Earth.

"It's a gundon!" Murlem shouted in terror.

The beetle started to chase after us, and Numigh slammed his foot to the floor. The half-track roared into life and dug its tracks and treads deep into the sand as it launched forward, throwing the rest of us off balance and to the floor.

"Battle stations!" Tinear ordered.

Saeui pulled a lever on the ceiling, and three seats lowered down from each of the turreted guns on the roof. Saeui, Colem, and John jumped into the seats and they were lifted up into the gunning turrets.

Tinear grabbed the radio. "All units, spread out. Drive to the side of the gundon's path to give all your gunners a clear shot. Focus fire on the eyes." He flipped a panel on the wall to reveal a monitor that showed him what the gunners were seeing. He scrolled through the gunners' different positions and observed the effects of the shots. "The shells are just bouncing off!" he yelled. "Connoneers, load explosive rounds! Take out its eyes!"

I watched over Tinear's shoulder as the beast's face was engulfed by repetitive fireballs. The creature reared up in pain. Then it came down again and pushed its head under the sand. It kept pushing, all the while chasing us until its entire body was covered under the sand, and it kept coming, like a wave. I watched the bulge in the ground chase after one of the other half-tracks.

"This thing isn't going to leave us alone," Tinear said.

The beetle was right under one of the vehicles. It burst from the sand, tossing its head sideways and catching the half-track in its massive, pincer-like jaws. It lifted the vehicle from the ground and clamped down around the armor plating again and again. The vehicle's armor held, for the moment.

"Numigh, stop the half-track!" Tinear ordered.

We came to a sliding stop. Tinear threw open the doors to the floor compartment and pulled out something very similar to a rocket-propelled grenade launcher.

"These are armor busters. Very expensive and very effective," he explained as he pulled out three launchers and three small rockets. "They are rocket-propelled and use a proximity sensor to know when to fire a depleted uranium core that punctures the armor

137

just before the rocket strikes with the high-explosive part of the package deal." He handed a loaded launcher to both Ron and me. "Point, pull the trigger, and don't miss. Not here!" He stopped Ron from trying a dry fire practice, with a loaded rocket. "I will shoot first. If my shot is ineffective, Mike will shoot next, then Ron. Get into your cherub-suits, and let's get out there!"

We quickly jumped into our cherub-suits and lined up at the airlock. Tinear was the first to go out. I went next. The door to the cabin closed behind me and the door to the outside opened. For the first time in several days, the sun shone down on me. I ran out and was engulfed by the glowing, yellow sand and brilliant, blue sky. I followed Tinear. He was already a good distance away and I raced to catch up. The giant beetle loomed before us, tossing and crushing the colossal half-track in its powerful jaws.

Tinear stopped, dropped to a knee, placed the launcher on his shoulder, and took aim.

"Eat crack, you soggling saggot!" Tinear yelled at the bug before he fired the rocket.

The rocket ignited and raced away with an angry hiss. The projectile hit its mark with spectacular effect. We could hear the bug's shell crack when the rocket's core punctured the gundon's head, as advertised. Then the payload detonated, and a shower of bug juice poured down. The enormous corps crumpled to the ground with a crash that gently shook the unstable sand around us.

"Nice shot," I said.

Then we heard a loud hiss and a roar from behind us, and we watched another rocket fly over the sand and hit the dead, giant beetle in the rump with another resounding crack and a spray of bug juice. We turned around and stared at Ron, who looked back at us with large, surprised eyes and an empty launcher.

"You too," I said.

"I'm sor-. I didn't mea-." He shuffled awkwardly. "Thanks," Ron said, still looking stunned.

I turned back to Tinear, and then I asked, "What's a soggling saggot?"

Tinear looked at me with a sheepish grin and said, "Just don't tell my mother I said that."

We quickly ran to the damaged half-track. Numigh drove alongside us. He slowed down to let us jump onto the running boards and hang on to the outside grab handles to catch a ride. We met the other half-tracks at the jaws of the beetle. Other soldiers from the other vehicles had put on their cherub-suits and were already working on getting into the crushed half-track, which was now on its roof in a crater of sand.

"Which crew is this?" Tinear asked.

"Colossal four, sir," one of the soldiers replied.

The tracks dangled from their rollers crookedly. Oil blacked the sand around the engine. The axles were bent up into the air. The armor had been badly dented and a few tears had me worried that the crew may have been exposed to the blistering heat, or worse. One of the soldiers had a plasma cutter and was working his way through the mangled airlock. The hatch fell free and a couple of other soldiers rushed in. They soon emerged again, helping a few crew members of colossal four to get out. To my relief, they were in their cherub-suits.

One of the better fairing soldiers from colossal four approached Tinear. "Sir, crew commander Azer, reporting."

"How is your crew?" Tinear asked.

"Minor injuries, sir. I had the crew get into cherub-suits when it was clear the gundon was after us. Its jaws broke the windshield when it picked us up. Then the heat rushed in and the air in the cabin glowed like fire for an instant. It was a wild ride, sir!"

"You saved your crew, Azer. Good work," Tinear said. "Alright! Salvage what you can from colossal four. We need to abandon the vehicle. Transfer the remaining water to the other half-tracks. Crew four will ride with colossal three. I want this gundon to reimburse us." Tinear announced. "I want as much of this animal's shell and meat as we can carry. Reinforce the vehicles' armor and make some flak jackets with pieces of its shell. Use the meat to restock our provisions. Let the meat sit out for a few minutes on the vehicles' hoods to cook before packing it up. Let's cut up this gundon!"

Soldiers with plasma cutters began cutting out portions of the giant beetle's shell. The smaller pieces were taken into the vehicles to be fitted into combat armor, and the larger pieces were fitted to the tops and sides of the half-tracks where they were tied down using the sinews from the bug's leg joints. The sinews were laced through small holes cut into the shell pieces and tied to the half-track's many tie-down points. Once the armor was fastened to the vehicles, then the outer layers of the sinews were carefully slit open. The inner sinews dried out in the heat and tightened their hold as they shrunk.

Ron and I helped cut and carry the exposed meat from the areas where the shell had been removed. We threw the raw meat up to a soldier sitting on the hood of the nearest half-track where he placed it on the hot hood and threw down the meat that had finished cooking.

"Just like a barbeque," I said.

After we had cooked and packed as much bug meat as the vehicle's compartments could hold and the outer armor had been covered in the beetle's shell, we began filing back into the half-tracks. I removed my cherub-suit and sat down. I had enjoyed the little break from the confines of our half-track. I looked toward the windshield and noticed a black spire mounted to the front of our half-track like a hood ornament.

"What's that?" I asked, pointing at the big, black spike.

"That's our hunting trophy," Murlem replied as he kicked his feet up onto the dashboard and reclined. "I cut the tip off the gundon's horn and mounted it up there. I thought it completed our half-track's new outfit."

141

I smiled and reached for a piece of the cooked bug meat. I bit into it and chewed thoughtfully.

"What does it taste like?" Saeui asked.

I thought for a moment. "Like fast-food chicken," I replied.

Ron laughed.

"What is 'fast-food'?" Saeui asked.

"It's like regular food, but gross. Some people like it." I looked at the chunk of meat. "It needs sauce."

Our convoy began moving again, and it would be several Edengone days before anything besides mile after mile of gentle rolling sands would appear through the windshield.

Chapter 10 – The Gates Of Hail

Several Edengone days later, lethargy was the epidemic, and it was plain that the lack of activity was wearing down the other crew members. John stared wide-eyed at the wall across from him. Tinear disassembled a rifle, reassembled it, and repeated the process over and over, with his eyes closed. Murlem spun a magnetic compass and watched the needle continue to point the same direction. Numigh drove with one hand and rested his head on the other with his elbow on the armrest. Saeui twirled a pen through his fingers, over, under, over, under, and then back again. Colem looked around the cabin through the wrong end of a pair of binoculars. And Ron was making a piece of paper levitate just above the chair next to him with his mind. It wasn't hovering high enough for anyone else to take notice. The paper gently pulsated with the little explosions I could only imagine Ron was using to keep the paper from touching the chair.

The half-track reared up as we began climbing the next sand dune. It was a particularly high dune, and I felt the need to prop myself up because of muscle fatigue from trying to stay in my seat. As we reached the top, Numigh raised his head.

"Whoa," he said.

"It's alright. We were expecting this," Murlem said as he stopped spinning the compass.

Everyone else arose and gathered behind Numigh and Murlem. We looked out through the windshield across the sandy waves in a golden, desert sea of dunes and saw something that looked like a thick, brown fog churning across the horizon.

"What is that?" I asked.

"A never-ending sand storm," Murlem replied. "The cool air from the arctic region moves across the habitable zone and into the desert where the heat causes it to rise rapidly. The winds we've been experiencing are just the air coming in to fill the low-pressure regions caused by this," he pointed at the storm. "This is where it gets hot enough to really shake things up. Combine the heat with all the air that was spread out across the circumference of the planet as it comes together toward a concentrated point and we get a storm with an attitude."

"All the winds of Edengone are crashing together," Saeui said in wonder.

"That is the beginning of uncharted terrain," Murlem stated. "We suspect it will get worse before we get to the Bull's Eye. Safe zones are going to be difficult to find. We will need to make the most of them when we find them."

The half-track bucked a little as we began our descent. We continued staring at the storm ahead of us until we descended below the tops of the other dunes.

More days passed by as slowly as we passed dune after dune. After a few days, we noticed the sand was snaking its way across the surface of the dunes, like a ghostly sidewinder blown by the growing winds. About a day later, we noticed that the sand was lifting off the ground and somersaulting through the air. The brown fog of the never-ending sand storm peaked over the dunes in the distance more often. Then, many more miles later, the sand was whirling about us, and visibility was reduced from the horizon to only a few miles.

Murlem's predictions were correct. Safe zones were difficult to find and constantly changing. After stopping to let the condensers catch up on reclaiming water for the engine, we often needed to put on the cherub-suits to get out of the half-tracks and dig away the sand that had blown in around the tracks and rollers.

Within another couple of days, we were driving through the dark, brown storm, with dust and dirt rushing all around us. We were nearly driving blind.

Murlem had a sonar screen in front of him that gave him a rough idea of the terrain ahead, which he relayed to Numigh. The brown became so thick and uniform that Numigh had given up trying to see anything through the windshield, and he just looked over Murlem's shoulder at the sonar to know where to go.

"It's like driving through a cesspool," Ron said, squinting into the brown screen ahead of us.

"Do I want to ask how you know that?" I asked rhetorically.

A loud thud overhead startled us, and we looked up.

"What was that?" I asked.

A moment or two passed before there was another heavy thud on the roof, shortly followed by another, then another, then a few more. Soon, the cabin was filled with the sound of rapid and repetitive thuds.

"It sounds like river dancers wearing iron diving boots," Ron said.

"Where are you getting these similes?" I asked. "They can't be from actual experience."

"What the hail!?" Ron shouted.

"Whoa, calm down. I didn't mean any offense."

"No!" Ron shouted. "It's hail!" He pointed past me and out the windshield, which Numigh and Murlem were not looking through, because they were studying the sonar to see where we were going.

We all watched small clumps of sand fall and dash against the gundon shell we had used to reinforce the armor.

"It's hailing sand," Murlem said with surprise.

"I take it this is as unusual on your planet as it is on ours," I said.

"I don't think this happens anywhere on our planet," Ron corrected me.

"Yes," Murlem replied. "It must be the sand that has been lifted into the upper atmosphere and collected together with the cooler moister up there until the sand is too heavy for the rising air to hold it up. Then the sand falls in clumps, with the water drying out of the clumps once it reaches the lower, hotter altitudes."

"I was thinking almost the exact same thing," I lied, completely uninterested.

"Almost like a regular hail storm," Ron noted.

"Except I could see this becoming really dangerous," Murlem said with concern. "Water expands when it freezes and becomes less dense, meaning it weighs less than a ball of liquid water of equal volume."

"What's your point?" Ron asked.

"The sand isn't changing states, which means its density isn't changing."

"Which means…" Ron implied a question.

Murlem turned around in his seat and looked at Ron. "Which means these sand-hail stones could get very heavy and do a lot more damage."

Ron's eyebrows jumped up his forehead as he suddenly understood, and he nodded in agreement. "Oh. A sharp decrease in the surface area to mass ratio would mean less air resistance per weight unit on a falling body, permitting a higher terminal velocity and increasing the kinetic force of the falling bodies to a greater magnitude than they otherwise would be, and within a more focused area nonetheless."

"Careful, Ron," I cautioned sarcastically. "You could hurt someone with talk like that."

"It's a good thing we are inside," Ron said, acting like he hadn't heard me.

"Maybe you've forgotten how often we've needed to go outside to dig out the half-tracks," Murlem reminded us.

We all stared at him in sober silence. We realized how dangerous our plight was becoming.

"We need to figure out a way to protect ourselves when we go out, as well as a way to minimize how often we go out," Tinear stated.

"We can make some shields from the remaining gundon shells and use them like umbrellas," Colem suggested.

Murlem turned in his seat. "We can reduce our average speed to cut down water consumption. That would help bring our water usage rates as near to equal as possible to the condensers' replenishing rates to reduce how often we will need to stop to let the condensers refill our tanks. That means we will be in this storm longer, but we should be able to cover more ground before needing to stop, thereby reducing how often we need to leave the safety of our armor," Murlem said casually.

"I like it," Tinear said. "Pass that info on to the other crews and have them do the same. The rest of you, take whatever rigid, flat scraps you can find and strap them to the shovel blades to broaden them so we can move more sand and cut down the time we need to spend outside."

We began digging around under the seats and through the storage compartments for anything that would move dirt and lashed them to the shovels with rope and bug sinew. All the while, the thudding overhead from the sand-hail grew louder.

A sudden, high-pitched thud with a fragile ring to it caused us to stop and look around. Both Numigh and Murlem were hunched down in their seats with their arms blocking their faces.

"What was that?" Saeui asked.

Numigh slowly peeked over his arms and said, "It was some of that sand-hail stuff hitting the windshield. We should put a gundon shell on the windshield, too, just to be safe. Covering the side windows couldn't hurt either. I can't see anything out there anyway."

"Right. We need to get some cover first," Tinear said. "Murlem, radio the other vehicles. Tell them we will be stopping in five to fit gundon shells on the windshields and they need to have shields ready to go out. Everyone else, get your umbrellas ready."

We lashed handles to the smaller bug shells and then began preparing a larger piece to be mounted to the half-track's windshield. Once everything was ready, Tinear stood up.

"Alright! Suit up," Tinear ordered. "We're going out. Stay right against the vehicle. Visibility is near zero and we don't want anyone getting lost."

We put on the cherub-suits and armed ourselves with bug shields and tools. The half-track slowly stopped and we filed out of the vehicle one at a time, as fast as the airlock would allow. My turn came up, and I stepped into the airlock. The door shut behind me. I could hear the cabin air being drawn back into the cab and the scorching desert air entering with an angry, seething hiss. The airlock door opened and sand blew around me. I exited the airlock with my bug shield held over me. I felt the sand-hail strike the shell with heavy blows. I fought to stay upright in the raging, swirling winds as it rushed around the half-track, making it unpredictable and difficult to know which way to lean. I could hear the sand scratching against my suit as it rushed around me in thick, brown airstreams. With the same shade of brown all around me, it would have been difficult to say which way was up. I stayed close to the half-track and ran my hand along its side to keep me stable while I made my way to the front. I met some of the others, who had already begun mounting the shells.

We worked in two-man teams. One handed over their shield to the other and worked on mounting the shell while the other held both shells over both of themselves. I teamed up with John and held the shields while he quickly went to work mounting the pieces to the half-track. If staying upright hadn't been difficult already, holding the shields in that fierce desert wind was like trying to hold on to an umbrella in a storm, but with dangerous consequences, if I lost the fight.

The gundon shells mounted over the windshield were suspended above the windshield like a visor or the bill of a baseball cap. The shells on the side windows were laid flat against the glass, blocking them completely.

"I'm finished," John announced.

He took his shield again. We moved around the vehicle to help the others when Colem's voice came over our suits' radios.

"I need help," he said calmly. "I got blown over, and when I got up... I can't see the half-track. I can't see anything."

"Just stay put," I quickly said. "You can't be far. We'll find you."

"What do we do?" Tinear asked.

"The same thing we would do if we were pulling him out of a fast river," I replied. "We make a human chain." I got on the radio so everyone else, including Colem, could hear my instructions. "Everyone, put your shields in your right arm. With your left arm, hold on to the person next to you by their right elbow. Saeui, hold on to the half-track. The human chain starts with you," I said, noting that he was the largest and probably the strongest among us. "We will stretch the chain out away from the half-track and walk around the vehicle. One of us is bound to walk into him. When you do, do not let go of the person next to you. Tell us you have him, and we will all pull back to the vehicle. Clear?"

"Yes, sir," came the unanimous reply.

"Let's go."

According to my instructions, we made a human chain. I was the furthest link from the half-track, and I could not see the colossal vehicle that I knew stood only a few yards away through the blowing sand. My arm was growing tired and sore from holding my shield up against the constant barrage of pounding sand-hail. We walked slowly around the half-track. It was one of those moments in life that lasts only minutes but feels so much longer. At last, I heard Ron shout out that he had found Colem.

"Saeui, pull us in," I ordered.

We pulled together until we were all back against the half-track. We made our way back inside the vehicle through the airlock. We removed our cherub-suits and settled back into our seats. Suddenly, a loud bang forcefully pulled our attention to the front of the cab where Numigh and Murlem were both hiding behind there raised arms again. The gundon shells over the windshield had swung down under the beating of the sand-hail, completely covering the glass the same way the side windows were covered.

Numigh slowly peeked over his raised arms. Then he let his arms drop to his side. "You know what? That's fine. That's just fine," he repeated, raising a hand toward the blocked windshield and shrugging his shoulders. "There wasn't anything to look at out there anyway." He took hold of the steering wheel, looked down at the sonar screen, and pressed the accelerator. We were on the move again.

Ron studied the outsides of the cherub-suits carefully and said, "Let's hope we don't need to go out too often." He held up the suit. "I don't know how much more wear and tear these suits can take. They've been badly sandblasted."

"Maybe we can put flak jackets over the outside and wrap the arms and legs in… something," Colem suggested as he looked around the cab. "What do you think?"

I looked at John. He caught my stare and stared back. "How about you, John? What do you think?" I asked.

John silently stared at me.

"About the suits," I added, thinking that maybe he wasn't listening to the conversation. "What do you think we should do about the suits?"

He shrugged his shoulders.

I nodded and wondered how he could be so silent. Was he indifferent? Was something wrong with him? Was he planning something?

Tinear folded his arms and leaned back in his seat. "That's something to think about," he said carelessly, and he closed his eyes.

"Is no one concerned about the suits?" Ron asked.

A few of them looked at Ron with blank expressions.

Murlem spoke. "Professor Litona designed those suits. She's very good at what she does. I think she considered the sandstorms when she made those."

John almost smiled.

"Oh," Ron said meekly.

Chapter 11 – The Eye Of The Bull

Two more Edengone days had passed since we had entered the sand-hail region and covered the windows with bug shells. Thanks to our slower pace, we had only needed to stop once more. And thanks to our slower pace, we felt like we had been cooped up for longer than usual. The sand dunes had become less extreme, and the howling wind more so. The pounding from the sand-hail beat steadily. The engine of the half-track gently purred. The wind, engine, and sand-hail all came together to make a symphony of melancholy.

Boredom was the illness that took its course within our cab, and peculiarity was the symptom. Saeui lied in a hammock and slowly ran the zipper back and forth as he watched the zipper's teeth interlock and break free again with each pass of the pull. Murlem was asleep in his upright chair with his head tossed back and his mouth opened toward the ceiling, gurgling. It sounded like he had a pool of spit in the back of his throat. He inhaled through his nose and exhaled through his mouth with a bubbling sound. Numigh carefully studied the sonar screen to know what kind of terrain lay ahead. John was re-reading a book that I had seen him already finish two other times on that trip. Tinear was also reading. I bent down and acted like I was scratching my ankle so I could get a look at the title, but when the title came into view, I was disappointingly reminded that though the Edengonelings spoke our language, they did not write in our language. All I could gather from the green and black cover was a series of squiggles. I sat back up and looked at Ron. He had a sheet of paper that looked like it had been folded several times already, and he was folding it crossways, unfolding, folding diagonally, holding that fold, and so forth until he had made a small origami cube. He placed a flat hand out with the palm up and set the little, paper cube in the middle of his palm. Then he concentrated. He stared at the little cube for a few moments. The cube suddenly heaved and unfolded into a flat piece of paper again. He was improving at controlling his new abilities.

154

The half-track rolled lazily over the gentle dunes. Colem was lying on his back in the middle of the floor, staring at the ceiling with a glazed look in his eyes.

Then he spoke. "There was a girl back home…"

"Uh-oh! He broke." Tinear said excitedly, as he looked up from his book. "Who bet Colem would be the first to talk about girls?"

"That's mine. Pay up," Saeui said. He reached a hand out from his hammock. Everyone else passed their lost bets to him.

Colem continued. "I can see her there, standing on the shores of Lake Tacala; a vision, a dream, and the envy of angles. She had eyes like fire-stones, hair like the rolling brook in a golden sunset, and the touch of her hands… Her hands were soft…" he said dreamily as he looked at his hand, "so soft." He gently touched his own face.

"Snap out of it," Saeui said, and he threw a pillow at Colem.

Colem looked up with a sheepish grin. "What about you, then?" he asked. "Tell us about your girl."

Saeui sighed with a scowl directed at no one and retreated into his hammock. "She was a chronic liar," he said with a glum grumble.

"Uuuooohhh," everyone said sympathetically. "Wow," "Ouch," "That's too bad," "Sorry, mate," and other such half-hearted condolences were offered from around the cab.

Colem sat up and looked around. "Hey, wake up Murlem. He's always chasing some girl," he said.

Numigh reached over and gave Murlem's shoulder a few rough shoves. Murlem awoke with a cough and a sputter of spittle. "Ahem! Eh? What?"

"Tell us about your girl," Colem requested.

"Oh, yes. My girl. Hmm. She was a girl," Murlem said and then yawned.

"Well, that's a good start," Tinear said with a chuckle.

Murlem continued. "She was the girl of my dreams. Mmm," he said dreamily and with a slight smile. "She was the girl *in* my dreams before you interrupted. I hope I can find her again," he said sleepily, and he settled deeper into his chair.

"Oh, come on!" Colem protested. Murlem didn't respond. "Fine. Go get her, tiger," Colem said, disappointed.

"Mmm. Thank you," Murlem mumbled as he began dozing off again.

"What about Mike? Do you have your eye on anyone? What are the women like on Earth?" Numigh asked.

"Well," I said musingly. "Nah. There's no one."

"Yes, there is," Ron announced with a mischievous grin.

The others egged me on.

"Alright," I conceded. "There is this girl... No, not a girl. 'Girl' is too weak for her. There is a *woman*.

Man!" I exclaimed. "There is a *womanly* woman," I said emphatically. Then I paused and acted like I was reflecting upon this vision.

"You cheesecake! Go on!" Murlem shouted, sounding annoyed at first and then eager, and suddenly very awake.

"Light-brown eyes," I began in a sultry tone. "Rich, chestnut hair. Fair complexion. Graceful in form and movement. Intelligent," I nodded. "Very intelligent. Impressively intelligent. *Magnificently* intell-"

"Go on!" a few of them shouted.

So I continued. "Attitude. Sassy, knows-she's-right sort of attitude. And she is; she's right. And when she's angry, she is both beautiful and terrifying, like a storm rolling in from the horizon over a still sea."

"Wait," John sat up. "Does she wear glasses?"

"Yes, actually, she does."

Colem jumped to his feet with a smile of triumph across his face. "It's Professor Litona!"

I raised an eyebrow and huffed as though that were ridiculous. They all stared at me. I put on my best poker face, but, despite my best efforts, something must have given it away. They all erupted with boisterous laughter. I looked at Ron, and he shrugged.

Colem started dancing mockingly as he sang, "Mike and the pro-fess-sor, nothing more and nothing less-er!"

Some of the others made kissy noises while Colem continued dancing amidst the laughter.

157

I took hold of Colem's shirt and pulled him into a chair. "Sit down before you embarrass yourself," I said in good humor, and I laughed with them. "'Nothing more, nothing lesser'?" I repeated. "What the halibut is that supposed to mean?"

Colem had that deer-in-the-headlights look. "Nothing. It just – It just rhymes with 'professor'," he confessed with a shrug.

Then something jarred the vehicle, and we all jumped.

"Numigh?" Tinear inquired.

"Hang on." Numigh turned some dials on the sonar as the vehicle jarred again. "Just rocks, sir. Looks like we are running out of sand," he reported.

I listened. "It sounds like the sand-hail is letting up a little," I pointed out.

Murlem studied some gauges and dials on the dashboard. "The temperature is rising quickly. So is the barometer. Wind speeds are increasing. We were expecting this as well, but not to this extreme," he said.

"Will this be a problem?" Tinear asked.

"I don't think so, but I won't know what to expect from this point on until we are heading back to the habitable zone," Murlem replied.

Tinear nodded. "Keep a close eye on changing conditions and let me know of anything that may be a problem."

"Yes, sir," Murlem answered.

The colossal half-track trundled on with the pounding from the sand-hail slowly letting up and the jolts from running over rocks becoming more frequent until the pounding had stopped completely and the dominating sound was the vehicle's suspension working hard to get us over the rocky terrain.

"I think I preferred the noisy sand-hail over this," Ron said, while the jolts and vibrations jiggled the softer parts of his face.

I smiled. "This isn't bad," I informed him. "This is nice compared to some other things I've been in. This floats like a broken Cadillac."

Ron rolled his eyes. I picked up a folded blanket and handed it to him.

"Here," I said, offering the folded blanket. "Set this on your seat. Military chairs are for toughened rumps. These chairs were never intended to carry an office bum," I said with a smirk.

"I'm not an office bum," he protested. "I walk to the cafeteria and back every day, at least twice." He put the folded blanket on the seat and fluffed it up a bit. Then he sat down. He raised his eyebrows with surprised approval. "Better," he said. "Thanks."

"Whoa," Numigh uttered. He studied the sonar closer and made adjustments to some dials.

"What is it?" Tinear asked.

"I'm not sure. It looks like the bottom of a cliff or maybe just a large ledge. Either way, I can't see past it and I can't see a way around it. I'll need to get out of the vehicle to see what it is," Numigh explained.

Tinear stood up and rummaged through one of the storage compartments until he pulled out two coils of rope.

"I'm going with you," Tinear said to Numigh. "We'll tie these to the half-track so we can scout out a little ways and still find our way back."

They both put on cherub-suits and exited the vehicle. The rest of us just sat and waited. It wasn't long before Tinear came back through the airlock.

"Give me the tool bag," he ordered, "and look out through the windshield. We're going to remove the gundon shells, and you'll want to see this." Then he left with the tools.

A few moments later, we heard some scuffling near the front of the cab. The bug shells that covered the windshield lifted and pulled away as Tinear and Numigh removed them. The view it suddenly revealed was nearly unbelievable, like we had gone to another planet – one other than Earth or Edengone. There was a ledge, the one Numigh saw on the sonar, of red stone in front of us that barely peeked over the hood of the half-track. But above and beyond that lay an unworldly landscape, miles and miles, maybe hundreds of miles of sand and more red stone in forms and structures I had never seen before. All of the bare stone was smooth, like it had been polished. If the sun had been permitted to shine there, I'm sure the stone would have had a glossy sheen.

Dominating the scene was a looming mountain of golden sand that must have stood well over two thousand feet tall from base to peak. Surrounding this mountain was a field of tall, meanly jagged stone outcroppings, the sharp points of which all pointed away from the mountain of sand. Across this forsaken field of leaning spikes and spires were rivers of blowing sand, all running toward the mountain. And then the rivers of sand flowed *up* the mountain through its several ravines until they met at the peak. Atop the peak swirled a twisting funnel of sand, a tornado, that seemed content, maybe even proud to be on its throne of chewed up, infertile dirt. The twister rose to the heavens where it broadened out to meet the dusty blanket of brown clouds above. The air was clear, except for in the rivers of sand and across the sky above us, so that we could see clearly across the red, rocky fields from our point all the way to the other side where a wall of sand indicated the edge of the never-ending storm, which wrapped all the way around the central mountain of sand and its tornado-crown.

"It's like the eye of a hurricane," Ron stated. "The storm rages all around us, but here, the air is still."

"It looks more like we are in a dome than an eye," Murlem added. "See how the sand is drawn to the mountain where it's lifted into the atmosphere and spread out and away until it falls back down, probably as sand hail? And it leaves this eerie, very brown, dead dome."

"Where does that mountain sit in relation to the rest of the planet?" I asked suspiciously. I already had a good idea about what the answer would be.

Murlem checked a few instruments. Then he looked up in amazement. "That's the Bull's-Eye, the center of the Demog Desert," he said.

"So the Bull's-Eye is not a bottomless pit like General Kulek had believed," Ron noted. "Which means this planet is not a flying doughnut, but more like a, uh... a Death inducing Star with an outie bellybutton." Ron's words bumbled out of his mouth.

I huffed. "Just because you *tried* to avoid using a pop-culture movie reference that no one else here would understand, I will act like that wasn't the weirdest thing you've said on this planet," I joked.

"Thank you," Ron mumbled.

"Don't mention it... ever again."

Tinear leaned over and peered in at us through the windshield. "Why don't you all come out here and get a better look?" he suggested. "Besides, we're going to need everyone scouting for a way around this. This is a bigger problem than we thought. In fact, make that an order." He turned on his suit's radio to contact the other two vehicles. "Everyone out."

In a few minutes, everyone was out of their half-tracks and had split into teams to scout out a way around the stone ledge. Some went back the way we had come to see if there was another path we could take. Some went off to the flanks, and some tried going ahead to

162

find a path that would lead back to the vehicles, like trying to solve a maze by starting at the end instead of the beginning. A couple of military engineers were standing by the ledge, deep in discussion and using a lot of hand motions to communicate their ideas. Numigh and Murlem had climbed on top of the roof of the half-track and, from their vantage point, they tried to read the land to plot a course through the jagged terrain.

I had teamed up with Ron and Colem, and we were one of the teams that went ahead to find a promising path that would take us deeper into the field of red stones.

"Why do you think all these spires and spikes point away from the mountain?" I asked.

Ron was quick to answer. "I was wondering the same thing. I think if you look at the direction the sand is flowing," he pointed around at the landscape and the rivers of sand, "you will see it's caused by erosion. The blowing sand has slowly worn away the softer parts of the stone and left these sharp, harder parts. And since the sand is blowing toward the mountain it would... make sense... that... No, wait. That doesn't work." His arms slumped in defeat. "I don't know."

Colem looked around. "I think it looks like an explosion; a really big explosion, centered on the mountain," he said gravely.

"Do you think the mountain had something to do with it?" Ron asked.

163

Colem shook his head. "No. Whatever caused an explosion this big, if it still exists, is *under* that mountain," he pointed an accusing finger at the mountain of sand. "And it has been buried by the sand in the wind, as though the planet was trying to bury a bad memory."

"That gives me goose bumps," Ron said.

We walked a little further and stopped at the edge of a stone shelf. We looked down from our red, stone ledge at the brown and yellow, racing sand that sped along in a channel before us. The sand came right up to the edge of the shelf we were standing on and was as thick as a muddy flashflood, but we knew this river was only sand and fierce winds in the channel. The river hissed like an angry snake as the rushing air scraped the sand against the sides of the channel. The illusion of it being a fast flowing river was so convincing that Ron bent down to put his hand in it, but I quickly stopped him by grabbing his shoulder and pulling him back. Without explaining, I took a coil of rope I had brought with me and I tied a knot in it a few feet from the end. Then I lowered the rope into the river of sand until just the knot was above the surface. It was only there for a moment, but when I lifted the rope again, the part of the rope below the knot, or the part that had been submerged into the rushing sand, was gone, stripped and eaten away by the raging, sandblasting current.

"I think that stony ledge is the least of our worries," I said. "How are we going to cross this?"

Then we heard Tinear over the radio. "All units, return to the half-tracks."

We turned around and marched back to the waiting half-tracks. When we arrived, we found that the engineers had built ramps from extra pieces of the bug shell and some large stone slabs to let the colossal half-tracks drive up on top of the ledge.

Numigh was back behind the steering wheel in our half-track. Murlem stood on top of the ledge, guiding Numigh with hand signals. After slow progress and many engine-roaring complaints from the half-track, Numigh mounted the top of the ledge amidst cheers and cherub-suit-muffled clapping.

After the other half-tracks had also driven up onto the ledge, we helped the engineers disassemble the ramps, and we packed the pieces of gundon shell back into the vehicles.

Progress from that time forward was slow going, even slower than crossing through the sand-hail because instead of soft, rolling dunes that gave little resistance to our crossing, there were now unforgiving, sharp spires of hard stone that demanded we solve their puzzling maze to gain passage.

"Murlem," Numigh said, leading to an inquiry, "this may sound crazy, but are the wind speeds low enough for you to put out a kite?"

"A what?" Ron asked, confused. Then he remembered what they meant by "kite". "Oh," he quickly caught himself, "you want him to put eyes in the sky to scout out a path."

Murlem checked the gauges and dials before he responded. "No," he answered contemplatively. "It's still too windy for a kite. However, I can get a balloon up, and that will give us a better idea of our closer surroundings. I won't be able to scout ahead like I could with a kite, but it's better than what we've got."

"Good," Tinear said. "Get it done."

"Yes, sir," Murlem replied as he got out of his seat and went to the storage compartments at the back of the cab, where he began assembling and preparing a balloon.

He pulled the balloon's limp form out of its foam-lined carrying case. He attached a cable to a harness on the underside of the balloon. The cable had a wiring harness strapped along its length with a connector at both ends. Murlem pulled out a tank with a hose dangling from it and attached the hose to the balloon. There was a whistling of air as the balloon began to inflate and float off the floor. It wasn't the kind of balloon I had expected. It didn't even look like a weather balloon. What it did look like was a really chubby model airplane. When the balloon had inflated, Murlem disconnected the hose and plugged in the wiring harness to a sensor module mounted at the bottom of the balloon. Then he and Saeui got into cherub-suits and exited the vehicle with the balloon and cable.

"Where are they going to put it?" Ron asked.

166

"They're going to attach it to the roof of the vehicle, and it will float along with us where ever we go, like a little, pet tallakete on a leash."

Ron nodded. Then he jiggled his head side to side and looked at Numigh. "Wait. A little, pet what?"

A bright beep from the dashboard stole Numigh's attention before he could answer Ron.

"Wow. They've already got it connected. Picture is good. Sonar is good. All systems are good," he said, satisfied.

Murlem and Saeui entered the vehicle a few moments later.

"How does it look?" Murlem asked as he returned to his co-driver seat.

"The image is good. I was thinking about going along this route," Numigh replied, tracing a path on the screen with his finger.

I noticed that the path he suggested crossed one of the sand-rivers. "Those rivers of sand are vicious," I informed them, "We dipped a rope into one while we were scouting, and the rope was shredded and gone in a moment."

"We'll see how hardened steel holds up when we get there," Tinear said confidently. Then in a more humble tone, he added, "But I see your concern, and we'll assess the situation at that point. Numigh, does that route minimize how often we cross those rivers?"

"For as far as the balloon can show us," Numigh answered. "But if all these rivers flow up to the mountain, then we can't get across this field without crossing a few of them."

"So we have a short term path chosen," Tinear said, as he mentally took inventory of our situation. "Any ideas or strategies on how to get across this rocky field?"

"I think those sand-rivers are our biggest concern right now," said Colem.

"I agree," Ron chimed in. "And we know that the rivers flow towards the mountain. I think we can minimize how often we need to cross if we follow one of the rivers to the mountain, rather than crossing it. I suspect that just as a watery river flowing *away* from the mountains and into the sea is joined by other rivers flowing the same direction, these rivers of sand will do something similar as they flow *toward* the mountain. So, the rivers we cross near the mountain may be wider after being joined by other rivers, but there will be fewer of them. However, that presents its own challenges."

"Yeah. What if they are too deep for us to cross, or too wide for us to build a bridge?" Saeui asked.

"That's a good point," Tinear said as he pointed to Saeui.

"What if we go around?" Numigh suggested. "We could skirt around this rocky field and stay close to the storm wall. We may have to cross more rivers, but they would be smaller."

Tinear nodded while he deliberated. "I'd rather take one big chance instead of a bunch of little ones, and every crossing is going to be a gamble. I say we get it over with all at once, or as close to it as we can. Taking one big chance seems better than taking a bunch of smaller chances."

Ron held up a hand, "Actually, statistically speaking, it really doesn't – "

"I say we follow the rivers to the mountain," Tinear interrupted. "Set a course for that mountain," Tinear ordered.

"Yes, sir!" Numigh said as he spurred the colossal half-track into action, straight for the towering mountain of sand with the swaying twister at its peak.

Chapter 12 – In Stone

The half-track's pace had slowed as the terrain became more difficult to traverse. We slalomed at a snail's pace around great, leaning, sharp spires of red stone and navigated our way through a maze of red walls and ledges. The mountain of sand slowly loomed larger, and the wind of the twister became faintly audible. It wasn't long before a river of sand crossed our path, and we began following the direction it flowed. Unlike the sand river we had come across earlier, this river lied deep in a straight-sided chasm. We drove alongside the river with the river to our right, or in other words, with the river on Murlem's side of the vehicle. A rising ledge on Numigh's side of the vehicle pushed us closer and closer to the ravine as we continued further along the bank.

Murlem uttered a panicked groan as he looked out his window and down into the ravine and the ravenous sand-currents below.

"Don't sneeze, Numigh," Tinear cautioned. "This is getting really narrow."

"Yes, sir," Numigh responded. He let off the throttle, and the vehicle slowed down even more.

Murlem uttered another groan.

"Are you alright over there?" I asked.

"Murlem doesn't like heights," Colem explained.

"I thought you were a kite flyer," Ron said curiously.

Murlem looked back at us. "The kite flew. I stayed on the ground," he said in his defense. He looked back out his window. "Can you move any more to your side of the road?" he asked Numigh.

"I can't," Numigh replied. "There isn't any room."

"There's not much room over here either. Can't you move, just a little?" Murlem persisted.

"I don't have any room over here," Numigh repeated, with tension building in his voice.

"Well, I can see how much room I have over here, and it's not much. So that means there has got to be more room over there."

"There is NO more room over here!"

"Let me see. I know there's got to be –"

"Hey!" Tinear snapped. "Are you two married to each other?" he asked.

Neither one of them spoke.

"That's an awkward silence," Tinear said after a moment. "I said: are you two married to each other?!" Tinear repeated in a more demanding tone.

"No, sir!" Numigh and Murlem answered in unison.

"Then stop acting like it!" Tinear commanded. Then he rolled his eyes.

"What if they had said 'yes'," Ron asked quietly, with a childish smirk.

Tinear pointed a finger at Ron and looked sternly at him. "You're not helping," he said.

I couldn't help but laugh quietly to myself and I managed to suppress a grin, but Tinear heard my laugh.

"What's so funny, soldier?" he asked me.

"This reminds me of car trips when I was a kid," I answered. Then I quickly added, "Sir."

Tinear narrowed his eyes. "I should hope we didn't bring any *kids* on this mission because there's NO ROOM," he looked up front at Numigh and Murlem, "for kids in this half-track or any of the other half-tracks. Any more nonsense out of any of you and you will be riding on the roof! Am I clear?!"

"Yes, sir!" we promptly replied.

"Good! I left headquarters with soldiers, and I intend to reach Death's Grave with soldiers. Anyone who has a problem with that can ask to get off at any time and they can walk back home."

Just then, the radio chirped. "Colossal two to colossal one, come in colossal one."

Murlem picked up the radio. "This is colossal one. Go ahead."

"Colossal one, you are very close to that edge. Could you move over just a little?"

"I knew it!" Murlem hissed. "Colossal two, how much room do we ha-?"

Tinear snatched the radio from Murlem and spoke into it. "Colossal two..." He struggled for words as his temper flared. "Mind your own business!" he roared into the radio. Then he threw the radio at the receiver and sat back down with an agitated sigh.

We rolled on steadily and in silence for many, many hours, with the only sounds being the droning of the engine, the whirl of the approaching twister atop the mountain, and the rocks scraping along under our iron wheels and tracks.

I had been staring out the front window at the red terrain in front of us for a long time; a very long time. My mind was nearly empty and void of thought or feeling as I watched the rocks move past us. The horizon tipped and tilted as the half-track rolled over larger obstacles on one side or the other. I looked at Ron, and his face appeared to be a little blue, like he had been holding his breath for a long time.

"Are you alright?" I asked.

172

"Yeah," he replied, puzzled. "Why?"

"Your face looks blue."

Ron's eyes roved around, looking for something that could be amiss that would cause this oddity. "I feel fine," he said.

I rubbed my eyes and laughed. "Ugh. My eyes are saturated with red!" I looked around the cab, and everything had a blue hue to it.

"It looks like we are coming to our first crossing," Murlem announced. "We have another river coming up on our left." He pointed to the screen that the balloon over our half-track fed data to.

A few minutes later, Numigh stopped the half-track at the fork where the two rivers of sand merged together. We all exited our vehicles and stood at the merge. The sand from both rivers rushed together and flowed in fierce whirls and swirls before one river was consumed in the other, and the force of both rivers continued toward the mountain.

Tinear knelt at the river's edge and firmly held a piece of iron over the sand by a corner. He slowly dipped it below the surface, and the sand grated against it with a metallic objection, as though it was offended by this offering. Tinear lifted the metal out of the sand and examined it. Then he stood up and tossed it to Numigh.

"Take a look, then let the engineers have their way with it," Tinear said.

Numigh looked at the metal piece. The edges were badly rippled and brightly polished. One edge had gone into the sand blunt but now appeared razor sharp.

I dropped a piece of rope on the sharp edge and the rope fell to the ground in two pieces. I whistled. "Swimming is out of the question," I said.

"I don't think it would be wise to just drive through these rivers," Numigh stated.

"I'm glad we agree on that," Tinear said in a serious tone.

"Even if the half-tracks wouldn't get chewed up, we can't drive through these rivers," Murlem explained. "The sonar showed that the banks are straight down with at least a twenty-foot drop. We will need to bridge these rivers."

"Any ideas?" Tinear asked.

No one said anything, and a few of us shook our heads.

We stood around for a few minutes, even wandered around for a few minutes more. The engineers and mechanic were arguing, presumably about how to get across. I found a narrow shelf in the stone ledge that held us close to the river. It was about the right height to sit on. So I sat, and I looked around at the landscape. I wondered at the size of our colossal half-tracks again, and I watched the other soldiers meandering about, totally at a loss on what to do.

I shifted my weight and the shelf I was sitting on broke away from the rest of the stone. I stumbled out of the way to avoid getting my toes smashed. Once I recovered my balance, I looked down at the flat piece that had broken off. Then I looked up at the rest of the ledge. After sizing it up, I looked across the river. Then I looked back at the ledge. I walked over to the engineers and dragged one away in the middle of his argument. I brought him to the stone ledge and pointed up.

"What if we cut a piece out of the stone wall large enough to span the river?" I asked. "How thick would it need to be?"

He thought while he looked up and down the red stone. "That's a silly idea," he finally said, "but still, it may work. Let me consult with the others." He turned to leave.

"Whoa. Hey!" I said, getting his attention. "What's your name, soldier?"

"My name is Pik, sir," he replied. I nodded, and he walked away and sought out his associates.

Tinear walked over to me. "What's going on?" he asked.

"I was wondering if this stone was strong enough to hold up a half-track. We may be able to cut out a chunk and let it fall right over the river. We already know how to get a half-track up a ledge, so the stone can be as thick as it needs and we can build a ramp to get on top, cross the river, and get back off."

"What if the stone breaks?" he asked.

"I think if it's ever going to break, it will be when it hits the ground. If it survives, then we have a way to cross. If it breaks, then it falls into the river and we are right back where we started. No harm done."

Pik returned with his fellow engineer and they debated for a few moments until it appeared some conclusion had been met. The other engineer walked up to the stone wall and broke off a sizable chunk with a hammer. Then he took the chunk of stone back to one of the half-tracks.

"He is going to run some tests on its composition to determine its integrity," Pik explained.

I nodded my head, pleased with the progress report. "I'm all about tests," I said. The idea of tests reminded me of Earth and my job as a university professor there. Then I got an idea. "Whoa! Brain wave! What if we could build boats or something and just ride the river to the mountain?"

"That's a cute thought, but it won't work," Ron said. "The river is made of mostly air. There wouldn't be enough buoyancy to keep us on the surface."

"Oh," I said, slightly dejected. "You already thought about that, didn't you?"

Ron just made an expression that said, "Of course." Then he walked away.

"You smug basset hound," I said, feigning disgust.

The engineer returned from the half-tracks with the stone sample and talked with Pik. Ron listened in and added a word or two here and there. Their conversation was hushed, almost secretive.

"Talk to me," Tinear said.

The three of them turned around. "It's doable," Pik replied, "but it's going to take a lot of time."

"How much," Tinear asked.

"A day, maybe two, depending on whether or not we can find a chunk large enough without any fissures or flaws that would compromise its integrity. It will also depend on how quickly we can drill around the stone to cut it free."

"Then we'd better get to it," Tinear said with determination. "Ron, I want you to help them pick out the chunk of stone. Help them with the physics end of it so we can land that rock right where we need it."

"Yes, sir," Ron replied, eager to put his expertise to work.

"You three are in charge of this operation. Tell us what needs to be done," Tinear stated.

Pik spoke. "We three are going to scout out a suitable chunk of stone. We will need tools; jackhammers, drills, chisels, ropes, and whatever else you think may come in handy."

And so we began. Tools were sprawled about and a section of the stone ledge had been selected. Markers had been placed where cuts and holes should be made. The ground beneath the stone was prepared to ensure the stone would fall the right direction. We worked in shifts, nonstop. Jackhammers powered by the halftracks through high-pressure hoses hammered endlessly. We carefully cleaned the drilling dust from our suits when our shift was over to keep the dust from abrading between the folds and wearing a tear in the suit. Work was slow and monotonous, but, eventually, we reached the critical point where the stone was ready to be broken free from the ledge. An explosive charge was prepped and dropped deep into a carefully drilled hole that would free the stone and send it falling.

We stood clear of the stone and watched with eager anticipation as one of the engineers counted down and pressed the detonator. A cloud of dust burst from behind the stone, and it suddenly dropped off the ledge with a deep thud before it began tipping away, making a grating noise as it fell. It gained momentum and smote the ground with a low, thunder-like clap. The stone held together and spanned the river. Now we had a bridge. We cheered. Then we got to work building the ramps that would get the colossal half-tracks on top of our rough, stone bridge.

The rest of the operation was just a rerun of the incident with the ledge when we had first entered the fields of red stoned spires and spikes. We built the ramps from smaller stones and pieces of gundon shell. The ramps were perpendicular to the direction the bridge ran because of the lack of space we had between the deadly river of sand and the rising ledge of red stone, so we had cut out a stone wide enough for our huge half-tracks to turn on the bridge once they were up the ramp. Then they crossed and drove down another set of ramps on the opposite bank. Once all three vehicles were across, we disassembled the crucial parts of the ramps and packed them away again.

Then our journey resumed along the riverside, without a ledge pushing us closer to the river, much to Murlem's relief. We drove toward the towering mountain of sand for a few hours until Murlem announced, "Another river merge is coming up."

"Already?" many of us asked in dismay.

"Can we possibly go around this whole thing? I know that means driving blind in the sand hail, but at least it was easy going," Ron asked.

"Our speed would be too slow and the distance too far," Tinear said. "This is still the fastest way across. I'm sure I don't need to remind you of our limited life-sustaining resources."

"Of course," Ron said in an exhausted tone. "The shortest distance between two points is in a straight line."

"Besides," Tinear said with a smile, "we are pioneering a new course across this planet. What if these bridges are the foundation for a future trans-desert highway called Ron's Pass."

Ron thought for a moment. "Sounds stupid, but, yeah, I see what you're saying."

A few hours later, our convoy came to another halt between two rivers of sand. We exited the vehicles in our now resented cherub-suits, which had begun to smell ripe after working in them and without having showered since we had left headquarters.

"How are we going to get across this one?" Tinear asked while we all stood where the rivers met and watched the sands swirl. "There aren't any ledges nearby to fell a chunk of stone from."

"As we say back on Earth," I said, "'There's more than one way to skin a cat'."

"Skin a cat?" Pik repeated with disgust. "Earth must be full of barbarians."

I shrugged. "It's home." I thought about Earth for a moment. Then I said, "Back on Earth, our military had mobile bridges - big machines that could drive to the edge and extend a bridge across whatever hole in the ground was stopping them."

"We have something like that, too," Tinear said. "But we didn't think we would need them. We've never seen so much as a canal on this side of the planet."

"I still think a stone bridge is our only way to get across," Ron said, getting us back to thinking about the current problem.

"How are we going to get a stone across that?" Murlem asked. "The last one was easy compared to this. It was close enough to where we needed it, and it just fell into place."

"I guess we will need to carve it out of the ground," I said. "Then we will need to get it over here."

Colem made a suggestion. "If we can find an outcropping or a small plateau that was the correct thickness from ground level up, then we could just slide it out and push it across the gap."

"The stone slab will be very heavy. How will we move it?" Ron asked.

Numigh leaned against the front roller of a colossal half-track. "I think we can handle it."

"Even with that, there will still be a lot of friction, and they will weigh much more than a half-track," Ron pointed out. "We need something the slab can roll over or slide on."

"We could carve out some stone rolling pins or use some spare axles or maybe cut up a push-bumper and use the pipes," Saeui suggested.

Ron shook his head. "Whatever we use to slide the slab needs to be expendable because it *will* be rolled into the river as the slab goes over. And, by the way, the slab will need to be more than twice as long as the river is wide for us to stretch it across without it tipping into the river. That's a lot of stone."

"What if we use sand?" I asked. "We could spread sand across the ground and it would be like a bunch of little ball bearings or marbles."

"Where would we get the sand?" Tinear asked. "We're not driving all the way back to the dunes to pick some up. The only place around here where there's sand is in that murderous, freak-of-nature river."

"We can channel it out of the river," I said. "We saw that metal holds up for a little while in the river. Fasten a metal plate to the end of a pole, reach out into the river so that the plate just skims the surface and deflects the sand out onto the bank. If we're talented enough, we may even get the sand to spread itself across the entire surface that we need to be covered."

"I like it," Tinear said. "Let's get it done."

"One problem," Pik elbowed in. "When we cut the stone out of the ground, how are we going to get it moving initially? When the stone is first cut, that is where it will have the most resistance to moving. It won't have any sand under it and we can't lift it up to spread sand under it. So, how will we move it in the first place?"

We thought for a moment. Then Ron spoke, "We're going to need to carve under it anyway to break it free from the ground. While we are carving, we can leave two narrow tracks of stone that run the length of the slab and carve out everything else so that the stone will be supported by those two narrow tracks. The tracks will act like skids under the stone until it is dragged over the sand. That will reduce the amount of friction involved."

"Will that work?" Tinear asked Pik.

Pik made some quick calculations in his head before he said, "Yes, I believe it will. We will start scouting for a suitable piece of stone."

"Good," Tinear said enthusiastically. "Now, Mike, show us how you plan to get the sand out of the river."

I went to the half-track to gather some parts for the contraption I had in mind, but when I came across one of the shovels, I realized I had what I needed. I took the shovel and a torch and heated the shovel's neck, where the spade attached to the handle. I held the torch there until the metal glowed red. Then I wedged the shovel head under our half-track's tread and bent the shovel head into a right angle. I walked to the edge of the river of sand and reached the shovel head out and downstream from where I was standing. I dipped a side of the shovel head into the river until it just began to skim the surface. The sand that hit the shovel head deflected off of it and sprayed across the shore I had faced the tip toward. I experimented with different angles until I had figured out how to cover the entire shore side where we planned to slide the stone. Then I focused the shovel on one point until there was a large enough pile of sand for us to collect and spread all the way from the shore to our little quarry, where the stone bridge was being carved out.

Again, a couple of days passed, and we worked in shifts to carve out a stone bridge. Once the stone was ready to be moved, we drilled and anchored hitch points to the leading edge of the stone to hookup the three half-tracks for towing. Then we let Numigh and the other drivers, with their half-tracks, do the rest of the work. They pulled together and slowly dragged the large stone across the sand we had spread out. I could feel the ground gently rumble as the stone slithered across the surface. When the drivers had brought the stone to the river's edge, we disconnected the stone from the half-tracks, and we retrieved the hitch points for future use.

183

Numigh and the other drivers maneuvered the half-tracks behind the stone slab where they carefully pressed the bumpers against the stone. Then they gradually pushed the stone forward with the half-tracks until the stone spanned the entire width of the river, and we were able to cross.

Again, we built ramps to get the vehicles on top of the bridge and off the other side. Once the stone was settled in place and the ramps were built, we all boarded our vehicles, dusted off our smelly cherub-suits, and drove over the river and on our way.

"I suspect river crossings will become less frequent the closer we get to the mountain and as the rivers become more established in their ways," Ron predicted.

He was right.

Chapter 13 – Buried Past

River crossings became less and less frequent, as Ron had predicted, and each time we simply repeated one of the two methods we had used before; we either felled a stone slab across the river or we extracted a slab and pushed it to span the river. We became quite proficient at working with stone after having built a few bridges with the stuff, and we made our way to the mountain of sand with greater ease.

Eventually, the sand rivers began to overflow and to blow thin layers of sand across the ground without any ill effects to our suits or our vehicles. Sand began piling up until we were driving once again across smooth, sandy dunes that steadily lead us up closer to the mountain. As we continued to climb the mountain, the rivers began to fan out more and more while still maintaining dangerous currents in the deeper channels and ravines, the same way a river of water fans out into a delta when it empties into the ocean.

"Are we going to keep climbing this mountain until we go up and over, or are we going to start going around it at some point?" Ron asked as he took hold of a grab-bar to keep himself upright when the vehicle reared up to climb another dune.

"We're hoping the rivers will thin out enough to make them shallow," Murlem answered. "Maybe they will be shallow enough to not do any harm to the half-tracks. Then we can ford our way across them."

Ron nodded.

The half-track crested the dune we had been climbing and began its downward descent when Ron swiftly rushed to the front of the cab.

"Did you see that?!" Ron shouted as he pointed a finger straight ahead.

"See what?" I asked.

"I saw a tunnel entrance!"

"Like a cave?" Murlem asked.

"No!" Ron said excitedly. "It was definitely man-made!"

We all stared out the window as Numigh slowed down to give everyone a chance to look. We didn't see anything. We all looked at Ron.

"I think you've been in the desert a little too long," Tinear suggested.

"No. No, it was there," Ron insisted. "Numigh, backup to the top of the dune."

"Can't do," Numigh said. "Gravity has us now. The only direction we are going is forward. We can take a closer look at the top of the next dune."

We all stood, holding on to something to keep our balance as the half-track tilted and bucked through the dip between dunes, and we started our next climb. We all leaned forward to get a better look through the windshield as we neared the top of the dune. Numigh stopped the vehicle once we reached the crest, and we all squinted out through the window. Tinear scanned the terrain with a pair of binoculars.

"Does anyone see anything interesting?" Tinear asked.

"Just a lot of sand, sir," Colem replied.

"The balloon isn't showing anything unusual," Murlem reported.

"Maybe getting on top of the half-track will give us a better vantage point," Saeui suggested.

The other two half-tracks pulled up alongside us and signaled that they wanted to know what was happening.

Tinear picked up the radio. "We may have seen something of interest. Standby," he told them.

Murlem, Ron, and I put on our cherub-suits, exited the vehicle, and climbed the side-mounted ladders to the roof of our half-track. I made it to the top first, and I looked through a set of binoculars.

"I don't see anything," I told Murlem and handed him the binoculars as he dismounted the ladder and got to his feet.

"What?" Ron objected. "I was sure I saw something." He scrambled up to the roof with us and then continued his climb up to the top of the front turreted cannon. He mounted the barrel and scooted along it until he was at the business end of it. He wrapped his legs around the barrel and turned on his radio. "Colem, could you point the front cannon up a little, please?" he asked.

Colem didn't answer, but evidently he was happy to do so because the cannon began to slowly point up.

"A little more," Ron encouraged as the barrel continued to rise. "A little more. A little more. Whoa! Stop! Stop! That's good! Thank you!" he shouted as he quickly grabbed the lip of the barrel to keep himself from sliding back down to the turret's base.

"What do you see up there?" I asked over the radio, so the others below us could know what was going on.

Ron steadied himself on the barrel and looked around. "Aha!" he shouted triumphantly. "I knew I wasn't crazy!"

"That's still debatable," I muttered with a smile.

"I see the tunnel!" Ron reported. "It's straight ahead!"

"Very good," Tinear said over the radio. "Numigh, set a course for straight ahead."

The half-track started moving.

"Whoa!" Ron clung tighter to the barrel. "Could you let me down first? Please?"

Several bursts of laughter burbled across the radio.

The barrel was mercifully lowered and Ron, Murlem, and I rejoined the others inside the cab, and we resumed our slow, steady, mechanical march across the rising dunes and higher up the mountain.

Several hours later, we crested yet another dune. This time Ron pointed our attention to what he was talking about.

"There! There it is!" Ron said emphatically as he pointed at what, indeed, appeared to be a man-made tunnel, far in the distance.

Tinear quickly picked up the radio. "All vehicles, get to the bottom of this dune as quickly as possible. Begin radio silence" He hung up the radio. "We need to know what this is and whether or not we've been detected."

The other vehicles broke our usual single file formation and were quickly beside us as Numigh sent the colossal half-track rushing down the dune. Ron emitted a few grunts of disapproval and distress as he stared wide-eyed at the ground straight ahead of us in our steep and fast descent. The half-tracks came to a sliding stop. Tinear put on his cherub-suit, and we followed his lead. Numigh and Murlem stayed with the half-track while the rest of us exited the vehicle and scrambled up the next dune, which was no small feat. The dunes had grown very large for a man to climb, but the half-tracks had made quick work of them.

We reached the top of the dune, and we carefully poked our heads over the crest. Ron had left his radio on and was panting heavily from the exertion of our swift climb. I reached over and turned off his radio for him.

Tinear and Murlem studied the tunnel and its surroundings through binoculars while John held up a device that looked like a small radar dish.

After a few moments, Tinear asked, "What do you make of it?"

"I don't see anything that indicates recent activity, or even old activity," Colem observed.

"I'm getting some kind of signal," John reported. "It's not a radio signal or any other kind of communications frequency, but it's not natural either."

"It seems like no one is home, but they left the lights on," I said.

"Right, let's get back to the vehicles," Tinear said.

We slid most of the way down the dune and entered our half-track while Tinear went to the other vehicles first to let them know what was happening. Then he returned to the cab.

"We'll proceed with caution, maintain radio silence, and be ready for a fight," Tinear said. "Arm up and man the turrets."

Colem, Saeui, and John jumped into the turrets while the rest of us put on our cherub-suits, checked our firearms, and packed extra ammo. The half-tracks advanced steadily up the dune alongside each other with a generous amount of space between the vehicles. As we crested each dune, we studied the tunnel intently for signs of activity or any indication that we had been detected. We advanced steadily. There was still no sign of life from the tunnel.

"Murlem, do you see anything that looks like surveillance or observation equipment?" Tinear asked.

"No, sir," Murlem answered after quickly double checking the readings from the balloon.

The half-tracks slowly crept up to the tunnel entrance, and Tinear ordered Numigh to stop. The other vehicles followed our lead. The half-tracks we rode in were colossal, as their class designation suggested, but the tunnel before us made our massive half-tracks look like toy cars. Sand had blown into the tunnel, and for as far as we could see into the dark, gaping mouth of the tunnel, sand possibly covered the ground throughout the entire structure.

"We are going to drive in there, single file," Tinear said, as he explained how we were going to proceed. "Mike, Ron, and I are going to exit the vehicle and march alongside. I will cover the driver's side of the vehicle, Mike and Ron will cover the codriver's side. Keep an eye out for any threats or hazards. Gunners will stay in their turrets, drivers will switch to night vision, and radios will only be used to identify threats and targets. Let's go."

Ron, Tinear, and I exited the vehicle. Soldiers from the other vehicles did likewise, with their gunners and drivers manning their positions while everyone else exited and joined the patrol. Then all three half-tracks slowly advanced deeper into the tunnel.

I turned a lever on the side of my cherub-suit's helmet and a night vision lens with false color dropped down in front of my face. The walls were straight and tall. The ceiling was flat and broad. The corners were beveled in, probably to strengthen the structure. I couldn't make up my mind about what the tunnel was made of. Was it concrete, or rough metal?

The tunnel continued going on, further and further into the mountain. I looked back at the entrance, a mere candlelight in the dark. The walls and ceiling ran on with no variation or deviation. The engines of the half-tracks quietly purred and echoed down the long corridor. I was sure that if anyone was in the mountain, they would have heard us by now and radio silence was vain. Still, there was no point being any more apparent than needed. I thought for a moment that perhaps we should have left the vehicles at the entrance, but I also wondered what would be in this mountain that needed such a huge tunnel. Then I was grateful to have the half-tracks' armor and firepower near at hand.

Murlem broke the radio silence. "Doors ahead, four hundred feet, one at nine and three at twenty-seven," he warned.

I was confused for a moment about what he meant. On Earth, I would have used the numbers on the face of a clock to give a more precise location of something in relation to the observer. Then I remembered that the Edengone clock had thirty-six hours. After some simple calculating and translating, I understood that he meant the doors were four hundred feet away. One door was to our right, and the others were to our left.

I raised my weapon. If anything was going to ambush us, it would be now. I heard the turrets rumble as they rotated to cover the entrances. I looked back and saw that the rear team and half-track had all their weapons pointing the way we had come, covering our rear. I also noticed that I could not see the light from the end of the tunnel. I assumed that meant that either the tunnel had curved without my noticing and blocked the entrance from our line of sight, or a large door had closed and covered the entrance. I turned my attention back to the path ahead and saw the doors on either side of the tunnel, facing each other. The one to the right was as tall as the rest of the tunnel and nearly just as wide as it was tall. The doors to the left were much smaller. One was just large enough for a colossal half-track to squeeze through, but the other two were only as tall as an ordinary doorway and twice as wide.

Tinear signaled the caravan to halt just short of the doors. Ron didn't see the signal and bumped into me.

"Soldiers, on me. Armor, cover the large door at nine," Tinear ordered.

We hurried with Tinear to the other three doors.

"Crew four, support the half-tracks. Crew three, guard the other two doors. Crews one and two, with me," he said as he stood to one side of the nearest small door.

We stacked up behind him, with Ron at the rear, and Tinear hit a button that opened the door. The door slid open with a whoosh, and we were in. A long, narrow hall stretched before us with more doors along each side. We swiftly and methodically began searching the rooms. Two soldiers advanced ahead and kept their attention and weapons directed down the hall while the rest of us searched each room behind them. Once we had confirmed the room was empty, we would call "clear!" and the two soldiers would advance just past the next set of doors and wait while we searched those rooms in like manner. Room by room, we searched. It was often difficult to tell what I was looking at, partly because of the night vision lens and partly because almost everything had been damaged by the raging heat that was even present deep in this mountain. The intense heat had destroyed anything not resilient enough. There were books that appeared to be petrified in black ash but crumbled to dust as soon as they were touched. Bedding peppered the bunks and the floors around them in the barracks. Charred chairs laid strewn about. Whoever had been here had left in a hurry.

We took care about where we stepped. Some materials had melted into boiling, silver puddles that could have easily done terrible damage to our suits and, consequently, to us. Other rooms spewed strange colors of smoke or steam when the doors were opened. Our steps echoed as we moved through the silent inferno. The atmosphere felt eerie and bizarre. It felt almost alien. Down the long hall, up a few flights of stairs, and through another hall full of doors, we swept the entire facility and did not find any living thing inside. The facility was vacant.

We returned to the half-tracks and stacked up behind Tinear at the giant door on the opposite side of the tunnel. My heart beat with nervous anticipation at what we may find behind such huge doors. Tinear hit the door button, and the door slowly lifted. A few soldiers dropped to their stomachs and aimed their weapons under the growing opening. We rushed in as soon as the door was high enough to enter, and we immediately stopped. There was no need to search the room further.

We could already see everything in it. We stood there, dumbfounded and stilled at what we *had* found. This room, in the heart of the mountain, was a cavity cut out into a perfect, spherical shape and lined with the clearest of mirrors. It housed the strangest assembly of titanic sized components that were also mirror plated. I would have estimated the room to be about two miles in diameter. This room was spherical; two miles across, two miles ahead of us, one mile up, and one mile down. The cavern spanned before us, and somehow the entire chamber was lit. I first thought that it was just the light from our flashlights reflecting off an entire chamber of mirrors, but it was too bright to believe that was the case. Somewhere, or somehow, light was entering and filling the chamber. I felt dwarfed. A glass catwalk ran around inside the circumference of the sphere. In the middle, seemingly dangling from the ceiling like a gigantic chandelier by a thick column of polished copper, was half of a sphere, or a dome, about half the size of the room itself, with the flat side facing up. On the flat side of that half-sphere was a second, smaller dome on top, which was half the size of the first dome. The two half-spheres, or domes, put together looked something like an avocado that had been cut in half around the pit, and the huge, copper column that the avocado hung by was like a skewer that had been thrust into the pit, perpendicular to the cut. At the top of the copper column was something that looked like an enormous ball joint. The parts that caught my interest the most, however, were ridges around the larger dome that started at the edges of the flat part and vortexed around the dome until they reached the bottom, all mirror plated, like the rest of the room, except for the flat part of the larger dome and the copper column by which it hung. It made me think of a motorized mixing bowl.

We all stood and silently stared.

Finally, Colem asked the question that was burning in all of our minds. "What is it?"

Again, we were silent. Then Tinear spoke. "One of the rooms we swept through on the upper floor, didn't it have an image of this?"

I raced through my memory. "It did," I confirmed.

"Let's go there. Pik and Ron, we'll need you two to work together to figure out what this thing is, what it's supposed to do, why it is under this mountain, and how in the blazes of the Demog Desert did it get here," Tinear said.

We returned to the room Tinear had mentioned. We turned on our gun mounted lights and retracted our night vision lenses to get a better look around. The image Tinear was thinking of was a faint and worn mural etched into the unusual surface of the wall. It may have had color at one time instead of smudged, burnt lines and smears to define the image. I imagined it was intricate and maybe even beautiful in its early days, but it looked like time and the constant exposure to the intense heat was cruel to it. At its center, it depicted the large spherical room with the large, hanging dome that we had found on the other side of the massive tunnel. In the lower corners were images of throngs of people boldly and cheerfully marching to some destination not depicted in the illustration. In the upper left corner of the mural were stars and planets moving in their orbits. In the upper right corner was the face of a man with strong and defined features, a pronounced chin, clean shaven, well-groomed hair, a strong brow, a high arched nose, and a sharp jawline. His face portrayed courage and determination, and yet, there was a craze in his eye. I felt like I had seen that insane eye back on Earth, in a history book.

"Who is that?" I asked, pointing to the prominent figure in the mural.

Tinear snarled. "That is ex-Major Dathfron, the most sadistic and heartless tyrant to ever blemish good Edengone, and the founder of the Forward Party. The Forward Party is the predecessor to the Advansynergist movement. If Major Dathfron was involved, I can guarantee that this facility has some wretched and foul history behind it. Alright, everyone spread out and gather anything that may give us a clue about what we are dealing with here. Place your findings on this table, where Pik and Ron will put the pieces together. Go."

We spread out and began rummaging through the piles of ash and melted goo. Almost immediately, Pik found something.

"I think I found a computer," he said.

"Wouldn't the circuitry have melted in this heat?" Ron asked.

"This model is made completely of silicon; very resistant to heat," Pik explained. "However, that being said, it doesn't look like it's unscathed. A few of the data storage units appear to be damaged. But let's see what we can find in the remaining few."

"Won't you need power?" I asked.

"John said he was getting a signal coming from here," Tinear recalled. "So there must be power."

"I think I found it," Ron said as he flipped a switch.

Several lights turned on overhead and a faint, steady whirring noise began.

"How did that survive?" I asked as I turned off my flashlight, amazed that this facility had power despite the harsh conditions.

"I actually do not know," Pik said, equally amazed.

We finished a thorough search of that room and expanded our efforts out to the rest of the facility while Pik and Ron continued to nurse the silicon computer back to life. I searched through several rooms and didn't find anything until I entered the barracks, where the lights didn't work. I turned on my flashlight and looked around the room. I noticed that there was a sizable lump at one end of a bunk where maybe a pillow would have been. All of the other bunks were flat and blackened. I poked at the lump with the barrel tip of my gun. It looked like a book, but unlike the other books I had come across, this one did not crumble into a pile of dust. I picked it up. It was not a large book. It reminded me very much of a journal I had kept back home. I gently brushed off the ashes and carefully opened it. To my amazement, the pages were intact and white; clean white. The pages didn't feel like paper. They felt more resistant, almost like thin rubber. I turned the page and was even more amazed to find writing that seemed to glow with its own light. I turned off my light, and the letters were still there. They were not reflective. They actually glowed. I couldn't understand the written language, so I closed the book and took it back up to where Pik was working on the silicon computer.

"Hey," I said. "Is this normal?" I opened the book with the pages turned toward Pik and Ron so they could see the glowing writing.

"Whoa!" Pik exclaimed.

"I'll take that as a 'no' then," I said, and I carefully put the book down on the table.

"Actually it is normal. I just didn't expect to find one here," Pik said. "They are silicon-based, which is why it hasn't disintegrated like everything else, and a charged stylus is used to write on them. As you can see, they are designed to last through the ages. Their writing doesn't fade. They are usually filled with information or knowledge that someone at some time did not want to die with them. They are often referred to as 'legacy journals'. I'll take a look at that as soon as I'm done here."

"I could look at it," Ron offered.

"It's written in Edengone, pal. Can you read Edengone?" I asked.

"Actually, I can," he said smugly.

"Since when?"

"Since Pik taught me while you were out searching."

"He taught you a whole language while I was gone?"

"Well, I already know how to speak Edengone. That's half the battle. He just taught me what sound the letters represent, and then it was a simple matter of applied phonetics."

"Well, good on you," I said, irritated at his haughtiness.

He picked up the book and read the glowing pages. I found something to sit on, and I waited. It wasn't long before the others returned from their searches. One by one, they entered the room, empty-handed. Then there was nothing to do but to wait for Ron and Pik to do their part.

"You got anything? Any ideas?" Ron asked Pik.

"No," Pik answered ponderously. "All I've learned so far is that the tunnel we came in continues through the entire mountain and opens again on the other side."

Ron tapped a page covered with something that looked like a hieroglyph of equations. "These figures look important, but I can't make out what they are referring to," Ron said as he studied the records with a scrunched forehead.

John looked over Ron's shoulder and examined the mess of figures. "They look like calculations for finding the hypotenuse of a sine beta wave from an ion pulsating bio-matter capacitor," John said casually.

Everyone stopped what they were doing, and we all stared at him.

"When did you learn to speak?" Ron asked. He stared at John curiously.

John stared back at Ron and just raised his eyebrows, almost as though he didn't recognize the sound of his own voice and was as equally surprised.

"Is he serious?" Ron asked. "You know, you really are a hard one to read. I can't tell if you are just making something up to fool with us or if you're being real," he said to John.

"He's always serious," Tinear said, answering on John's behalf. "John doesn't say much," Tinear explained, "but when he does speak, it's because he knows what he's talking about."

"Where did he learn that, though?" Ron asked.

"I've found it's pointless to ask," Tinear answered with a wave of his hand.

"Well then, please, go on," Ron encouraged John.

Then the three of them began putting the pieces together.

Chapter 14 – A Light Matter

Tinear had sent the other crews to scout further down the tunnel. Ron, Pik, and John had been pouring over the records for a couple of hours while Tinear and I waited.

Finally, Ron showed some signs of understanding. He stood, his face lit up, and his hands began to shake. I had seen this before, and I nudged Tinear, who had fallen asleep sitting up.

Ron looked up and around at the rest of us as he frantically pecked at a page with his finger. He seemed to have lost the ability to speak in his sudden, feverish excitement. He was in a state of intellectual shock. His finger just pecked faster and faster until his whole person was shaking. Tinear raised an eyebrow, and Pik shifted nervously away. John had the normal blank stare that I had come to expect from him.

"Anything good?" I asked calmly.

Ron took a deep breath and exclaimed, "Yeah! Yeah, yeah, yeah. Oh, yeah!"

"Good," I replied in the same calm tone. Then I waited, and he continued to peck at the page. "Would you like to tell us about it?"

"Yeah! Yeah! Oh, yeah!"

I calmly got up from my seat, walked over to him, took the legacy journal, and slammed it shut.

Then Ron blurted out, "It's a light particle propulsion engine!"

I nodded slowly and looked at him nonchalantly before I said, "Good. That's good work, Ron. I guess we can all go home now."

"Wait!" Ron panicked. "But there's more!"

"Of course there is, and we would like to hear about it," I said, slowly. The trick was to get Ron calm enough to be coherent. "You said the device is a propulsion engine. How does it work?"

Ron took a moment to gather his thoughts. Then he noticeably calmed down and began. "The device gathers light and compresses it until it generates enough pressure to propel an object; potentially to propel an object as big as a planet. That giant room with all the reflective surfaces was the collection chamber. And that giant thing hanging from the ceiling – they called it the pendulum - actually spun, like a blender, while an electric current at the correct alternating frequencies flowed through those outer ridges – the ridges that vortex around the lower dome; those kept the light active in the chamber through an effect they called 'electrophoton induction'. Then the light would enter through the bottom of the lower dome of the pendulum through a thin layer of black-body matter once the light reached an adequate frequency and intensity, where it would again be affected by the electric current flowing through the pendulum, and then the light would be exhausted through the copper column. That copper column is a thruster, and the entire pendulum can swivel to change the direction of the thrust."

"Wow," Pik said, astonished.

The rest of us just stared at him.

"Why is it so big?" I asked, after a respectable moment of silence for the loss of my weaker brain cells.

"Well, just like any engine," Pik said, taking a turn in the spotlight, "if you have a larger load to move, then you need an engine with a reaction chamber large enough to generate sufficient power to move the load."

"What do you mean 'reaction chamber'? I thought they were just gathering light."

"They were gathering light as part of creating power for this propulsion system," Ron explained, "the same way a jet engine gathers air to mix with fuel to generate thrust. To get more energy out of something, something more must be added to it. The reaction within the mixture creates opposing forces, which then can be harnessed to do work, whatever the work may be. In this case, they were using electrophoton induction to generate more energy." Ron was speaking in the best layman terms he could muster.

"Okay. So what were they trying to move?" Tinear asked. "What was the load?"

Ron opened the legacy journal. "Our friend here has the answer," he said. "And there are some references in here that perhaps you can elaborate on," he added, looking at Tinear. Then he began to read.

"I've begun to doubt Lord Dathfron's intentions and those of the Forward Party. At first, when he proposed this idea of propelling the planet out into space and using the planet itself as a spacecraft to discover distant worlds, I was elated. Here I thought this visionary man had discovered a way to keep humanity well and alive throughout time. As many like us have been saying for hundreds of years, the population of this planet will exceed its ability to provide. We will need to find a fresh world if our species is to survive. Our exploration of space has been limited by the limited supplies we can take with us. But instead of leaving the planet to discover new worlds, we would take the planet with us, and all the supplies and provisions and means of life with it. Our range of exploration would be unprecedented. I believed this was a new beginning, the pinnacle of humankind's advancement. But now, I believe a madness has taken Dathfron, or perhaps I have emerged from a madness myself. Either way, the more I see this project through, the more I believe this will destroy humanity. I had believed that all people would realize the need for this program once it was underway and that all people would be welcome to join us in the cities we would build near the core of Edengone as she carries us through the void between the stars to new, clean, fertile worlds. Now that has changed. I've seen the plans for the interstellar dwellings, that is, the cities to be built near the planet's heated core, and I can see they are not sufficient for the population of the planet, nor even a portion. My guess is that only a select few will survive in the interstellar dwellings while the rest of the people perish on the ever freezing surface. This is genocide. This is his idea of global domination. He will rule the world himself because there will be no one to oppose him. I must end this before we get any further with our plans. I'm going to relay our location to the enemy. I will most likely be killed when they invade our base, because, after all, I have become like Dathfron. At least I will die doing what I had intended to do by joining this project; I will save the world. I will divulge the details of what we are building here within this journal, and hopefully this device will never be used. In fact, I hope it is destroyed and forgotten."

Ron closed the journal. "From what I could gather from the historical references within the journal, the Forward Party was a radical movement, devised of some of the most acclaimed and renowned minds of their time. They were also devoid of any form of moral direction or guidance. They placed the progression of humankind over the wellbeing of humankind."

"I couldn't have said it better myself," Tinear smirked with folded arms.

"I take it they weren't too popular with the rest of the world," Ron deduced.

Tinear shook his head.

Ron continued. "Anyway, they were trying to take this planet out of its orbit and on a deep space voyage. I don't know where they were planning on going," he said with a hint of doubt. "I'm not even sure *they* knew where they were going. But that huge device was their means of propulsion, and it used light as its catalyst. They were going to turn Edengone into a planet-sized spaceship. No, wait. Let me rephrase that. They were going to turn the planet *into* a spaceship; a spaceship capable of faster than light speeds. Well, faster than visible light, anyway. Mike knows my thoughts on that."

"How was this device supposed to make anything, much less this planet, go faster than light?" I asked, confused and bewildered at the thought.

"Think about it. When you want to go faster than something, you push against it. If you want to go faster than the ground, you push against it with your foot or a wheel, usually. If you want to go faster than water, you push against it with a paddle, or your arms and legs, or a propeller, or a paddlewheel, or some other option. If you want to go faster than sound, or, as we have talked about before, we know that sound *is* air moved by energy – so if you want to go faster than the air, then you push against the air with a propeller, or a jet, or even a rocket. Even cars that try to break the sound barrier use..." He held his hand out to me and turned his head so that he looked at me out of the corner of his eye, indicating that he wanted me to finish the sentence.

"A jet engine," I said, playing along. "Which pushes against the air they are trying to go faster than."

"Correct," Ron said, taking back the baton. "So if you want to go faster than the speed of light, then you need some way of pushing against the light. As I have told you, I believe that light is matter; very fine matter. So if you want to move, you are going to need enough matter to push against to get moving. This machine was designed to gather and compress light, thereby creating opposing, material forces within the device. Then the force would be released through that giant copper tube, and the force would move the planet."

"Small correction," Pik interrupted. "Now that I know what this machine is, I believe I have the rest of the story. To rephrase what you just said: the force *was* released through the tube and the force *moved* the planet."

"Wait. 'Was'? As in past tense? As in, it actually happened?" I asked, astonished.

Pik nodded. "That device is the reason this planet is tidally locked. I believe it would be best if I let someone who was there when the device was fired explain the rest." Pik turned to the computer screen, opened a file, and began to read.

"It appears the damage has been done. We've managed to stop them in time to keep those arrogant fools from launching us and the planet out of orbit, but the planet has stopped spinning. We are tidally locked with the sun. It's getting hot. Really hot. We have cooling units working hard to keep things bearable, but they just aren't enough. My shirt is soaked with sweat. It has only been a couple of days since we got here. I worry that we won't make it; I mean as a people. I fear that this last act of the Forward Party has done us in. This planet may not be able to sustain life by the end of the week. Those fools didn't even have a plan for living on the planet. Their plan was to live underground for the rest of their lives, near the planet's core to keep warm. Would that have even worked? It doesn't matter. It was all foolishness. This isn't the only thing they did. They were doing worse. They were doing unthinkable things, and they had plans for other unspeakable… 'abominations' is the only word to describe such heinous acts. And all in the name of advancing humankind; all for their fanatic, delusional dreams of fame and glory from other zealots of this shameful faith in science. I don't blame them for wanting to learn more. I am, after all, a scientist myself. But what they didn't understand is that knowledge is a form of power, and unless that power has an adequate means of being controlled, it will wreak havoc, like the unstoppable storms of the Demog Sea (which has begun receding, by the way). Knowledge is a form of power, and it must be harnessed by wisdom, and wisdom is engendered by understanding correct moral principles. Wisdom would have told these idiots of the Forward Party that one should not do something just because they can. Wisdom would dictate that every action should have a good purpose, or else those actions are of no value. Moral principle would explain what a 'good purpose' is and what is not, what should be considered harmful and what is not. If those fools had lived by correct moral principles, then they would have seen the harm in this vain, ignorant, condemnable experiment! Curse my misfortune for not having another one to shoot at while I am burning with heat and fury and an everlasting resentment for their kind! Down with the Forward Party and all who adopt their ways hereafter!

"There is nothing more we can do here. We are leaving, and hopefully we will survive, if we are not burned to death first."

Pik stopped reading, and we stood in silence for a moment or two.

"Do you think they made it to the habitable zone?" Colem asked.

Ron solemnly shook his head. "It sounds like the temperature was rising too fast. You know how long it took us to get here. I'm afraid they perished in the fiery heat, which means no one else has seen this since then," he said in wonder.

"I wonder what it looks like when the device is working," Pik said curiously.

Ron was too eager to answer. "I imagine the inside would look like a black hole because all of the light around it would be drawn towards the center of the reaction chamber, and since we only see light coming *towards* us, there would be no light to detect around its center, thus appearing to be dark and void of light. However, the thruster must have been a sight to behold. Even if our journal writer hadn't given away the location, I'm sure that the thruster would have been seen, even far beyond the horizon. And it would have been really, really bright. But then it also would have been too late, and Edengone would have been floating through endless space." Then a familiar look crossed his face. He had an idea. "We can fix this planet," he said in almost a whisper.

"It sounds like they already tried that," Pik pointed out.

"And they failed, yes," Ron said. "But that was because they didn't have all of the pieces." He held up the legacy journal. "We could fire up the propulsion system right now and fix this planet," Ron suggested excitedly.

"That would destroy it," John stated.

"He's right," Pik said. "Putting this planet back into a normal rotation would mean this side of the planet would cool off and the other side, the side covered with snow, would warm up. That could have cataclysmic consequences for everything living in between; major flooding being one of them."

"But once it stabilized, there would be so much more room for everything living and for more life to live," Ron argued. Ron had a frenzied, glazed look in his eye; the kind of look he gets when his excitement clouds his judgment and his stubbornness solidifies his will.

"Ron," I said in a forceful but calm and controlled tone to get his attention, "you are right. But right now is not the right time. It would be better for us to finish our task, return to base, and then fix the planet. That way everyone living between the two extremes can prepare and be ready for this kind of huge, global change. It would be the wise way to do it."

I looked Ron sternly in the eye. The wild excitement in Ron's eyes faded until a more sensible and reasonable countenance replaced it. "You're right," he said. "We need to fix one problem at a time."

I thought for a moment because that was not what I meant, but it was good enough for now. "Exactly," I said.

Then a smile curled across Ron's face and he raised a finger as another idea took shape in his mind. "However," he said, "we can still use this knowledge to our advantage."

"How so?" I asked cautiously.

"We can equip the colossal half-tracks with smaller versions of the light propulsion engine and be knocking at the door of Death's Grave within a few Edengone days."

Tinear looked at Pik and John. "Is that possible?"

Ron opened to a few pages in the journal and pointed to sections of interest while Pik and John looked on. Pik took the journal from Ron and thumbed through it again while John looked over Pik's shoulder. Then Pik looked at John, as though they were quietly consulting. After a moment, they both looked at Tinear.

"Yes, it's possible," Pik stated.

Tinear smiled. "Good. Let's get it done. Pik, I want all the files on that computer backed up and locked up. Then I want both the computer and journal put in a safe box and safely stowed away to return to headquarters. Ron, you have permission to organize the teams how you see fit, within reason, to get the vehicles equipped. John, you shadow Ron and double check his work." Then Tinear pointed a stern finger at John as he said, "And make sure he does not try to fix this planet. Am I clear?"

"Yes, sir," John smartly responded.

"Good. Let's go."

The crew members who had been sent to scout further down the enormous tunnel had found other rooms that looked like they were used for constructing and maintaining the light propulsion engine. Pik repurposed the machines and materials stored there to help manufacture and build components for the modifications we would be making to the half-tracks.

Ron and Pik worked together to redesign the light propulsion engine, to reduce it to a more manageable package with lower power requirements. The first prototype we built was naturally a little rough and shot spurts of blinding light in sporadic intervals and chaotic streams. It was a beautiful sight to see, even through the lens of a welding mask. The device eventually exploded and charred the test chamber we had placed it in. But after a couple more prototypes and a few tests, we had a working light propulsion engine that we were satisfied with, except for Ron. He was absolutely beside himself, like a toddler in a candy store, shaking and quivering with uncontainable glee.

The light propulsion engines, which we started referring to as "LPEs", were surprisingly easy to assemble once Ron and Pik had calculated the proportion reductions in the original design and calibrated the more sensitive components. The spherical reaction chambers of each LPE were a little larger than a basketball, and each half-track had a total of four LPEs, one mounted at the lower end of each corner of the chassis, much like a quadcopter. The primary difference between our LPEs and the big one we had found in the mountain, aside from size, was that our little LPEs swiveled as an entire whole, rather than having an inner pendulum. This gave us greater control and flight stability.

Yes, I said "flight". We were going to get those colossal half-tracks airborne. When Ron had first suggested the idea of using the LPEs, I had imagined they would function like a booster and help us move along the ground. But Ron pointed out that the dunes would become jumps with that idea, and there would have been a very real chance we would get launched into orbit. To keep that from happening we just weren't going to touch the ground at all. As a matter of fact, we weren't going to be driving at all. The navigation and stability of the vehicle at the speeds the LPEs were capable of would have been nearly impossible to manage, even for a duo as skilled as Numigh and Murlem. So Pik and John worked on an automated flight system to do the dirty work for us. Theoretically, once the vehicles had been completed, we would simply enter them, drive them out into the open, punch in our desired coordinates, and then sit back and enjoy the onboard entertainment and refreshments. This brought my mind back to home, and the idea of automated cars. I remembered how bad of an idea it had seemed to me when I first heard about it. It still seems like a bad idea, mostly because you can't calculate how random other drives are or can be. But flying across the Demog Desert under the watchful care of an automated pilot didn't feel as risky to me, mostly because I knew we wouldn't be coming across anyone and their death-inducing incompetence way out here.

As Ron had predicted, we had the LPEs mounted and operational within a few days. Now we only needed to take our leave of the facility and be on our way.

"Alright people!" Tinear shouted. "Vacation is over! Saddle up!"

We boarded the half-tracks and rolled further down the tunnel for many hours until a speck of light poked a hole in the darkness. Eventually, the browned sunlight over The Bull's Eye tinted the inside of our cab and the red stones of the surrounding rock field filled our view. We emerged from the tunnel, and we stopped at the crest of the mountain slope just outside the exit. The other two half-tracks pulled up alongside us. Ron said it would be too dangerous for us to travel in a single file as we had done so far. He said there was nothing wrong with lateral expansion to prevent vertical calamity. We agreed with him.

Murlem picked up the radio. "Colossal one, initiating lift off," he said.

Numigh took hold of a throttle lever and gently pressed it forward. An unusual electrical hum emanated from the four LPEs and the vehicle felt like it was riding over rough terrain, but there was a strange rising sensation accompanying it.

Murlem looked at the dials with approval. "Colossal one is airborne," he announced joyfully.

The other crews radioed in and reported they, too, were airborne and ready for departure.

I walked behind Numigh and Murlem and leaned to look out the window at the other half-tracks. A brilliant, blinding, white light that veiled the lower half of the colossal half-tracks blasted from the LPEs. I held a hand up and blocked the light so I could see the vehicles. It was bizarre to see such a cumbersome, behemoth of a machine hovering like a dragonfly.

I noticed Murlem taking nervous glances out his window at the ground below.

"Are you going to be okay?" I asked.

"Yeah," he said with a jittery nod. "I'll just tell myself I'm not actually in the air. I'm just looking through the visor of my kite. Everything is going to be okay," he said weakly.

"You'll want to buckle up," Ron advised as he fastened the harness of his seat.

I sat down and Murlem checked some figures one more time before he said, "Course commands input to navigation system. Ready for departure."

Tinear picked up the radio and looked at his watch. "All vehicles begin flight command sequence at fourteen sixty-five hours." Then he hung up the radio and fastened his seatbelt as well. He looked back at his watch once he was settled in. Then he began the countdown. "Three... Two... One... Let it rip!"

Numigh jammed a large button down and then held on tight to his seat harness. The electrical whirring wound up and the vehicle started moving, slowly at first, but as the LPEs continued to swivel back, we began to accelerate at a tremendous rate. The seats in the back of the cab were faced inward, toward the center of the vehicle, so as we accelerated, everyone leaned sideways, towards the back. We struggled to stay upright. The force was so severe that Ron couldn't stay upright, and his head landed on my shoulder.

"Get back in your own seat! It's hard enough for me to stay up without trying to keep you up, as well!" I shouted over the sound of the LPEs. "He's touching me!" I yelled in a tattle-tail tone.

"I've fallen and I can't get up!" Ron shouted. "Is it going to be like this the entire way?!"

"No!" Ron answered. "Once we reach cruising velocity then inertia should equilibrate and everything should be normal!"

"Good!" I yelled, not really understanding what he had said or meant. "I like normal!" Then, after waiting for a few moments longer, I asked, "Are we there yet?! When is everything going to be normal again?!"

Just then, as though in answer to my question of distress, the invisible force that had us all in its clutches slowly released its grip, and we sat upright in our seats with many moans and groans of discomfort. The noise from the LPEs softened and maintained a bearable whirring sound. Numigh and Murlem were both laughing.

"That was awesome!" Murlem shouted. "Let's stop and do it again!"

"I've got a better idea," I said, slightly disgruntled, "let's turn the seats the correct way next time."

"Agreed," Tinear said as he held the side of his neck. "Check in with the other crews. Make sure no one else is injured."

I unbuckled as I looked out the windshield at the scene ahead and did not notice anything different other than the ground being far below us and moving quickly.

"Is this what it looks like to travel at the speed of light?" I asked, a little disappointed.

"No," Ron laughed. "We are using light to propel us, but that doesn't mean we are moving at the speed of light. It's like moving air with a jet engine without traveling at the speed of sound. The potential is there, but we don't need to go that fast. Actually, we shouldn't go that fast, for structural integrity reasons. I don't know if you've noticed, but the designers of these half-tracks were not too concerned about aerodynamics."

"That reminds me," I said tentatively. "We passed through some rough weather on the way here. How are these machines going to do in strong winds?" I asked.

"We compensated for that in the programing," John said.

Just then, the vehicle shifted hard to one side and fishtailed, throwing most of us to the floor with a thud. Numigh instinctively grabbed the steering wheel, but the wheel wasn't connected to the LPEs, so the act was futile. The half-track stabilized and we looked at John from our scattered positions around the cab.

"We could have compensated a little more, I suppose," he admitted.

"If worst comes to worst, we could always land and continue on wheels and tracks," Numigh pointed out as he still clutched the useless steering wheel.

"At least up here we don't need to get out and dig sand away from around the wheels and tracks every time the condensers need to catch up," I said. I got up off the floor and returned to my seat.

"Actually," Murlem began, prompting me to roll my eyes and regret speaking too soon. "We will need to make regular landings. The LPEs are powered by the same engine we've been using this whole time."

"So, business as usual?" I asked sullenly.

"Yep."

I buckled up again, thinking it was better to stay in my seat than to be sporadically thrown to the floor. I stared at the desolate, forlorn scene before us through the windshield and I studied the landscape as I tried to imagine what the area was like before the Forward Party had fired their giant light propulsion engine and stopped Edengone's spinning. While I thought, consciousness slowly drifted away, and I fell asleep.

Chapter 15 – Flight And Fall

Those devilish eyes stared, with his brow pressed together. His mouth was stern. He stood proud, in defiance. Blood dripped from his hands. Bodies lay strewn about him.

"You and I aren't different," he said in an articulate voice. "You kill hundreds. I kill thousands. I just do what we do better than you." He smiled, and his head swayed in a conceited way.

I ignored him. My team and I had him surrounded. He was as good as captured. We advanced on our prey, closing in to make the final capture or, if necessary, kill.

A whistling overhead warned us of falling mortar shells.

"Take cover!" I shouted. We scrambled behind vehicles and crates. We could only hope our shelters would shield us from the deadly shrapnel that would fly after the shells hit. I looked over the hood of the car I was hiding behind and saw our target standing with opened arms, welcoming the deadly rescue the shells brought. Then he was gone, in a blast of fire and dirt. Debris landed all around us with loud thuds. That was it then. It was done. Debris continued to fall around us.

I was abruptly awakened by the too familiar thudding sound of sand-hail striking the roof of the half-track. From the sounds of it, I guessed that we had just barely entered the hail storm. I looked out the windshield. We were back on the ground.

"Welcome back to the land of the living," Ron greeted me.

"How long was I asleep?"

"A few hours," he answered.

"Only a few hours?" I questioned in amazement. "And we're already coming across the sand hail?"

"Like I said, these light propulsion engines will save us a lot of time," he said casually.

Tinear stood up. "Okay. You all know the routine. Let's get that windshield covered."

We put on our cherub-suits. Then we gathered the gundon's shell pieces and other materials we would need to protect the windows from the relentless, heavy sand-hail. Again, we worked in pairs. One worked on fastening the bug shell to the vehicle while the other held up another piece of bug shell to shield both of them from the hail.

I had just finished fastening my part when a loud clang pulled my attention to one of the LPEs. I leaned closer and examined the device. I noticed an unnervingly sized dent in the upper part of the sphere. I turned on my radio.

"Tinear," I called, "we should also cover the LPEs. I've got a damaged one over here. It just took a hit from a hailstone."

"Copy that," Tinear replied.

"And while we are on the topic," I added, "I think we should drive on the ground through this part. If a LPE gets damaged in the hail and we fall from the sky, that could be a major setback for us."

"You're right," Tinear replied. "Murlem, tell the other half-tracks to armor their LPEs. We're getting through this the old fashioned way."

We finished fastening the gundon shells and settled back into our seat.

"How are we looking up here?" Tinear asked Numigh and Murlem.

"Eager to get back to the love of my life," Numigh said as he rubbed the steering wheel.

"All the sensors have been adjusted for blind driving," Murlem reported. "And the condensers are all caught up on refueling and running at peak efficiency."

"Excellent," Tinear said, satisfied. "Just like last time, Numigh. Nice and slow to give the condensers a fighting chance at keeping us fueled so we won't need to stop."

Then we began our slow, swaying, and noisy drive through the bizarre storm of hailing sand. The journey was uneventful, and a few days later we emerged on the other side of the hail storm. We stopped again once the hail had stopped beating the roof of our half-track, and we put on our cherub-suits and exited the vehicle to remove the gundon shells from the windshield and LPEs.

I shielded my eyes as the airlock opened to the bright, sunny outside, and I joined the others out on the golden sands and under a blue, clear sky. I looked back at the wall of brown we had left behind and wondered once more what secrets it hid. But my thoughts were interrupted before they got much further than that.

"Oh! Glorious sun! How I have missed you!" Colem exclaimed, with outstretched arms and a heavenward gaze, as though he were ready to embrace the glowing sphere in the sky.

Ron and Pik examined the LPEs while we removed the bug shell armor, and they soon determined that they were still flight worthy. Then we returned to the confines of the half-track's bowels and went to work

223

reorienting the seats to prevent repeating the injuries and awkwardness of our first launch. We removed the seats from their wall mounts and fastened them to the floor. Since the seats had been mounted to the walls and used the wall's structure to hold them off of the floor, there was nothing to hold them up when we moved them to the center of the cab and faced them forward. So the seats were resting directly on the floor, and our legs stuck out directly in front of us.

"Everyone ready?" Murlem asked after we had buckled up.

"Let's go," Tinear said.

Numigh pressed a lever forward. The engines began to whirr louder and louder, and the vehicle rumbled into the air.

"Entering course commands into navigation system. Ready for departure," Murlem reported.

Tinear looked at his watch and picked up the radio. "All vehicles depart at one hundred hours," he said

And in a few moments, we were speeding toward the horizon. This time, with the seats facing the correct way, the acceleration to cruising speed was like the first drop on a rollercoaster, except there was no ground or track bottom to know when the acceleration would stop. It was simply thrilling. After a few moments, the half-track had reached cruising speed and the accelerative force released us from the back of our seats. This time, everyone was laughing.

"Wow! We should stop and do that again," I exclaimed.

"I second that," Numigh said.

"We'll be getting plenty of that along the way," Tinear said. "Remember, we still need to stop to let the condensers refill the tanks."

"Great!" I said with a laugh.

"Alright. Everyone up. We need to get the seats back where they belong," Tinear said.

"Why don't we leave the seats where they are?" Ron asked. "We're going to need to put them back this way again anyway after we let the condensers refill the tanks."

"Look around you," Tinear said. "The seats are in the middle of our living space. I know our mobile home was never much to begin with and it just now sprouted wings, but I intend to make the most of it anyway. We need room to move. We need to keep from going stir-crazy. Now get up and mount the seats back where they belong."

We unbuckled and put the seats back on their wall mounts, and life went back to the way it had been over the last few weeks.

The rest of that day passed by without any incident, and the following day we began looking for somewhere to land and let the condensers refuel.

"What about over there?" Numigh asked. He pointed to a location in the distance.

"No," Murlem responded. "None of that is any good. Do you see how all of the dunes are swirled and running in different directions? We will get buried alive over there."

"Well, we're going to need to land somewhere," Numigh said with a sigh. "The tanks are nearly depleted."

Murlem scanned the horizon and pointed. "There, near that cone-shaped pit. It doesn't look like that sand has moved in a long time."

Numigh adjusted our course and we flew to the location Murlem referred to.

"Land as close as you can to the edge of that pit," Murlem advised. "That looks like the least disturbed spot. We shouldn't get buried there."

Numigh landed the half-track, and the other half-tracks landed on either side of us. Then we waited.

"Refill should be complete in about thirty minutes," Murlem announced.

"Maybe we should get the chairs back in the middle of the cab for launch while we wait," I suggested.

"Yep," Tinear agreed. "Let's get it done."

So we began dismounting the seats from the walls again and mounting them to the floors when Numigh suddenly hissed out, "Shhhh! Do you hear that? Where is that rumbling coming from?"

Murlem checked the gauges on the dashboard and said, "It looks like there's mild seismic activity. Not enough to worry abo-"

Numigh had looked out his window while Murlem was talking and something launched him into action. He snatched the radio and shouted, "Colossal three, move! Now!" Then he dropped the radio, started the engine and slammed the pedal to the floor. The half-track launched forward, throwing most of us and the dismounted seats to the back of the cab. Then he slammed on the brakes after a short distance, which threw everything and everyone back to the front. "The side of that pit is caving in!" Numigh yelled back to us.

"John, get up in your turret and get an eyeball on colossal three," Tinear ordered. "Murlem, get them on the radio! Saeui and Colem, battle stations! Ron and Mike, suit up. Numigh, leave the engine running. If the vehicle feels like it's going to fall in, then get us out of here, fast."

John leaped into the turret seat and rotated the viewer toward the pit. "No sign of them, sir," John reported.

Murlem picked up the radio. "Colossal three, come in. What is your status?"

There was no answer. Tinear, Ron, and I were quickly gearing up.

Murlem tried again. "Colossal three, do you copy?"

Then an urgent voice came back over the radio. "We're sliding into the pit! Something is trying to pull us in!"

"Numigh, get the canons a line of sight with the bottom of that pit! Murlem, tell the other crew to do the same! Ron, Mike, with me!" Tinear ordered as he opened the airlock and stepped in.

I stepped into the airlock after Tinear had cleared the vehicle and the cab door sealed behind me. The airlock depressurized. Just as the back hatch began to open, Tinear's voice rang urgently over the radio.

"Fire at the bottom of the pit! Now! Now! Now!"

I jumped from the back of the moving half-track and broke my fall with a roll in the giving sand. I quickly got back to my feet and ran to the edge of the pit where Tinear was standing.

Colem's voice came over the radio. "Negative! The cannons' depression won't go that far! No shot! Repeat, no shot!"

I made it to the pit's edge and looked down. The slope of the pit-side was about eight half-tracks long. Colossal three had slid halfway down the sandy slope of the pit and was struggling to drive back out. The engine roared, and the wheels and tracks sprayed sand in huge arches. The vehicle crabbed side to side as the driver searched for traction.

"Get the vehicles turned around!" Tinear ordered. "We're going to have to pull them out! Get in position and wait for my command!"

Just then, two giant spider legs sprung from the bottom of the pit and flung sand up the pit's sides and at

228

the sliding half-track, causing the side of the pit to avalanche a little more and the vehicle to slide a little further.

Tinear retrieved a heavy chain with two large hooks on either end from one of the half-tracks. I grabbed another such chain from the other half-track. We hooked one end of the chain to the rear recovery loops of each vehicle. Tinear stood at the pit's edge with the other end of his chain.

"Give me the other chain," he said.

"Nope. Not you. You have orders to give," I said as I snatched the hook from Tinear and jumped down the side of the pit before he could protest. I slid down into the pit toward the flailing half-track and clutched the ends of the chains that were attached to the vehicles above. The driver of colossal three stopped crabbing side to side and lined up with my slide to catch me with the front bumper. I should have slid under the tall half-track, but the vehicle had sunk its thrashing treads deep into the tumbling sand. It was losing the battle. I quickly slipped the chains' hooks into the front recovery loops of the struggling half-track. Then I climbed onto the hood of the vehicle.

"Go!" I shouted over the radio, once I was safely away from the chains.

I could hear the roar of the other two half-tracks as their drivers pushed them into action. The chains pulled tight with a clatter and a straining ring. The spider legs below threw another shower of sand, making it difficult to see and creating another small avalanche. But the half-track stayed steady. Its engine roared and its drivetrain whined while it continued to fight for its life.

"Pull us out!" I shouted over the radio.

I heard a renewed effort from the straining vehicles above. I looked up and saw Tinear and Ron standing at the pit's edge. A spray of sand from the other half tracks cascaded over the edge. Then Tinear's voice came over the radio.

"It's no good!" Tinear's voice cried over the radio. "Abandon the vehicle! Everyone in colossal three, get out and hang on to the chains! Mike, be ready to pull the pins on the hooks to free the chains from the vehicle!"

"Got it!" I replied.

"Colossal three," Tinear called over the radio, "Once everyone has their suits on, disengage the safety from the airlock so you can all get out quickly! Repeat, vent the cab via the airlock!"

"Copy that," Pik's voice answered.

A moment or two passed. I looked in through the windshield at the crew inside. The driver was still fighting to keep the vehicle from sliding any further into the pit, and everyone else was gathered at the back of the cab around the airlock entrance. Everyone had their suits on, but something was delaying them.

"What's wrong?" I asked urgently over the radio.

The driver looked at me and said, "The safety won't disengage. We're coming out one at a time."

I nodded, and another spray of sand from the spider legs showered down on us. "Make it fast!" I said.

Then another shower of sand sprung from the pit bottom, followed by another, and another. The creature below had also increased its efforts, and they were more effective than ours. The half-track again began to slide.

"No, no, no!" I shouted.

"Pull! Pull!" Tinear ordered the drivers.

But we continued to slide. I peeked over the roof of the half-track and looked at the pit bottom below. I was just in time to see the creature rear its bug-ugly head from the sand as it threw up more sand and reached out with sharp mandibles. Then I felt something violently push my whole body away from the pit bottom, like a blast of wind, or like the explosion in Doctor Dalmour's lab before Ron blacked out. Then I realized that it was *exactly* like the explosion in Dalmour's lab.

"Good thinking, Ron," I whispered to myself. I looked up toward Ron at the pit's edge. He had dropped to a knee and he held the side of his head in pain. Tinear did not notice. "Just hang in there a little longer," I quietly pleaded.

The half-track in the pit seemed to experience the same effect, because it, too, lunged just out of reach of the searching mandibles. The half-track and I began sliding back down into the pit again, and just when it seemed that the mandibles would snatch us, another blast struck me and the half-track, launching us just out of reach. It was painful, like getting checked in a hockey game by someone twice my size, but it was keeping us alive. The two half-tracks at the top of the pit also surged forward as I and colossal three were hit by each explosive push Ron emitted. Then they slowly slid back, succumbing to the weight of the falling vehicle.

A few of the crew members had exited the half-track and were climbing along the side of the vehicle, making their way to the front. The driver was still at the wheel, struggling to keep the vehicle steady.

"Come on!" I encouraged.

The creature below threw more sand and reached with its mandibles. Ron emitted another burst, and we lurched out of reach. The push nearly threw a couple of the crew members off the vehicle, but they held on. I looked in the cab, and only the driver remained.

"Come on! Get out here!" I ordered. "We aren't leaving you here!"

The driver quickly grabbed a rifle. He jammed it between the seat and the throttle to keep the vehicle going. He leaped from his seat and into the airlock. The trick worked for a little while, but the gun slipped out of place and released the throttle. The vehicle began to slide faster without the help of the engine. Ron emitted another burst. The driver emerged and scrambled along the side of the vehicle until he joined us at the chains.

Everyone was holding onto the chains and Pik and I fought with the pins holding the hooks to the chains.

"We can't pull the pins out!" I radioed. "You need to give us some slack to release the tension!" I shouted urgently. "Tell the other drivers to back up!"

"Drivers, prepare to reverse on my command!" Tinear ordered. "Now!"

The chain went slack for a moment before the sliding vehicle out-slid the slack chains, but that was all we needed. Pik and I pulled the pins, and the half-track tumbled to the pit's bottom, leaving its crew dangling on the pit's sides by two chains. The giant creature below wrapped its legs around the half-track and greedily sunk its mandibles into it before it disappeared below the surface of the sand.

"That's it!" I shouted over the radio. "Pull us out!"

The drivers above applied their throttles and carefully dragged us up and out of the pit. Once we reached level ground again, I got up and ran to Ron, where he lied sprawled on the ground. I kneeled over him.

"Ron," I said, gently shaking his shoulder, "Ron, are you alright?"

He slowly sat up with a groan. "Yeah. But I have got a whopping headache."

"Come on," I said, pulling him to his feet. "We can fix that."

We all stood for a moment at the pit's edge. We watched the slowly churning sand below and listened to the sound of bending metal.

"It's too bad all that ordnance is going to waste," Tinear said, almost mournfully.

"It's not going to waste," Pik said. He held up a remote detonator.

Ron smiled. "Bon appétit," he said.

Pik pulled the trigger, and the pit bottom exploded with a spray of sand and steam from the destroyed half-track's water reservoirs. The creature must have exploded, too, because slimy stretches of something meaty rained down around us and sizzled when it hit the hot sand. Of course, a piece landed on my helmet and draped over my shoulder.

I wiped it off and brushed off my gloves. Then I looked at the crew of colossal three and said, "You guys want a ride?"

Crew three joined us, and crew four that had been in our first colossal half-track casualty joined the rest of their crew in the other half-track.

"Thousands of miles, a few weeks, and we are down to two half-tracks with full crew numbers," I said, taking note of our inventory. "We've seen some action. We've made some unexpected discoveries. All things considered, we've done well."

Everyone settled into their seats and buckled up. Numigh pressed a lever forward and the LPEs engaged, lifting the vehicle from the sand.

"This is the last stretch, boys!" Tinear announced enthusiastically. "Let it rip!"

Murlem entered the navigation information, and, once again, the invisible force of aggressive acceleration weighed upon us as we sped toward the horizon. We were now on the fast path to Death's Grave.

Chapter 16 – Rules Of War

The dunes gradually grew smaller as we sped along above the desert, and eventually the dunes flattened and were gone altogether. The sand was soon dotted with patches of rugged shrubs, and those gave way to vast grasslands. The grasslands gave way to more inviting shrubbery, and then we encountered the forests.

"Alright. Land them here," Tinear ordered.

Numigh pulled back on a lever, and the vehicle slowly descended until it rested its enormous weight on the foliage below.

"Should we fly or drive?" Tinear asked, looking at me.

"You're asking me?" I asked in surprise. He hadn't ever directly asked for my opinion in the past, though that hadn't stopped me from giving my opinion anyway.

He nodded. "This is where your experience comes in. In fact, I would be willing to turn over full command of this operation to you right now if it will ensure the success of this mission. Your advice has proven effective, and your judgment seems sound. You will be taking command for sure when we move to invade Death's Grave, but as the senior officer on this side of the planet, I think it would be best to let you do your job from here." He tore off the patch designating his rank from his shoulder and slapped the patch on my uniform. "And that way if something goes wrong, at least it's not on my watch," he said with a wink. "Officer on board!" he announced. Both crews in the cab stood to attention and looked at me. "What are your orders, sir?" Tinear asked.

I looked around at the two crews and imagined the other two in the other vehicle. In some of their faces, I saw friends I had known from Earth. In other faces, I saw friends I had made on Edengone. These were the faces of friends. This was a band of brothers in arms; united, loyal, and determined. I felt the familiar weight of responsibility rest upon my shoulders.

"Murlem," I said, "get your kite out. We need to know the lay of the land, how dense this forest is, and where potential threats may be hiding between us and Death's Grave."

"Permission to speak, sir," Murlem requested.

"Granted," I replied.

"Now that we are out of the sand storm, we have a clear view from our satellite positioned over us. It will be able to give us a wider, further view without any risk of exposing our position, as long as the weather is clear."

"Good. Establish a connection," I ordered.

"Yes, sir," he replied and went to work at the controls on the dashboard.

I looked back to the two crews in the crowded cab. "Everyone else needs to be checking weapons and equipment. Weapons need to be cleaned and battle ready. We are in enemy territory. Numigh, forward that to the other vehicle."

"We have a connection with the satellite, sir," Murlem reported.

"Tinear, I want you to see this, too," I said as I looked over Murlem's shoulder at the image the satellite had sent.

Murlem pointed to the map. "There's Death's Grave."

"Can we get all of this in a portable hologram projector?" I asked.

"Sure. It will take a few moments," he answered.

"Good. We'll get the entire squad together outside and go over the plan," I said.

A few minutes later, all crew members were outside and gathered in a half-circle before me. Murlem turned on the hologram and a map of the city where Death's Grave resided appeared in the air above it. Then the image zoomed in on Death's Grave.

"Here is Death's Grave," I said, beginning the mission brief. "Our objective is to destroy the entire facility," I sighed wearily, "and everyone in it."

"That is genocide!" Ron erupted.

"Order in the ranks!" Tinear shouted.

"Why are you just now bringing this up?" I asked, a little annoyed.

Ron shrugged. "I guess it's just now hitting home. I'm just now realizing what we are about to do. This is mass murder. That is what this is," he said with vigor.

"No. It's war," I stated grimly.

"Maybe so. But there are rules in war, too; rules of engagement and such."

"Many may believe that, but the truth is, the rules of war are simple," I said. "The last man standing wins. Those are the rules. We're going to be the last men standing."

"Let us reason with them first. Perhaps we could save some lives," Ron pleaded.

"Reasoning has already been tried, and it failed," Tinear stated irately. "When speech is ineffective, when all other forms of communication are rendered null, when reason has been drowned by either delusion or resolve, then the force of war becomes the arbitrator. And like the ancient civilizations, let the involved forces call upon whatever power they believe will sustain them, and the victors win the knowledge that they were right, and their principles of living will rule supreme."

"Winning does not mean you are right," Ron said angrily.

"No?" I challenged, raising my eyebrows. "Evolution teaches survival of the fittest. Religion preaches strength through righteousness. Any way you look at it, being strong is a desired attribute, and the society that cultivates strength the best will win."

"Thereby proving that their way of living is better and, therefore, more correct," Tinear added.

I continued the argument. "Think of almost any war. The winning army was backed by a society that was strong enough to sustain their armies and give its forces either the resolve and determination, or the firepower to subdue the enemy. History will back me up on this one." Then I remembered Ron was not familiar with my military background, and I saw the confusion and worry on his face. He had always known me as a mild-mannered philosophy teacher.

"Who were you back on Earth, really?" he asked.

"Ron," I said in a friendlier tone, "I was your friend. I still am. I watched your back and protected you from dangers you didn't know existed. I've fought battles that the rest of Earth will never know about. I fought those battles to protect you, my family, and everyone. I'm not proud about it, but it has taught me that the right course of action is not always pleasant or comfortable, and sometimes our choices take us places we do not expect to be." I saw him review the events of the last few weeks, and he seemed to peacefully capitulate. "I would have told you," I added, "but I was under oath and forbidden from mentioning my military 'dealings' to anyone on Earth. Now that we aren't on Earth, I would tell you, but I hope we will return to

Earth. So to keep you safe and to preserve the integrity of my honor, all you need to know about me is that I'm not a stranger to warfare."

A look in Ron's eye told me he understood.

I continued with the briefing. "The facility consists of several buildings on the surface." A square on the hologram highlighted the area of the facility. I pointed to each building as I listed them. "The barracks are the long narrow structure on this edge. There is a manufacturing building here, along this edge near the barracks, where components for the implants are produced. The infirmary is this 'L' shaped..." I noticed a few confused glances. Then I remembered that their alphabet was different, and they didn't know what an "L" looks like. "...I mean this corner shaped building on the opposite side from the barracks. This is where the undying implants are installed, wounded are treated, and where soldiers recover before being redeployed. Then there's the heart of the whole outfit; the laboratories, here, in the center of it all. There is a labyrinth of connecting infrastructure beneath the surface, leaving a massive cavity under all of the key structures. And here is our objective." I highlighted the point I was referring to. "This is the Achilles' heel of-"

"They don't know what that means," Ron reminded me.

"This is the weak spot," I reiterated. "The main support pillar is right below the labs in this giant underground... place."

"What's in there?" Saeui asked.

"We don't' know. However, power draw and activity levels suggest it may house a bank of computers. It could be a giant server or a huge data bank. Whatever it is, we are here to destroy it." I pointed to the pillar in the hologram. "If we take out this foundational structure from within, then the rest of the facility will crumble to its destruction.

"As for what we can expect from the opposition," I continued, "this facility is concerned with the production of soldiers, so the only firepower we expect from the enemy will be from light arms. The facility has a minimal garrison. Most of the soldiers at Death's Grave are in the recovery section of the infirmary. However, given what we know about the enemy's resilience to pain or injury, the few that are present and battle-ready are not to be taken lightly, much less ignored. Automated security systems are simple and rudimentary, consisting of alarms and automatic locking doors. The enemy seems confident that they are safe from invasion, and, much like your base," I indicated to Tinear and the rest of the squad, "they rely primarily on staying out of sight to ensure their security.

"The method of execution will be overwhelming-force going in, and rapid exfiltration. We will divide into two smaller squads. Squad one will be composed of the primary drivers of the four half-tracks and the gunners of the remaining vehicles. They will be commanded by Tinear, and they will be in the half-tracks. The rest of you will be with me, and we will be attacking the facility on foot.

"The first target will be the control tower at the top of the laboratories. That tower controls the gates and the main communications. One of the cannons on the half-tracks will target and fire upon that structure, thereby giving us time to get into the facility before the rest of them can figure out what is going on. We need to get to our objective before they initiate a lockdown. Destroying the control tower first should delay their response time for scrambling troops and keep the doors unlocked for a little longer. We will be carrying door-breach charges with us in case the doors are locked after we get inside. However, locked doors will slow us down and increase our chances of failure. We need to move swiftly to avoid that situation.

"The shot fired at the control tower will be the signal for the rest of the plan to commence. The other cannons will concentrate fire on the barracks to neutralize any possible reinforcements before they can be deployed against us. Once the control tower and barracks are destroyed, the gunners will fire at will at anything they may believe to be important. The bombardment will divert attention from our attack of the facility and minimize resistance. The half-tracks will patrol the perimeter during their bombardment to ensure no one escapes. They will remain until my team has placed the charges, after which they will retreat using the LPEs to get to the rendezvous point. After the bombardment has begun, my team will storm the front doors of the lab building, neutralizing any and all personnel we encounter."

Ron raised his hand. "Everyone?" he asked.

I gave a single, stern nod. "Our orders are to eliminate everything associated with the development, production, and maintenance of the 'undying'. That includes knowledge. Those are our orders."

Ron lowered his hand.

I continued where I had left off. "My team will push on to the staircase that leads to the primary pillar and place the charges around it. There are maintenance panels to their systems around that primary pillar. The charges will be placed inside those panels to avoid detection," I pointed to where the charges needed to be placed. "While the charges are being placed, we need to hold off any enemy counterattack or other interference at points out of eyesight of the primary pillar. We don't want the enemy knowing the charges are there until they are detonated. After we place the charges, we will rapidly retreat to this lower section here, where we will enter the sewer system through this grate and escape back into the city to rendezvous with the vehicles. Once we are clear of the blast radius, we will detonate the charges remotely and go home. Are there any questions?"

"Why don't we use the sewer to get in and then use it to get out?" Murlem asked.

"Because that would break not just one, but two rules of infiltration. One, don't be predictable. And two, never use the same route twice if another one is available," I answered.

"Then why don't we use the sewer to get in and leave through the front doors? Wouldn't that draw them away from the charges we will be leaving behind?"

"Once they know what we are up to, they are going to come after us through the front doors, whether we went in that way or not, and by then they will have figured out how we got in and will have blocked it. That would leave us trapped. Our entrance would be shut tight and our exit would be overrun with enemy forces. They would expect us to use the doors once they know they are being attacked. So, we will use the doors to get in, while we have the element of surprise. We are going in through the front doors with guns blazing, and we are escaping through the sewer. Go in with a grand entrance, and leave with a discrete exit, just like going to a party. Furthermore, we want to draw them *into* the facility and *closer* to the explosion for maximum effect."

"You mean to kill more people," Ron said bitterly.

"However you want to word it, it is what it is," I replied coolly.

Tinear raised his hand and asked, "How are we going to get near enough to the facility in these half-tracks without being detected?"

"According to intelligence, their factories are turning out new and different vehicles on a regular basis. The enemy also seems to believe that they are safe, far away from the war. Their forces have the ways blocked on either side in the habitable zone, and the extreme climate conditions protect their flanks. They don't have any reason to suspect enemies are at the heart of their territory. With that false sense of security and the frequent sightings of new military vehicles traversing their roads, no one would be surprised or even raise an eyebrow if we simply drive down the middle of the street. We expect them to assume we are one of them."

"Isn't that risky? Shouldn't we at least try to remain unseen?"

"Sometimes the best hiding place is in plain sight. If we were caught snooping around then they would have a reason to be suspicious, but if we look like we belong there, then they will believe we belong there. Just stay cool and act like you've never been anywhere else other than Death's Grave. At the same time, remain discretely alert and aware of your surroundings."

"What if we used the LPEs and flew to Death's Grave?" Murlem asked.

I focused the hologram of the map on a few key points and said, "Because it looks like they are expecting your forces to launch missiles or a long-range air force strike. These ground-to-air defenses would shoot us down before we got within sight of Death's Grave. In fact, it looks like their entire territory is dotted with these weapons. I'm assuming that's why General Kulek didn't have us fly here."

Ron spoke up. "Why can't one of us sneak into the facility, place the charges, and then sneak out. No one would know we were there, and if something goes wrong then we don't risk losing as many of our own people."

The others raised their eyebrows in surprise and others nodded their heads in agreement.

"That is an excellent tactic, and under normal circumstances that would be the best option," I said encouragingly. "However, we all came on this mission because we are all needed here. If this mission could have been done with one man, then I would have done it alone. But as you know, I could not have crossed the Demog Desert alone. None of us could have. Furthermore, if I were to fail and be discovered by the enemy, then they would be aware of our capabilities to cross the desert, a feat they currently believe to be impossible. They would also know that the location of their base is known by us and they would move operations to a different location with greater efforts to conceal it. We would be back to square one, and more lives would be lost on the battlefront. By going in with a force like this and following the plan I have laid out, we have a much better chance of completing the mission the first time, because this time we have the element of surprise, we know where they are at, their defenses are weak, and we won't need to make a second trip. This time, the first time, we deliver a crippling blow to the enemy. This time is our time. This time is our only chance, and this time we won't need another." I looked around at the squad and asked, "Are there any other questions related to the current plan, and not an inquisition into why a different plan was not chosen?"

No one replied.

Tinear clapped his hands once and said, as he circled his hand over his head, "Alright! You heard the man! Let's get back in those half-tracks and do this! Next stop: Death's Grave!"

Back in the half-track, I reviewed the map of the local area with Numigh.

"We need to get to that road," I said, pointing to the map. "It's the fastest way to Death's Grave. Follow the ridgeline as closely as you can. There are fewer trees along it."

"Should we fly or drive?" Numigh asked.

"Hover just above the ground at low speeds. That will be faster than driving and more discreet than outright flying. We don't want to draw attention to ourselves any more than we have to."

Numigh pressed forward on the lever to get the vehicle off the ground, and instead of the usual, painful explosion of acceleration, we moved forward gently and hovered through the forest of aspen and cottonwood, which slowly gave way to oak and elm and maple, which then continued to grow thicker and thicker. The vegetation changed until we were navigating our way through thick, choking, tropical-like rain forests.

We wound our way around the trees and across the rivers until Murlem announced that the road was a half-mile away.

"Okay, land here," I ordered. I studied the map and watched the steady flow of glowing dots representing military movements. "It looks like they have a steady stream of convoys along this road. If there is a time to be sneaky, this is it."

"I thought you said the best hiding place was out in the open," Colem inquired.

"I did," I replied. "But to every rule, there is an exception. This is one of the most likely places we could be stopped and questioned, especially if we just pop out of the jungle and drive into their convoy. If they are going to believe we are one of them, then they need to think we have been with them the entire time. If they see us just drive out of the jungle and into the convoy, then we had better have a really good story to explain ourselves, or be ready to put those LPE's into a hasty retreat, or… Well, I'd rather not have to deal with that anyway. Once we are on the road, then we will essentially become a part of their society and there should be few places we can't go. Until then, we are strangers to them, and they will want to know who we are and what we are doing."

"So, how do we get on the road?" Tinear asked.

"I'm not sure yet. Colem, John, Saeui, come with me. We're going to go get a closer look," I said.

We pulled the safety on the airlock so that the doors would stay open and all four of us could exit the vehicle together. The air was damp and heavy with that sweet smell of flourishing vegetation and rich earth. We worked through the shrubs and undergrowth toward the road until we could hear tires and tracks rolling over pavement and the steady hum of many engines. We crouched low and stayed beneath the lower foliage as we continued advancing until the road was in sight. We could see the convoys passing steadily in both directions. We watched vehicles of many different designs and sizes pass by.

"Are you sure we can't just drive onto the road and be on our way?" Saeui asked.

"Not without raising suspicion," I answered. "We need some excuse for coming out of the jungle, something that will either be questioned that we can explain or something that they would take for granted and not give a second thought about. Keep an eye out for anything in their movement patterns that would give us a predictable opening to get on the road, like checkpoints, an intersection, or machine repairs."

We watched the traffic for a while and gazed down the road for as far as we could see in both directions, but nothing seemed to offer a chance to get into the convoy line.

"This isn't looking too promising," I said. "Let's head back to the vehicles, check the satellite maps again, and see if we can find an intersecting road that is less busy."

We carefully moved back into the thick jungle and were about to make our way back to the half-tracks when the sound of a large, breaking branch caught my attention. I looked in the direction of the sound and saw not two large eyes staring at me, but eight, closely set, black, gleaming eyes. And beneath all those eyes were two large mandibles, dripping with some foul, thick fluid.

"Not another," I moaned quietly. "Everyone," I said a little louder, "fast retreat, back to the vehicles. Go."

Everyone saw the eyes and promptly obeyed my order, except for Colem. He had become petrified where he stood.

"Colem!" I hissed. "What are you doing?"

"I'm hiding," he mumbled as he stood rigid and wide-eyed.

"It can see you!"

"But I'm hiding in plain sight."

"That doesn't work if it wants to eat you! RUN!!" I roared.

It was enough to shake Colem back to his senses, and he ran. It was also enough to urge the enormous spider to chase after us. I fired a burst of rounds at its face, and it recoiled for a moment. I ran after Colem, and the spider ran after me. Saeui and John fired at the spider as Colem and I ran past them. Then Colem and I stopped and fired while Saeui and John retreated past us. The spider flinched and hesitated with each burst from our guns, but the rounds were ineffective. Again, Saeui and John provided suppressive fire while Colem and I retreated. We carried on this leapfrog tactic through the jungle until we were closer to the half-tracks.

"Tinear!" I shouted over the radio, "We have another gundon chasing us! Our weapons are ineffective! Get the cannons ready to fire!" I tapped Saeui and John on the shoulders as Colem ran past them. "We're almost there! Run to the vehicles and don't stop!" I ordered, just before firing another burst at the pursuing beast.

We crashed through the jungle at a full run. We reached the vehicles and rushed through the open door. I mashed the button to close the hatch once we were all in.

"Where is it?" Tinear asked from the gunner's seat. Colem jumped into the other gunner's seat and looked around through his viewer. He suddenly jolted and fell out of his seat onto the floor.

"Twenty degrees off driver's side!" he shouted from the floor.

Tinear swung the turret around. "There you are, you big ugly!" he said with a smile, and he pulled the trigger. The half-track rocked with the blast. Tinear sprung down from the seat and announced, "All clear!" with a satisfied grin.

We opened the rear hatch and went out to take a look at the strange creature. Tinear had struck it in the abdomen and it laid split in two, front and back. It had all the same appearances of a spider, but it was the size of a small car and had very long legs.

Ron looked at the giant bug in disgust. "I'm getting really tired of seeing these giant bugs," he said.

"That's not a bug," Murlem stated. "It's another kind of gundon."

"I hear vehicles!" Tinear shouted and raised his gun.

"Everyone, stand down!" I ordered. "Just stay calm. Let me do the talking. This is what we want."

We stood around the dead spider as three Advansynergist armored vehicles pulled up and stopped. A soldier stepped out from the foremost vehicle and several others followed with their weapons lowered.

"We heard gunfire. What's going on here?" the first soldier demanded.

I slammed the butt of my gun on the shell of the giant bug's back-half and casually said, "Just finishing our patrol." I sauntered toward the soldier that seemed to be in charge, and I stuck out my lower chin. "And we just landed another kill," I said with a big, arrogant smile as I placed my foot on the dead gundon's head and leaned on it.

The soldier looked around at the two giant half-tracks covered in gundon shell pieces and the huge horn we had taken from our first encounter, still mounted to the front of the half-track. Then the soldier looked around at us.

I noticed the soldier glance past me nervously. I turned around to see what he was looking at and noticed Tinear was glaring at the Advansynergist soldier while tightly gripping his rifle and grinding his teeth together.

"Have we met?" the soldier asked Tinear.

"Don't mind him," I said calmly, jabbing a thumb in Tinear's direction. "He's still a little tense from the fight. Now, we would love to continue these pleasantries, but we've got to get back to base. Our navigation equipment was damaged in the scrap. Is the road still that way?" I asked, pointing a little off of where I knew the road to be.

The soldier corrected my intentional mistake and pointed us in a different direction. "Just follow us," he said.

"Thank you, sir!" I said cheerily, with a brief salute. "Company! Move out!"

Without another word to the other soldiers, we entered the half-tracks. The Advansynergist soldiers returned to their vehicles and turned around to get back to the road.

I walked up behind Numigh's driving seat and said, "Those soldiers are our ticket onto the road. Follow them to the road and head for Death's Grave. The other convoys will see us with this familiar group and accept us into their ranks."

"Yes, sir," Numigh replied.

"How do you know he isn't leading us into a trap?" Tinear asked, still glaring toward the enemy soldiers.

"They have an entire convoy of soldiers just a stone's cast away. If they wanted to capture us, they would have done it by now," I answered. "Oh, be sure to use the wheels and not the LPEs, Numigh."

He turned around and stared at me with a face that asked if I thought he was an idiot. I grinned a little to suggest I was joking and gave a single nod. He turned back around and coaxed the half-track into moving through the dense underbrush.

"We're actually lucky they didn't notice that there weren't any tracks behind our vehicles," Numigh mentioned casually, "otherwise they may have wondered how we got here and asked more questions; very awkward questions."

That thought twisted my stomach, and I sat down.

Chapter 17 – What Matters

We cruised along the road, amidst the enemy convoy, towards Death's Grave. We abruptly emerged from the jungle into a vast plain of tall grasses and rotting stumps. The vehicle we had been following turned off the road and into a camp. The rest of the convoy followed.

"Stay on the road, Numigh. Drive like no one matters and you know where you are going," I ordered.

The road was now empty and clear. Numigh pressed the throttle a little further. We passed more camps of soldiers, tents, vehicles, and makeshift repair yards crowded around the road and filling the grassy fields.

"Why are there so many soldiers here?" I asked. "Why aren't they camped closer to the battlefront?"

"They are probably being redeployed from one battlefront to the other," Tinear said. "That means we must be winning on one of the fronts."

"Could it also mean your forces are losing on one of the fronts, and so the Advansynergists don't need so many soldiers on that front?" Ron asked.

Tinear looked at Ron as though he was a fool. "Let me explain it from our perspective - what we would do if we were winning. If we were winning on either front then we would not pull troops away and risk losing our advantage. We would continue pressing our attack with everything we had," Tinear explained in a condescending tone.

I looked around for something to change the topic and ease the tension, and I found it. "What – is – that?!" I exclaimed, pointing to an enormous metal sphere rolling far behind the tents of the camps. I was enthralled at its unbelievable size and ease with which it moved. The vast amounts of dirt it uprooted and dispersed in its wake was as mesmerizing as the Vshaped, iron tread going round and round as it rolled along. It was like watching a small hill gather itself together and just move across the landscape.

"That is a line-breaker," Tinear stated with a grim expression. "They use them to, well, to break our lines at the battlefront."

"It looks unstoppable," I said in wonder.

"It's not. We stop them... sometimes."

We continued watching the line-breaker until it was out of sight. Then we continued driving on the long, straight, and flat road until we saw what looked like a city in the distance. As we drew closer, we saw that there were buildings of many kinds; apartments, factories, stores, and such, but all of them were void of life and decaying. Their roofs were sunken in. The walls were crumbling and leaning. The windows were empty and dark. Yards were buried in dead weeds. Doors were missing. Nothing moved beyond the road.

"What happened here?" Ron asked.

"The same thing that has happened to the outskirts of our cities," Saeui replied. "Their population has been whittled away by this war, and there aren't enough people to occupy all of the space. These buildings are no longer needed, except to stand as a memorial to the families and friends who lived here long ago, a token of happier times."

We drove for hours with abandoned and dreary buildings passing by on both sides, like we were traveling through a worm-eaten chronology of past people's lives. Low clouds began to spread in a thick, gray blanket across the sky. A smell lingered in the air, something like decay and stagnant dirt, the vague aroma of filth. Then, all at once, the buildings changed, and there were doors, clean roofs, rows of trees along the roadside, windows with light pouring out from them, and walls that held their form. And all the buildings, which now all looked like apartment fronts, were the same and filled the entire block. One side of the street looked like a mirror image of the other side. Each door and window looked exactly like the previous door and window. The roofline was the same across the entire city block, and from one block to the next. There were also fences, miles and miles of tall, black, iron, rail fences with small spear tips at the top of each rail. The fences ran down both sides of the road and separated the sidewalk from the road. There were no crosswalks and no people bridges to get from one side of the road to the other. The sidewalks were pitted with subway tunnel entrances at regular intervals on both sides of the street.

I looked down the side streets as we drove by, and the same seemed to hold true for those roads as well. It appeared that each city block was isolated from the others by the fences, and aside from our two half-tracks, there was no other traffic of any kind. Even the sidewalks were empty, and yet the buildings seemed occupied. I looked further down the road, much further down the road, and it appeared to be the same all the way to the flat horizon. I pulled out a pair of binoculars and peered through them to be sure that it all looked the same.

"This is really creepy," I said.

"Yeah. My skin is crawling," Numigh shuddered.

"Where does it end?" Saeui asked.

Tinear took the set of binoculars from me, put them to his eye, and peered into the horizon. Then he lowered them with a bewildered look. "It doesn't," he replied.

And so it seemed. We drove for hours upon hours without the slightest change in the buildings or the road.

"This street reminds me of a treadmill," Ron said lethargically. "I can run and run and run, but when I'm done, I haven't gone anywhere, and everything looks just the same as when I had begun," he looked down at his stomach, "including my paunch."

"That's odd," Murlem muttered.

"Isn't it though? Maybe it's my diet," Ron said.

"Not you," Murlem said, annoyed.

"What is it?" I asked Murlem.

"The weather patterns and atmosphere composition don't make sense. It looks like there is a cloud propagator working nearby, but it's not seeding to make rain," he answered.

"What? You have cloud seeding on this planet, too," Ron asked, surprised.

"We do," Murlem replied proudly. "It's usually used in our farming sectors, but a few of the largest cities use it to help clean the air by propagating clouds and seeding to induce rainfall. Then the water that is drained from the streets goes through a treatment process to remove toxins and impurities before being evaporated back into the atmosphere for reseeding. But this," he waved a hand at the sky. "This looks like it was intended to just be cloudy, nothing more."

I looked in through the windows of the apartments we passed and noticed they all emanated a warm, cheerful light.

"It's to keep people indoors and under control," I said. Everyone in the cab looked at me strangely.

"I sense something philosophical," Ron said.

"It's more psychological," I said. "If it's dreary outside but cheerful and warm inside, then people will want to stay indoors. People who are willing to box themselves in are easier to control."

"Why would-" Ron started, but stopped. His forehead scrunched together between his eyes and he leaned closer to the windshield as he looked out. "What is going on?" Ron asked, staring out through the windshield.

I looked, and saw all of the doors on the third floors of the apartments along both sides of the road, for as far as I could see, open simultaneously, and one person from each door emerged. At the same time, we heard a cheerful, female voice from an unseen source.

"It's another glorious day of advancing our synergy, citizens!" the voice announced.

Then with one accord, all of the people who had stepped out from the doors faced the same way and marched to the stairs.

"Today is another day you fight for what you believe in," the voice continued. "Today is another day you strike against the enemy."

They walked down to the sidewalks. They continued their march to the nearest street corner where they turned and continued marching down into subway tunnels.

"Remember, the future of this world is built by you. What you create today will scourge the enemy tomorrow," the voice promised.

The people flowed into the subway tunnels until the street was once again empty and void of life.

"What was that?" Ron asked.

"I don't know," I said. Then people suddenly emerged from the subway tunnels and flooded onto the sidewalks.

The voice spoke again. "Well done, citizens! The enemy has felt the fire of your resolve today. We will not back down!"

The people walked along the sidewalks to the first floors of the apartments, where they paused, one person in front of each door. When the sidewalks were clear and every door had a person standing in front of it, then all of the doors opened simultaneously, and the people vanished into the apartments. The doors shut, and the street was empty again. During this strange event, no one seemed to have taken notice of us.

"I take it back," I said. "I don't think the weather is what's keeping people indoors." Then a thought crossed my mind. "I think we just saw a change in work shifts," I said. "How long do your people work in a day?"

"A full work day is about twelve hours."

"Then, if a full Edengone day is thirty-six hours by your mode of reckoning and there are six floors of apartments, and if they overlap shifts, then we should see the doors open about every six hours. And all the people from the second floor are still at work. They will be the next to return home."

Numigh looked back and forth at the buildings on either side, horrified by the thought of living like that. "Like livestock being put away in the barn," he grimaced.

"How about that cheesy propaganda?" Ron asked dryly.

"I recognize that voice," Tinear said. His voice dripped with rancor. "It was the voice of a vile and sadistic she-devil known as Isthaelia. She is the madness that drives this faction, the delusion that blinds their reasoning. She blares her lies through loud speakers at the battlefront whenever the firing slows down. I prefer the sound of mortar shells to her wretched squawks."

Colem applauded. "That was beautiful, sir. Pure poetry."

"Why would she want her people living like this?" Ron asked.

"Control," I stated. "If you want to enslave someone, then you put them in chains. Some types of chains are longer than others, but they are still chains, as long as it limits a person's ability to move or act."

"But I don't understand *why*," Ron reiterated. "Why would she or anyone want this?"

"It's what I said earlier," Tinear said with a snarl. "She is not just mad; she *is* madness. It is all madness." Tinear stopped and looked intently down one of the sidewalks. "Speaking of madness; Colem, get a scan on that person down the road. I want to know what they are made of."

"Yes, sir," Colem responded as he jumped into the front gunner's seat and swung the turret around.

"What are you looking at?" I asked.

Tinear pointed. "There is something unnatural about that person on the sidewalk, aside from being the only living thing outside right now, they are walking like… There's just something wrong."

As we drove closer to the person in question, I looked closely, trying to understand what Tinear was talking about. There was, indeed, something odd about how they walked, but there was something odd about their face as well. They were too far away to make out details, but as we drove closer, some of the oddities about this mystery person became obvious. It was a man, with his head and brows shaved bald. A steel mask covered his nose and mouth. Something metallic and sprouting small fins clung to his forehead over one brow. Perforated metal plates pressed flat against where his ears should have been, and his eyes – something was very strange about his eyes. I focused on the stranger's gray colored eyes as we passed by. One of his eyes looked like a goat's eye, with a sideways pupil, or maybe it was two pupils in the same eye; I couldn't tell. The other eye looked like a chameleon's, cone-shaped and protruding. And he didn't blink, not even once.

"What the devil was that?" Saeui asked emphatically.

"I think the answer was in your question," Murlem responded.

"Colem, did you get a scan?" Tinear asked.

"Yes, sir. Sending it to the dashboard now."

"What's this 'scan' you are talking about?" I asked Tinear.

"Professor Litona had Doctor Dalmour install a compact and simplified version of Dalmour's scanner in these half-tracks. It can't get as detailed as the one in Dalmour's lab and it can't do surgery, but it will let us know what lies behind a wall, or in this case, if someone even has a soul left."

A blurred image of color appeared on the dashboard screen, and Murlem worked through settings and filters until we were left with just an image of the person.

"Go internal," Tinear ordered.

Murlem pushed a button and the image turned into a skeleton, but there was something else in the abdomen of the bone structure that I did not recognize as a bone.

"There!" Tinear said forcefully as he jabbed a pointing finger at the strange object in the stranger. "He's an undying! He has the implant! I knew there was something wrong with him."

"Zoom in on his head, Murlem," I requested.

Murlem did so, and the face we saw was not the face of a human.

"What happened to this… thing?" Saeui asked in horror. "And where are its eyelids?"

I pointed and signaled for John and Pik to come up to the screen. "John, Pik, I want you to analyze this scan and report what you learn. If the undying are supposed to be the Advansynergists' super soldier, and this thing is supposed to be one, then we need to know what they have done differently to this one. We may be dealing with a second generation of the undying."

John and Pik went to work on the scan, and we waited with nothing to occupy our minds but the unchanging road before us and the undying horrors we would yet encounter at Death's Grave.

An hour passed, and Pik finally turned away from the screen. "We have a report," Pik said.

"Good. Let's hear it."

"This is an older undying," Pik said. "This man has an older version of the undying implant. The version of his implant suggests that he is old enough for all of his senses to have failed long ago, as all implant hosts experience."

"You're saying, then, that this guy should be blind, deaf, mute, numb, and unable to smell," I suggested. I waved an upturned hand in front of me and asked, "So what is he doing walking around? Why isn't he...? I don't know. Why isn't he with all of the other retired undying?"

"His senses have been replaced," Pik replied. "All of his sensory perceptions have been replaced with artificial components to imitate the organic parts."

"Wait, so this guy is back in business?" I asked with surprise. "So they can return to battle?"

"Actually, we aren't sure this man is really alive," Pik said timidly.

"Please, don't say they're zombies," Ron pleaded with a pitiful expression of fear and terror. "I hate zombies."

"Pik," I said, "we saw him walking down the street. He looked pretty alive."

Pik pulled up the scan of the stranger and pointed to a region around the forehead. "A part of this man's brain has been removed and replaced with a computer."

"Meaning this guy is also smarter?" I inquired.

"Maybe. The part of the brain that was removed is responsible for moral reasoning and rational thinking."

"So, are you saying this guy is now insane? Talk to me, Pik. Stop beating around the bush, and just say it."

Pik took a long breath before he spoke. "We believe this man is no longer functioning as himself. For all practical purposes, this man is dead, and his mind has been replaced with an artificial intelligence. He is, in essence, a robot."

Several eyebrows were raised.

"And what was he doing out here?" I asked.

"He's patrolling. That's what we assume, anyway. We can't know for sure."

"Okay. Then what can we expect from an artificial intelligence, assuming we are going to find more of these things at Death's Grave?"

"If they are like any other computer," John said bitterly, "we can expect them to freeze, lag, get a virus, overheat, and crash."

"Or we can expect them to be superior in every way," Ron suggested.

"Nonsense," I retorted. "Nothing can create something greater than itself; not even God can do that. And these were created by other humans. So even at their best, these 'robots' are no more than equal to us. They may be a little different, but they are not superior," I said firmly.

"But they can do things we can't," Ron argued.

"So they have a little more power than we do," I said, unimpressed, "just like a regular, ordinary man driving a tank. But even a man driving an armored vehicle has weaknesses and limitations."

"Then what do we do?" Tinear asked.

"We level the playing field. Exploit their weaknesses. Artificial intelligences are programmed to learn, right? So, if we need to, we'll teach them all the wrong stuff. Something at its best is only as good as its creator. Humans created these, so we should view them as though we are fighting humans, and not robots. We will use the same tactics as we would use against any other human: deception, diversion, stealth, force. Then we'll hit them so hard it'll knock their artificial socks off," I said, holding up a clenched fist.

Ron spoke. "If these things are no longer human, then they may no longer possess a sense of self-preservation, remorse, compassion, or restraint. We don't know what exactly has or has not been programmed into their 'personalities'. How do you deal with an enemy like that?"

"First of all," I said, "you don't 'deal' with an enemy like that, because an enemy like that is always trying to mess you up. There's no point in 'dealing'. Second, the senses missing in a robot are no more than how some people function. It just goes toward proving my point; these robots can't be superior. If your speculation is correct, they are missing key human character traits that make us effective in battle."

"What are you talking about?" Ron asked, looking very puzzled. "Where do compassion and remorse fit in war?"

"Let me ask you this," I said, becoming very serious. "Let's imagine you are thrown into a gladiator arena, and a bear is let loose to fight you. Would you rather fight a starving bear, a wounded bear, or a cub?"

Ron huffed and smiled at the ridiculous scenario. "I suppose the cub would be the easiest to – "

"The cub is with its mother," I added.

Ron's expression sunk, and his eyes roved around apprehensively. "Oh," he said timidly. "I would rather fight the wounded bear," he answered.

"You would expect the mother to fight more fiercely for its cub than you would expect a starving bear would fight for food or a wounded bear would to save its own life. Likewise, our human compassion for each other is our most powerful weapon," I said soberly. "Our compassion is our driving motivator. It banishes all fear. It spurs courage. It destroys selfish desires. You picture someone you care about, and picture them in danger. Think about what you would do to help them, and you will know how much you care about them. If you do not enter a war with compassion, then you are fighting for the wrong reasons." I looked around the cabin. "You all need to figure out what you are fighting for, and, more importantly, what you are fighting with. Are you fighting with anger against the enemy, fear of being invaded, hatred for different ideas, revenge for fallen comrades, or are you fighting with a stronger, more potent, more faithful purpose; a purpose that won't abandon you when you need it the most? Because, believe me, when you need motivation and a reason, feelings like fear, hate, and anger *will* abandon you, and you will be left on your own. You are going to need a reason that will stay with you. So I ask you, what do you fight for?"

There was a pause, maybe even a hesitation.

"What do you fight for?!" I repeated, more intense than before.

"I fight for my friends," Tinear stated boldly.

"I fight for my sisters and brother," said Saeui.

"For my fiancé," said John.

"For liberty," Numigh chimed in.

"For the future of the people of Edengone," Colem announced.

"For Edengone," Tinear nodded with approval.

"For Edengone!" I repeated.

"FOR EDENGONE!" the soldiers roared.

"Now, we will take that to the enemy!" I asserted. "We will take that purpose to Death's Grave."

Chapter 18 – Death's Grave

"There it is, boys. Death's Grave," Tinear said.

At long last, the unchanging road had finally ended, right at Death's Grave's doorstep. We had stopped just out of range of the casual observer and we viewed the facility through binoculars.

"The middle of a giant city is a strange place for a military base," Ron stated. "Where are their defenses, or even just fences?"

"The fences are on the sidewalks throughout the entire city," I said. "And the defenses are the legions of nearly immortal soldiers going in and out of there."

"Yeah, but this place sounded like it would be the Area Fifty-One of Edengone. I thought it would be more hidden or secretive. They don't even have a guard at the entrance."

"When every soldier is given an undying implant and nearly every citizen is required to fight at some point in their life," Tinear said, "there isn't anything left to keep a secret."

"Whoa, whoa. Do you see that?" I asked Tinear. I pointed to a large movement of vehicles and soldiers entering the perimeter of the facility. "Is that a convoy?"

Tinear looked at where I pointed through his binoculars. "It looks like a convoy from the battlefront. It's probably the latest shipment of wounded to be patched up before redeploying."

"Right, let's get the whole squad in here," I said. "We need to make a few changes to the plan."

A few moments later, the entire squad was crowded into the vehicle. I put a map of the facility on one of the screens.

"We've just seen a convoy of soldiers enter the facility," I explained. "This doesn't change the main idea of the attack plan, but it does require a few adjustments to avoid complications. We aren't sure what the turnaround is for mending an undying soldier, and if this convoy just brought in a batch to be fixed up, then it's likely they are also here to pick up a fresh batch of battle-ready soldiers. That means we may face stiffer resistance than we expected."

"What if we waited for the convoy to leave, and all the fresh undying with them?" Ron suggested.

"Every moment we wait nearby," Tinear answered, "is another moment we may draw unwanted attention."

I nodded in agreement. Then I continued. "The first target is still the control tower, and that first shot at the tower is still the starting signal for the rest of the attack. The other gunners will still target the barracks first, but after that, priority targets are enemy soldiers, and not the structures or vehicles. If you run out of soldiers to shoot at, then fire at will, but I doubt that will happen. We need the gunners to keep enemy soldiers from getting to my team when we go to place the charges. Once my team has entered the laboratory, we will collapse the entrance behind us with explosives to prevent enemy soldiers from following us. However, the buildings are connected through the underground tunnels and they may try to use other entrances to reach us." I looked sternly at the gunners. "Make sure they don't get there." I pointed to the map. "The convoy is positioned between the manufacturing warehouse and the barracks, in this corner, opposite from the infirmary. Colossal one will position here on this side of the infirmary, aiming between the laboratory building and the barracks. Colossal two will position themselves on the other side of the infirmary and shoot between the laboratory building and the manufacturing warehouse."

"Why don't we put both vehicles next to each other?" Saeui asked. "It will strengthen our position."

"Because this is no longer trench warfare like you are used to seeing. We have more options here. With the guns focusing fire on the same point from two directions, the enemy will be confused and caught in the crossfire." I thought for a moment before I continued. "And there is a tactic I want you to use, which I will leave to Tinear's discretion to overrule depending upon its effectiveness. If the soldiers have artificial intelligence…" I grimaced, "…*installed* and if they begin to charge towards the vehicles, then I want the vehicles to alternate firing in three-second intervals."

The squad looked confused.

"Why would we do that?" Colem asked.

"That's exactly what we want *them* to be thinking. I suspect the designers of the AIs designed them to fight in a trench war, and I also suspect the AI will be programmed to eliminate the highest threat first. The firing half-track would be the higher threat of the two. Alternate which vehicle is firing and they won't know which way to go. It may slow them down for a bit. Now, let's move."

The soldiers from the other half-track began leaving the vehicle.

"Would it be better for the rest of your team to stay here so you can all deploy together?" Tinear asked discreetly.

"Once the first shot is fired, it will alert the enemy. If we've miscalculated their response time then it will be better for us to rush the building from two directions to divide their attention."

Tinear nodded, and we checked our gear as Numigh put the half-track into motion. We were making our final approach to our long awaited objective.

The buildings seemed so simple, with simple walls of metal on the manufacturing building, wood on the barracks, stucco on the infirmary, and reinforced concrete on the laboratory. There was nothing extraordinary about them, and yet there was something that echoed from their bowels, something of horror, fear, and terror. A foul feeling of dread settled in the pit of my stomach as we approached the facility. I closed my eyes, and I sensed a nightmare laid waiting beneath us.

Numigh parked the half-track at the designated point, and we waited for the other vehicle to report in.

"How do you think they do it?" Saeui wondered aloud. "How do they make ordinary people into senseless killers? Are they awake for the process, or do they sedate them? Are the subjects willing or compelled?

Who would be willing to go through the ordeal? What must be going through their mind? I almost want to join the invasion group just to see inside."

"I'll bring you a souvenir," Murlem ribbed.

The crackled voice of the radio brought news. "Colossal two is in position. Awaiting your signal," it said.

I looked up at the square, concrete tower with its long, sideways slits for observation windows. "There must have been some point in their history when they thought this building would be attacked. Those walls look really thick," I said worriedly. "We need to make sure we destroy their communications and their system controls with the first shot, because we may not get a second one."

Tinear turned to Colem and asked, "Can you fire a shell through that window?" He pointed at the observation slit at the top of the building.

"That window?" Colem asked, pointing to the impossibly small window in question. "Halibut! We didn't need to come all this way for that! I could have made that shot from the headquarters' cafeteria back home. It hurts that you asked," he replied, while feigning injured pride.

"That's what I like to hear," Tinear said. "Get it done."

I picked up the radio. "Gunners, take aim and wait for the signal," I ordered over the radio. "Fire when you're ready, Colem," I said.

"Years of planning, weeks of traveling, and the lives of us all rest in your hands," Ron said in a narrative voice.

Colem glanced curiously at Ron.

"No pressure. Take your time," Ron quickly said.

Colem sighed and turned his attention back to the scope of his cannon. I unlocked the rear hatch and waited for the signal from the shot. The moments slowly ticked by. I could hear my ears ringing. My thoughts dragged out and slowed nearly to a stop. My heart steadily thumped through my neck. The adrenaline built up pressure. My sight began to tunnel as the anticipation neared its peak. I watched Colem's finger slowly squeeze the trigger.

Then the silence was shattered with a ground-shaking boom. I threw open the hatch and ran out with half of my team following me. We raced to the front doors of the laboratories under the deafening booms of the other cannons and the explosions of wood and twisted metal from the barracks. The control tower above us billowed black smoke and flames leaped from the narrow windows. Colem had scored a direct hit.

The other half of my team rushed across the facility's yard from their half-track, and we stacked up at the doors. Again, time seemed to stop as I positioned myself for the strike.

I took a deep breath. I tightened the grip on my weapon. I took my thoughts to the deepest parts of my mind, and I tightened the grip on my senses. I didn't just hear what was around me. I didn't just smell. I didn't just see. I reached out with a sense that is difficult to explain, as difficult as explaining a color to someone who has been blind their whole life. But I reached out and took hold of my surroundings. I sensed my comrades in arms. I sensed their fear or anticipation. I sensed the fiery power of the capsules in our weapons. I sensed the lives that would be laid down when we entered those doors. And I sensed the consequences that would ensue. Then I joined those senses to an imbued strength of resolve and adrenaline, and I kicked in the door.

At that moment, I was no longer Michael. I was no longer intellectual or diplomatic. The time for that was gone. Now it was the time to act. Now was the time of reckoning. I became a force. I became death and destruction. I became blood and fire. My heart pounded to the beat of an instinctive, primitive, and intrinsic war drum. I was prosecutor, judge, jury, and executioner. I was the tribunal. The crime had been committed. Justice required punishment. And I was there to deliver. Deliver I did. My battle cry delivered the accusation. My weapon served the verdict. And the rounds fired from my gun executed the sentence.

Do I look back on my actions with pride? No. Would I have spared them if there was another way? Yes. I wish I could have spared them. I wish I could have let them be. But they would not let Edengone be.

Then can I reflect on my choices and look virtue and justice in the eye with confidence? Yes; a resounding and emphatic yes. The correct action is not always a pleasant or happy one, but it is necessary and always the best action. How do I justify my actions? That is between me and the powers I answer to. Let the world think of me as they will. I was trained to destroy, but more importantly, I was trained to know *when* to destroy. I do not reflect on my actions with any pride, but I do not reflect with any doubt, either.

The entrance was cleared, and charges were set to collapse the doors. We moved further down the hall, dropping anyone who came in sight. Murlem pressed the detonator and the hall echoed with the blast and snapping metal, followed by the crash of debris. We moved through the facility methodically, until we entered one room with a man in a lab coat, wearing a cloth mask, and holding a scalpel in his hand, leaning over a cadaver. He looked up at us, as though we had surprised him, as though he hadn't heard the gunshots and screams further down the hall.

"No! Don't shoot! I haven't hurt anyone! I'm a doctor!" he pleaded.

"Don't shoot!" Ron shouted and rushed out in front of us. "You see?" he asked, accusingly. "Not all of these people are bad. Now we just need to-"

I saw the doctor reach under the operating table and pull out a gun. He aimed it at Ron. "Ron! Look out!" I shouted as I pulled him out of the way.

Murlem and several of the other soldiers opened fire on the deceptive doctor. A storm of bullets raced across the room, pushing the doctor against the wall. The firing stopped. The doctor straightened up and raised the gun again. We quickly opened fire again and did not release the triggers until our target had hit the floor. A bullet from the doctor's gun grazed Ron's leg as he went down.

"OW!" Ron shouted. He slumped to the floor. "Shoot them! Shoot them all!" he groaned in pain.

I grabbed some bandages and quickly bound the wound. "That was a quick change of heart," I said as I tightened the bandages. The bandages turned crimson.

"Yeah, well, a near-death experience makes you look at life in a whole new way," Ron said as he winced in pain.

Murlem dug through the cabinets and pulled out a syringe. "This will kill the pain and get you back on your feet," he said, just before plunging the needle into Ron's other leg and depressing the plunger.

"OOWW! Now I've been shot in both legs. I'm lame!" Ron wailed.

"I won't argue with that," Murlem said.

"Why did he shoot me?" Ron asked in confusion. "These people are monsters. Why would a doctor need a gun at the operating table? He probably wouldn't have batted an eye if someone asked him to murder a child, I would venture." Then he paused. "'I would venture'? I never use that language." He looked at

Murlem suspiciously. "What did you say you injected me with, again?"

"You're fine," I reassured him. "You're just going into shock. You always get emotional when you're in shock, weirdo. Come on. We need to keep moving." I helped him to his feet and put his arm over my shoulders.

Murlem walked over to where the doctor had fallen. He raised his gun at the fallen doctor and fired another round. "This one was an undying," he said, as he pushed back the lab coat with his gun barrel and exposed the soldier's uniform underneath. The uniform was light gray with silver stripes along the seams. "That's why it took so many bullets to drop him."

"He was trying to ambush us," Ron said with horrified surprise.

"Yep. Let's go," I said. I pushed Ron toward the door.

Ron pushed me away as he said, "Whoa, I'm good. I don't feel any pain. That was fast."

"Are you sure you are okay?" I asked doubtfully. "It may just be a surface wound, but some are worse than others."

"Yeah, I'm fine. Let's go."

We left the room and continued advancing through the building. The rest of the team moved ahead, clearing rooms as they went until we reached the stairwell.

I threw open the door to the stairwell and the squad began its descent. "Regroup at the bottom," I ordered.

"Why don't we take the elevator?" Ron asked.

I chuckled. "Do you remember the *last* time we took an elevator?" I asked. "And there are a ton of other reasons that we don't have time to discuss," I said as I urged him through the doorway.

Around and around we spiraled down the stairwell until I was feeling slightly dizzy. We reached the first door in the stairwell. There were still many more flights of stairs, but this door was our first stop. I moved through the gathered squad to the door and gripped the handle. I opened the door slowly, with my gun ready. After the door swung open, we looked out over an enormous room, second only to the reaction chamber of the giant light propulsion engine found under the mountain of sand at the Bull's Eye.

We looked over a forest of glowing pods, each with a single human occupant. I looked through my scope at the glass pods and noticed that these "human" occupants were equipped with the same sensory replacements as the artificial intelligence we encountered in the city. We looked down over the countless pods, each containing the mechanized face of an undying artificial intelligence. Each seemed to be held in storage, or stasis, floating in a liquid, unconscious. Several tubes attached to the masks of the undying AI, which I assumed were for sustaining the bodies of these hybrid robots. They were clothed in something that resembled a wetsuit, but it had circuitry running through it.

"Those aren't computers," Ron said soberly. "Those are people."

Workers moved through the forest of pods. Some recorded readings from the pods. Others assembled new pods. Even more went about cleaning and maintaining the existing pods. And beyond all of this, lined along the far walls and stacked to the ceiling, were more pods, all holding human occupants. Here was an army of human hybrid robots in storage, waiting to be deployed. In the middle of it all was the giant pillar we needed to destroy.

The doors had given us access to a high catwalk. I watched the movements below. There were not so many workers that we couldn't sneak to the pillar, undetected.

"It looks like they don't know we are here," I observed. "Crews three and four, continue going to the bottom of the stairwell and secure our exit." Crews three and four left and continued down the stairs. "Crew two, guard this doorway. Take a few charges and place them around this door so we can collapse it when we are ready to go. Crew one, with me. We'll set the charges around the pillar, and then we run for the sewers. Stay close and stay silent. Do not fire a shot unless we are detected. Let's go."

We moved quietly onto the catwalk. I looked out over the hundreds of undying soldiers beneath us. We had gone a couple of hundred yards and were about to take stairs down to the floor level to start our advance towards the pillar, but just then, an alarm began to blare, and red lights strobed from all around.

"Stay cool," I said. "They still don't know where we are. We don't even know if the alarm is about us. There could be something else going on, a practice drill or something."

A large screen down below flashed and showed a video of us entering the building in slow motion.

"Okay," I said, beginning to feel less confident. "At least they don't know where we are."

A worker down below looked up at us. Then he pointed and shouted. Immediately, everyone in the room was looking at us. One of the workers below ran to a control panel. I shot him, and he lurched, confirming a hit, but he kept running. I fired repeatedly. He received hit after hit. The rest of the crew had also begun firing on him and the other workers. All the workers responded by running to different control panels.

"They are undying!" Murlem yelled over the gunfire.

"Shoot the control panels!" I ordered.

All of the control panels in sight erupted with sparks as our bullets tore through them. But it was all in vain. Naturally, in a space so large and full, we could not see all of the control panels or all the workers. The flashing red lights turned yellow, and the alarm changed its tune. The entire room filled with an eerie green glow as all the pods containing undying AI lit up and activated. The fluid inside the containers began to drain away, and the bodies inside the pods twitched as they slowly revived.

"Abort! Abort the mission! All units, head for the rendezvous!" I ordered over the radio. I pointed to my team. "Get back to crew two and help guard the doors! Leave the explosives!" I ordered.

The team turned and quickly set up a firing line at the entry points. I grabbed Ron's arm and signaled for him to stay. The hundreds of AI that had emerged from their pods were now flooding in our direction and making their way up other stairs to the catwalk. Thousands more were coming out of their pods. The team opened fire as they retreated toward the doors, leaving Ron and me where we were.

"Ron," I said, grabbing his shoulder, "can you boost these explosives toward the pillar when I throw them? Make it look like I'm really good at throwing."

Ron nodded. "I'm ready," he said.

I grabbed the bag of charges and hurled it over the railing. The bag sailed through the air, but it wasn't going to fly far enough. Then a burst of air hit me. I saw the bag jump in midair and soar toward the main pillar. The bag landed at the pillar's base.

"Good work," I said as I took aim at the bag with my rifle.

"Thanks," Ron said, holding his head in pain.

"Now run." I pulled the trigger, and the bag detonated with all the intended force that was supposed to be distributed around the pillar to buckle it. Fire billowed, and deadly debris screamed through the air. The ground shook, and portions of the ceiling fell, crushing everything and everyone beneath them. The damage was significant, but the pillar still stood. I watched in horror as mutilated soldiers dragged themselves from beneath the debris and rose from the floor with whatever limbs remained, and still, they rushed after us.

We raced back to the doors. We pushed the doors shut and ran down the stairs.

"Blow the door!" I ordered.

Pik triggered the remote detonator just as the enemy soldiers were pressing in through the doorway. The explosion rushed through the stairwell, showering us with dust and debris. We pushed through the blinding dust until it settled.

Gunshots from below filled the stairwell with deafening echoes. The stairs bottomed out in an intersection of halls where the other crews were firing at the pressing torrents of enemy soldiers.

"Let's go!" I shouted over the sound of the battle.

We turned and ran down the hall opposite from the stairs.

"Place charges here and here!" I ordered, pointing to the walls on either side of me.

The charges were placed, and we continued running.

About a hundred feet later, I shouted, "Detonate now!"

Pik triggered the remote, and the hall filled with the sound of the explosion and more dust. We kept running. We could hear the AI hybrids breaking through the rubble behind us. We passed several other halls and wound our way through the labyrinth of turns and corners, down more stairs, and into the underbelly of the facility where pipes and wires lined the walls and ceilings.

"In here," I said, as I turned into a side room. "This is the drain system in case of flooding," I explained. Saeui and I lifted a large grate from the floor.

Members of the squad were still trickling into the room as the first soldier lowered himself into the hole in the floor and into the sewers below.

"How many more are still out there?" I asked Murlem, who was counting at the door.

"It's just Ron now. He's right here," Murlem replied as he entered the room and pointed with a thumb over his shoulder.

Just then, a heavy door slid into place over the doorway, locking us in and Ron out.

"Hey!" Ron banged on the door. "I'm still here!"

"Toss me the charges!" I shouted.

Pik reached down into the sewer and ran the bag over to the door. We placed a couple of charges on either side of the heavy, steel door.

"Step back, Ron!" I shouted through the door. Then we went to the other side of the room and faced the wall. "Fire in the hole!" I pulled the trigger on the remote, and the door rang with the blast. I turned and looked, but the door still stood. "We need more charges!"

"That was all of them," Pik said.

"Ron! Ron, don't move. We'll find a way to get you out of there," I reassured him.

"Forget about it, Mike," Ron said through the door, his voice betraying the first signs of despair. "There's no way through this door, and you can't come back in through the entrance. There are too many of them."

"We're not quitting like that, Ron! Not on my watch! Christopher Columbus had a plan for getting back!" My voice cracked as I realized I had led Ron into the same kind of trouble he had led me into when we jumped to this planet. Bitter guilt swept over me. "He did not abandon himself and the crews of his ships to die in some foreign, new world! No... There's got to be a way," I said to myself as I searched frantically around the room, but there was nothing else there. "We're getting you out of there and going home! That's the plan!" My voice faltered through subdued tremors. I waited until I regained control over my fear and frenzy.

"But if you come up with a better plan," I said calmly, "you let me know, and I will help you get us home."

There was no reply from the other side.

"Ron?"

"I've got a plan," I heard Ron say.

"Okay. Good. What is it?"

"I'm going back."

"Whoa! Hold on! What's the rest of that plan?" I asked as I panicked again.

"I'm going back and destroying this place."

Murlem hit the door and spoke through it. "Don't be a hero, Ron! Just stay put. We'll get you out!"

I knew Ron didn't have any explosives, but I understood what he was saying. He was going to use his mind, the same way he did when he had the seizure in Dalmour's lab, the same way he shook our vehicle and made everyone think there was something wrong, the same way he practiced making paper float without anyone noticing just to stave off boredom, the same way he saved me and the crew of colossal three from falling into the jaws of that creature in the sandpit. I knew he could do it. I knew he could throw aside any who opposed him. I knew he could clear the halls we had damaged. And I knew he could buckle the primary pillar that held the facility.

"Wait! Can you break down the door the same way?" I asked.

"What are you talking about?" Murlem asked, looking annoyingly confused.

"No," Ron answered. "Not without collapsing the tunnel. We would all be trapped."

"You know the facility will come down on top of you if you go back!" I shouted.

"Then I trust you will get me out!" he replied.

I thought for a moment, and I raced through my mind for any other options we may had missed. "That's right!" I finally said with determination. "I will get you out! That's the plan! Good luck."

"You too," he said. Then I heard his footsteps disappear down the corridor.

"Come on," I said to the others. "We need to hurry!"

The others quickly jumped down the hole into the sewers. I took one last look at the door before I, too, jumped down and entered the tunnel that would take us to safety.

I turned on my flashlight and looked around. A large, steel tunnel encased us. Water flowed in a shallow stream. There was no side path or maintenance access to keep us out of the sludge and reek of the running flow of refuse. The consistency of the flow was certainly liquid, but much too thick and tainted to be called water.

I ran through the middle of the tunnel, sloshing through whatever was underfoot without a care. The others struggled to keep up. The only thought and goal in my mind was saving a friend who had been a friend for a large part of my life. Then my thoughts roamed and returned to Ron and his situation. My thoughts went with him, and in my mind, I was there with him. I imagined he turned from the room with the sewer access. He ran back along the halls and back up the stairs. He encountered the first wave of undying artificial intelligence hybrids. He boldly faced them. A shock issued from Ron and exploded through the wave of AI, throwing them to the walls and stunning them. Ron ran on. Each group of artificial enemy soldiers met the same fate as the first. At some points the enemy throngs were so thick, Ron launched burst after burst while he continued to run, creating a tunnel of tossed soldiers through which he passed. Ron threw them through the air, clearing a path back to the room of now empty pods. He ran to the giant pillar and stopped before it. He thrust his hands against the pillar and groaned under the exertion. The pillar made popping sounds as the metal began to bend, and then buckle. Then he gave one, last, mighty burst.

A deep rumble rolled through the sewer tunnel, and the ground shook. We stopped and looked back, grim-faced and silent.

"Come on," I said. "We need to hurry."

"Mike, he couldn't have survived the collapse," Murlem said.

"You would be surprised at how resourceful he can be," I said in a calm and level tone.

We continued running through the sewer until we reached our exit point where we climbed a ladder to the surface. The manhole cover had already been removed and Tinear looked down at us as we made our ascent. He reached a hand out and helped me out of the hole.

"What happened?" he asked.

"The alarm was raised, and there were too many of them to get to the pillar. They had a stockpile of AI soldiers under there. They all woke up. Ron got locked out from the escape route, and he went back to finish the job," I explained.

"Alone?" Tinear asked, surprised.

"There was nothing else we could do. We tried blowing the door open to get him out and there was no way we could mount a rescue."

"So he went back to do as much damage as he could," Tinear nodded solemnly.

"Yes. We need to go back, at least to assess the situation there and give a report to General Kulek, if not to see if we can get Ron out of there."

"Alright," Tinear agreed. "You heard him! Let's go!"

My team and I rushed into the two waiting half-tracks. The rear hatches closed and Numigh pressed the lever forward. The vehicle rose from the ground and sped back to Death's Grave, foregoing all secrecy and discreetness. I looked out over the rows and rows, street upon street of apartments, one not varying from another in any way. I looked for the concrete tower of Death's Grave.

"We should be seeing it any moment now," Numigh said.

"There," I pointed. "That gap in the rooftops. Do a flyby to see if it's clear."

Numigh slowed down as we made our approach so we could get a good look, but he maintained our altitude. We glided over the last apartment roof and we looked down through the windshield at the rubble-filled crater beneath us. Concrete walls lay shattered, wood splintered, metal twisted and torn. Water sprayed from broken pipes in some places while fires burned in others. Smoke and steam rose through and around from beneath the debris. Vehicles lay tossed and turned, crunched and buried across the debris field. Death's Grave had been destroyed.

"He did it," Murlem said in amazement.

"Land the half-track," I ordered.

Numigh gently set the half-track down, and the other vehicle landed next to us. We opened the rear hatch and everyone except Numigh exited the vehicle. The crew of the other half-track also exited and looked over the crumbled and twisted wreckage of Death's Grave.

"Keep the engine running," I said to Numigh. I walked out. "Alright, listen up!" Everyone looked to me. "We are here to find one of our team members. He's the one responsible for the success of this mission, so it's the least we can do to rescue him," I paused, "or to recover his remains. I want the Dalmour scanners from

291

both vehicles scanning this wreckage, starting from opposite sides and working toward the middle. Everyone else, break into teams of three or four and sweep the area you can see. Listen for calls of help, and be careful."

The half-track drivers drove to opposite sides of the crater and a gunner in each vehicle began scanning. The remaining soldiers teamed up and carefully traversed across the rubble. The scanners proved to be more efficient than I had hoped because it wasn't long before Numigh radioed that they had found Ron.

"We have his location. Colem will point him out," he reported.

Colem, who was in the gunner's turret operating the scanner, used his laser sight to point to where Ron was.

I followed the glowing red dot to the location and looked around. "Let's get the engineers over here!" I shouted. "We need to know how stable this is or if we are going to collapse this even more on top of him. Get the half-track rigged up to pull some of this larger debris out of the way!"

Just then, the ground rumbled. I felt the rubble beneath me heave slightly. It pushed a bit more, and I backed away. Then bricks started shuddering and shaking about.

"Everyone take cover!" I yelled as I leaped across the wreckage in a hurry.

There was a massive blast where Colem had shined the laser. Rubble showered down. I dove under a broken, overhanging concrete wall as heavy debris fell all around me. Once the shower of debris had stopped, I jumped to my feet and ran back to the location. I looked down in the shallow hole where the raining debris had come from and saw a hand sticking out of the rubble.

"He's here!" I shouted.

The others ran over, and we began unburying and freeing Ron from the wreckage. We lifted him out, unconscious, and carried him to the crater's edge. Ron was covered in dust and scratches. The squad's medic checked for signs of life, but that was soon abandoned as Ron suddenly began coughing.

"Ron," I said, once he had caught his breath and had a chance to look around. "Are you alright? Anything broken?"

"My ankle hurts," he replied with a wheeze. "And I have a massive headache. Oh yeah, and I've been shot."

"Again?!"

"No. Same one. Pain meds just wore off. Can I get some more?" He grimaced.

The medic checked his ankles and reported one was only sprained. I helped Ron to his feet and started walking back to the half-tracks.

"Good job, soldiers," I said to the squad. "We started this together. Now we have finished this together. Let's go home."

The other soldiers cheered, "For Edengone!" They clapped and walked on ahead, congratulating each other.

I continued helping Ron walk to the vehicles as the rest of the squad entered the half-tracks.

"This is it then," I said. "We're going home."

"It's been quite a ride," Ron said with a smile.

"It really has," I agreed cheerfully.

Just then, a rustle of branches and the clatter of rifles stirred behind us. I turned around and saw a flood of Advansynergist soldiers rush from the foliage and tanks smash through the trees. They were too close. Ron and I were too far away from the vehicles. There was no way we could make it.

"GO!! GO NOW!!" I roared back to the half-tracks. "GOOO!!"

Tinear slammed the button to close the rear hatch shut. The enemy tanks fired and their rounds merely splashed against the armor of the gundon shell pieces. The LPEs on the half-tracks glowed to life and emitted a blinding, white light as both half-tracks lifted into the air and fled into the distance in the blink of an eye, leaving Ron and me behind.

"Halt!" a voice barked from behind us.

We stopped and turned around. The Advansynergist soldiers were lined up, side by side, with their guns facing us.

"You guys are clearly linear thinkers, with absolutely no imagination," I chided. "You are supposed to surround us! What is going to keep us from running away? I suppose you could shoot us, but clearly you want us alive!"

"What are you doing?" Ron whispered.

"Having some fun," I whispered back. Then I turned my attention back to the soldiers. "So what if I just turn back around," I slowly turned around, "and started running again?" I acted like I was running in slow motion.

A soldier stepped out from behind the others and raised a small, light rifle at me. He fired, and a dart stuck in my rump. I quickly felt my limbs grow limp and consciousness fade.

"Oh," I said, just before I slumped to the ground and blacked out.

Chapter 19 – A Matter Of Courage

It was difficult to move. My arms and legs tingled with ensuing numbness from the tight ropes that held them to the chair. It was dark and stuffy with the heavy bag over my head. Then the bag was abruptly yanked off, pulling my head back. I looked around. A single light shone over me. Darkness lay beyond.

"You will answer questions," a heavy Bulgarian accent said from the darkness.

"I will do what I want," I said.

A heavy fist hit me from behind. I turned to see my assailant, but nothing was there, nothing but blackness.

"You have no choice," the voice baited.

"I always have a choice," I answered. "Even with my hands tied, there is always a choice."

Another strong blow struck me from the right. I looked, and again there was nothing.

"No," the voice said from the darkness. "Not this time. There is no escape. You are under my control."

I threw my head back with loud, defiant laughter. "You can take away all my belongings. You can take away my family. You can take my name and reputation. You can sever my limbs from my body. You can cut out my tongue. You can take from me whatever comes to your putrid, worm-infested mind, but you cannot take away my will! You may leave me with fewer options, but there will *always* be a choice to be made." I smiled at the blackness. "I will do what I want, and I don't want anything to do with you."

There was silence for a moment. Then the voice spoke. "Nice speech. Too bad this is just a dream."

I woke up with a moan and a splitting headache. I blinked and saw only a bright, white blur. Then the room came into focus.

"You know, if you were clever, you would not have let yourself get captured," said a woman's voice that was easy on the ears but soiled with sassy, baiting undertones, and yet I thought I had heard that voice before.

I glanced up and saw a slender woman, wearing something similar to a woman's business suit. The suit was light gray. A plume of lace under her chin adorned her white shirt. Her hair was blonde and short, hanging just below her earlobes. High cheekbones perched beneath her blue eyes. A slender nose – the kind people aren't born with – sat above bright red lips and a small, round chin. Her high heels clicked on the concrete floor as she swayed into the light.

The light still hurt my eyes. I let my aching head hang down again. "My sincerest apologies," I said snidely. "If you let me go, I promise it won't happen again."

"I don't think so," she said.

"Well, *you* shouldn't be kidnapping people with tranquilizer darts!" I snapped. "So let's call it even, and you let me go."

"Ah-ha," she laughed awkwardly. "Let's try this again. My name is Isthaelia."

Isthaelia. I knew I had heard her voice before. It was her voice we heard over the speakers when the citizens strangely left their homes at exactly the same time, and when they all returned to their homes again. It was her voice that Tinear, Colem, and the others despised hearing at the battlefront.

Isthaelia straightened her posture. "I am the supreme chief head-president of the Advansynergists."

"That title isn't at all presumptuous. I don't think they appreciate you enough," I said, with sarcasm oozing from every syllable. "I think if you added 'big cheese' in there somewhere, it should finish it up nicely."

She ignored my remark. "We have rescued you from *them*."

"Rescued, you say. Then why am I cuffed to a chair, and who is '*them*'?" I asked.

"The enemy, of course."

"Do you have a name for '*them*'?"

"Why would we bother naming such backward, ignorant, pigheaded baboons such as *them*?" she asked with an air of arrogant resentment.

"There you go. You just gave *them* a name. From now on, *they* will be known as 'the backward, ignorant, pigheaded baboons'. Was that so hard?" I asked maliciously. Then I puzzled over a thought I had. "Do you have pigheaded baboons here? What do they look like? Are they indigenous, or genetically engineered?"

She sighed, as though she was already weary of this game, and she said, "I just wanted to introduce you to our side of the story, from our point of view."

"Your point of view?" I asked, being sure to sound surprised. "I'm not sure I could shove my head that far up my – "

"Just hear me out," she pleaded.

298

"It sounds like I'm going to get an earful, whether I want it or not."

"We are the Advansynergists," she began.

"Here we go," I said, rolling my eyes.

"We are the evolved child of the Forward Party, which was established centuries ago by the great Major Dathfron, who – "

"If he was so great, then why was he just a major?" I interrupted.

"It was a display of humility. He never changed his title, no matter what heights he climbed."

"How silly of me to ask," I grumbled, with more sarcasm, "because *displaying* humility is exactly what *humble* people do, obviously." Then I asked, "Is this the same Dathfron who planned a worldwide genocide by launching the planet into space and away from the sun?"

She looked at me with wanton eyes, with covetous eyes, with savagely hungering eyes, with evil eyes.

"You found Dathfron's Legacy, didn't you?" she asked. "You found the planetary engine that was supposed to launch this entire world into a glorious future. Tell me where it is. It belongs to us. We are Dathfron's heirs." She loomed over me. The light behind her made her face dark, menacing, and fearsome.

I endured the evil glare in her eye. I stared back at her and resolutely declared, "No."

"How did your comrades fly away so quickly in those cumbersome vehicles?" she asked accusingly.

"You figured out how to replicate Dathfron's technology, didn't you?"

"That's 'Major Dathfron' to you," I said with a taunting and careless chuckle.

She stepped back. "We will find them, and the engines you stole. Major Dathfron had a dream," she said, beginning a monologue, "a dream that would change humanity forever. He worked to bring about a greater unity among us, a combined energy, and a single, efficient head of command. He dreamed of one being, superior in every way, who would lead the people through whatever course was necessary. This great leader would have the power over the lives of everyone. This leader would decide the smallest decisions for the people, for the benefit of the people. This way, the people would be more efficient, and they would be able to achieve more within their lifetime. They would be able to leave a greater legacy for the next generation than they otherwise would have been able to."

"They? Not 'we'?" I asked curiously. My hands discretely felt for the lock that bound them together.

"I am that leader now," she said exultantly and with a dominating tone of authority.

"Hold on," I interrupted. "You, being this superior leader Dathfron dreamed of, make all of the decisions that would ever need to be made… for everyone?"

Isthaelia nodded with a proud smile.

"So, things like retirement savings, the care of my health, where I live, what I should believe, what shirt I wear, who my girlfriend is, what charitable acts I want to donate to, whether I should have a low-fat sandwich or a double-decker cheeseburger for lunch... all of that is decided by someone else?"

She nodded again, with the same smile.

"And the people are okay with this?" I asked in amazement.

"Of course they are. They suggested it."

I looked at her doubtfully, and her smile changed to one of playful secrecy.

"Well, they voted for the structure. We just helped it along," she held up her thumb and finger in a pinching action as she added, with a slight shrug, "a little."

"Wait. It's 'we' now?" I inquired.

"We, the leaders of this nation, in order to establish unity and to further the progression as a whole, founded this organization to bring humanity under control of the intellectual elite and commanding supreme. By this means, we will benefit the many, at the meager cost of the few," she said proudly.

"Hold on, again. Who is included in 'we'? I thought you said there was one superior leader."

"Yes," she replied. "That is correct. But I can only be in one place at a time. I work through - let's say 'others', to help me with my duties."

"Who chooses these 'others'?" I asked. "And what do the people think about this?" I had found the lock, and I began feeling my way around it to deduce its design.

"The people wanted this," Isthaelia explained. "They don't want to think. They don't want the responsibility. Otherwise, they wouldn't be going along with the program so easily. They *want* this. They want someone to take care of them. They want someone else to make the hard decisions for them. This," she threw her arms out wide, "this is better for them."

"Then what is this war about? What are you trying to gain?"

She sighed. "There will always be people with a shortsighted vision, people who can't see the benefits of big investments. There will always be people opposed to progress. They need to be convinced of their errors. They need to be made to see that this is the better way."

"Then what will happen if you win the war? Will you change your policies? What can this world expect from you once there is peace?"

"Policies won't change," she stated. "What works during wartime also works during peacetime," she said smugly.

"Buffalo pucky," I said defiantly. "I've heard that before."

"It's all for progress," she said in a mockingly sweet tone. "We've seen great improvements in our society since we began. I could show you the statistics, and you could see for yourself. Numbers don't lie."

"No. But *you* do."

She sighed and placed her hands on her hips. "What would you like to know about us? What question would you have me answer to convince you that this system is better for everyone?" she asked with a hint of frustration.

"I do have one question." I paused and looked her in the eye to be sure I had her complete attention. Then I asked, "Why don't you drop dead?"

Rage flashed across her face, but only for a moment. Then she was smiling again.

"You're wasting my time," I laughed. I had quietly removed my watch from my wrist and was using the pin of the clasp to pick the lock that held my hands together. "I won't be convinced by you, not after seeing what you do to your people. You force them to fight in this war. You force them to take artificial implants that destroy their senses. Then you take their lives and turn their bodies into robots. Why don't you just make robots and be done with it? Leave everyone else out of it."

"Robots and materials to make robots can be accumulated only so quickly," she answered. "To produce an overwhelming force, you need to use whatever resources are available to you at the time. It has to do with the law of diminishing returns and production possibility frontiers. But there is another reason, a reason I would bring to your attention by asking you a question." There was a glint of anger in her eye. "Why didn't you send robots to destroy Death's Grave? You could have avoided the humiliation of being captured."

I knew the answer, and I was too proud to keep it to myself. "There are some things you cannot program a robot to do."

"Such as improvise, for example," she said.

"Exactly," I responded.

"Then you know why robots will only ever accompany and assist our human soldiers, and not ever replace them. Soldiers will always have a job."

"Then why are you turning your soldiers into robots?"

"Just like anything, when something wears out, you either throw it away or recycle it. When a human wears out, then you replace them with a robot," she said in an exhausted tone.

"But you said robots would never replace people," I reminded her.

She stared at me, appearing to be unmoved by the contradiction I had caught her in.

"You aren't recycling your soldiers," I stated. "You are working on mind control. You want to control not just everyone's choices, but also their thoughts, their wills, and their actions. You are power hungry, and you just can't seem to get enough."

"What I can't seem to get enough of," she said in a raised voice that signaled the end of her patience, "is information out of you!"

"You said you were here to answer *my* questions," I reminded her. "You said you were here to tell me why your society is better. Now you're saying you are looking for information?" I asked, feigning annoyed surprise. "Will you make up your mind, *woman*?" I asked, cantankerously.

"Enough of this," she said in a commanding tone. "I have a device that will give me access to your mind. If you won't give me the information I want, then I will have to take it from you."

"Sounds like a policy you live by," I said.

She suddenly crouched and put her face very close to mine. "I will get inside your head, and I will rake through your every memory. I will find the information I want. Then I will focus the device to dwell on every pain, every regret, and every disappointment you have ever experienced. I will degrade you with your own deeds, pester you with your own past, and maul you with your own mistakes. You will be your own tormenter," she snarled.

I looked at her carelessly. "You sound like my ex-wife," I said. She snarled, almost like a barbarian. I wasn't impressed. "I am no longer the same person who made those mistakes," I stated boldly. "Those mistakes are no longer regrets. Now they are memories of lessons

I have learned, and I have learned what to do in cases like this."

"Really?" she challenged through narrowed eyes.

"Really," I replied coolly. Then I smiled. "You people don't get many prisoners, do you?"

She looked at me curiously but did not reply.

"I didn't think so," I said as I threw off the lock that had bound my hands, and I launched from the chair I had been bound to. I forcefully shoved Isthaelia and threw her against the concrete wall. She bumped her head against the cold concrete. Before she could recover from the daze of the bump, I violently struck her forehead with the heel of my hand. Her head hit the wall again with a resounding crack. She slumped to the ground, and her lifeless eyes stared into the floor. Her blonde hair slowly turned bright red.

I turned to the door and was about to work on making my escape when I heard a voice. It was Isthaelia's voice.

"Hypocrite." The voice had a rancorous tone with a metallic timbre to it, like it was coming through a cheap speaker. "You killed me. *You* made a choice that affected *my* life. You didn't even ask me if you should. It was *my* life that *you* took. Or at least, it was a copy of my life." The door opened, and Isthaelia walked in, alive, well, and with two guards.

I looked down at the Isthaelia on the floor, then back to the Isthaelia that had just walked in. They appeared to be exactly alike.

"Don't look so dismayed," she chided with a gentle laugh, "or surprised. She was just a clone." She swung her arm toward the corpse. "They only have a useful lifespan of two or three years. This one was going to expire soon anyway. She's no real loss to me." Then she looked cruelly at me through squinted eyes and a maliciously curled smile. "But you lost something," she said, as she raised her hand close to her face and pointed a wagging, mocking finger at me. "You've lost your innocence by taking an innocent life. Tell me, how does it feel? I always hear the first one is the hardest. Is that true?"

"I don't answer to you, witch!" I growled. "But at the same time," I said in a calmer tone, "an innocent life? That's debatable. Is a clone as evil as the original? It's definitely a thought to philosophize about."

She put her hands on her hips and nodded her head in exaggerated bobs, mocking an agreement. Then she opened her mouth with a loud smack of her lips and said, "Yeah, good luck with that." She folded her hands behind herself and twisted back and forth at the hips like a flirty school girl. "But maybe seeing your friend again will cheer you up. What was his name? Ronald McPhearson, is it? That's a strange name. It's almost like he isn't from this planet. You see, we need information from him, too, and he isn't willing to give it.

We would have interrogated him properly, but he fainted at the idea," she giggled. "As you can imagine, it's very difficult to get information from a man who swoons at the mere thought of pain." Her sassiness was wearing on my nerves. "We thought we would be able to convince you about our cause, and then you would convince him to tell us what we want to know. But you had to be so difficult," she said with a pouty face. "So now I'm thinking…" She shifted her weight to one foot and tapped a finger on her chin. "I'm thinking we could torture *you* and let your friend watch."

"Why didn't you start with torturing me?"

"Because I can see that you won't break. You can take it. But your friend doesn't know that."

"That's not happening," I said defiantly.

She scoffed. "Whatever. Typical male; overconfident… Or is it arrogant?" she pondered. "It doesn't matter. I'm going to let these two soften you up before we take you to your friend." She spread her hands out to either side of her, indicating to the guards. "We can't let him see you like this."

One of the guards clenched a fist and smiled. The other snapped his own head to one side with a swift twist, and his neck let out a sharp pop.

"I'm mean, it's only fair," Isthaelia said. "You did kill my clone, after all."

"Until good people are free to make their own choices of their own will, she won't be the last to die by my hand," I stated firmly. The smug look on Isthaelia's

308

face withered, and the guards hesitated. Some say that weapons kill people, as though the weapon has a mind and will of its own. I didn't need a weapon. I only needed a reason. "For Edengone," was the last thing they heard me say.

I will not disclose in detail what followed immediately after, but a passerby outside the door would have heard a few moments of slamming and crashing, ending with a stomach-churning crack. I opened the door, and I walked out, leaving a total of four bodies in that room, two of them looking identical in every way.

I moved down the hall, and with nothing but intuition and luck to guide me, I searched for Ron. I moved swiftly and silently. I was nothing more than a shadow in the dark, a forgotten memory in an empty room, a solitary moment in a sea of events. No one knew I was there. No one knew I had come, and even fewer knew I had left. From what I could gather of my surroundings, I assumed I was in a large, underground bunker. I worked my way through the facility until I heard the faint but strongly familiar voice of Ron giving a lecture, traveling through the halls.

"You destroyed Death's Grave!" roared a woman's voice, interrupting Ron's. "You destroyed valuable lives that were critical to the function of this civilization! You don't want that burning your conscience for the rest of your life, do you? Make amends, and tell us about the suits you were wearing and how you crossed the desert. You owe it to us," the voice demanded. I recognized her voice. It was Isthaelia…again.

I moved in the direction of the voices and peeked around the corner of an open door. I saw Ron, bound to a chair, and Isthaelia looming over him. I realized I had only destroyed another clone, and, for all I knew, this Isthaelia was nothing but another carbon-based copy. She was accompanied by several soldiers. All of their backs were towards me.

Ron glared at Isthaelia. He discreetly raised a finger and wagged it. He had seen me. "The attack worked, didn't it?" Ron asked Isthaelia. "They flanked your forces and broke your line. They are on their way here, and you want a way to escape into the desert."

"It would be the right thing to do," Isthaelia reasoned with him. "It would be the merciful thing to do."

"You don't really believe what you claim to believe," Ron huffed. "You change your beliefs by what is convenient at the moment. A moment ago, you claimed that the process of evolution, natural selection, and survival of the fittest was the ruling law. Then you discovered you were losing and about to become extinct. Now you beg for mercy from me. I've tried being merciful to your kind. I offered mercy to the commander at Death's Grave, just before the whole place came down. Just before the pillar collapsed, I told them to surrender and to abandon their projects. But he refused and made threats; vile, cruel, shocking threats. And what

I have seen of your people, I don't doubt he would be true to those threats if he had a chance. I didn't give him the chance after that," Ron explained somberly. "What is happening will continue to happen," Ron continued. "You have revealed your true nature and you have judged harshly, without mercy. Now, with the same judgment you have given, you are being judged. Your kind will not survive. Whether this is the divine decree of an omnipotent being or the course of natural selection, it doesn't matter. You – will – be – destroyed," Ron said with conviction.

Ron's eyes rolled back in his head. I pulled back and retreated a little ways down the hall. A tremendous shock issued from Ron, slamming the other occupants against the walls of the room, where they fell to the floor, unconscious.

I ran into the room and was about to free Ron, who was also unconscious. But then I paused, and I looked around at the people who had captured us, who threatened to kill us, who were sworn enemies of the people we were trying to help. Would they continue their fight, or would they surrender and give up their psychopathic ways? Or would they feign surrender and then continue working undercover until they had built up a large enough following to rise up again? Would they ever change? We had been sent to eliminate this threat, but I thought about what Ron had said about offering mercy to the commander of Death's Grave. Could I also offer mercy? Half of my mind was made up to destroy our capturers where they lay and fulfill Ron's foresighted event. But the other half of my mind tethered the violent half and spoke humanely to it. It sued for mercy. I thought about all the lives I had destroyed in the past, all of them justified. And, yet, I had often found myself wishing I could have spared them if I was given the option or a way. Here, I found myself in such a situation. I fought within my mind because fear was getting the better of me. I was afraid these people would continue hunting us, and that they may successfully capture us again. Fear told me to execute the enemy here and now. But courage stated that we would prevail again if we came to conflict once more and suggested that these people may even change if they were given time. They were presently not a direct threat. They were, as I had come to call such situations, neutralized. I never would have suspected before, but I was discovering that it took more courage to spare a life than to destroy one.

Without further thought, I freed Ron and threw him over my shoulder, leaving the other people where they had landed, to their own fates. I carried Ron into the hall and onto an elevator. I set him down while the elevator began its ascension to the surface.

The elevator stopped at the top floor and the doors opened.

"Where are we?" Ron asked as he regained consciousness.

"We're getting out of here," I said.

I helped him to his feet and assisted him down the hall. We reached a set of doors, and I opened them. Sunlight bore down upon us. I blinked through squinting eyes and held up a hand to block the light. Our eyes adjusted, and we looked around.

"We're still at Death's Grave," I said in surprise as I viewed the rubble-filled crater.

We stood for a moment, looking around, unsure of where to go next. Then a group of blinding lights flew over the treetops. Again, we shielded our eyes. I heard a familiar whirring sound and realized it was the sound of several light propulsion engines. I remembered what Isthaelia had promised, and I feared that the others of our squad had been captured and that the engines were now in her possession. The engine sound slowly wound down and fell silent. I lowered my hand and looked. I saw both half-tracks, still covered in gundon shells. One half-track still sported the gundon horn from our first encounter. I heard the rear hatch open, and Tinear peeked out from behind the half-track.

"I thought you two would be goners for sure," he said.

I smiled, relieved to see a friendly face. "Then what are you doing here?"

Tinear shrugged and walked towards us. "Just figured we would come to clean up the remains, admire our handy work, and say a few words for the honorably fallen," he said with a grin as he clasped his arms around us. "But I guess we won't be saying anything about the

313

honorably fallen. No one who is honorable has fallen here."

Colem's head peeked from around the rear of the half-track. "Ha!" he exclaimed. "You see! I told you they wouldn't need rescuing! Pay up, suckers!" he shouted back into the half-track.

"Come on. Let's get you home," Tinear said, walking back to the half-track.

"No," I said. "Isthaelia is here and alive, and there is more to Death's Grave than we thought. She is in another, deeper facility beneath us. Gear up. We aren't done here."

A few moments later, the entire squad stood ready at the doors that Ron and I had escaped through. Ron and I were no longer escaped prisoners. Now we were invaders.

I approached Murlem, who had done another scan of the area using Dalmour's scanner to map out the facility below. "We hadn't expected another facility beneath Death's Grave that would be shielded from radiation, so we hadn't made the adjustments to the scanner to compensate for the lesser light density," he explained. "But now Isthaelia has nowhere to hide." He pointed to the map on his handheld computer. "Isthaelia is here, and we are going to bury her in her own house," he said emphatically.

"Good work," I said. Then I turned to the rest of the squad. "Alright, listen up! Isthaelia is here. She has clones of herself running around causing all sorts of problems. We need to find the real Isthaelia. We didn't know she would be here when we first attacked. We can't let this opportunity pass us by. Move out."

And with that, we entered the doors, boarded the elevator, and descended into the depths of Death's Grave.

Chapter 20 – The Monster Within

The elevator doors opened and we cautiously entered the hall. Murlem led the way, following the map on his device. We wound through the halls and passed empty room after empty room.

"Where is everyone?" Numigh asked.

The hallway opened up into a large rotunda with many, many other halls leading away from it in every direction. Murlem stopped.

"Where do we go next?" I asked.

"I don't know," Murlem replied in a worried tone. "Something is interfering with the scanner."

Saeui shifted the weight of a large gun he carried over one shoulder.

Ron glanced up at the gun Saeui carried. "Did you tear that gun off one of the half-tracks, or is that standard issue?" Ron asked.

"Don't be jealous," Saeui replied casually.

"I'm not," Ron said, equally as casual. "Why would I be?"

"Mine's bigger," Saeui answered.

I looked around at all of the vast halls surrounding us. "I don't like this," I said. "Let's pull back into the hall where we aren't as exposed."

Before we moved, a maniacal laugh rolled through the rotunda.

"You have hit the hornets' nest," Isthaelia's voice said. It seemed to come from everywhere. "And now you must suffer the swarm."

The lights in the facility went out, and we found ourselves in complete darkness. We quickly turned on our gun-mounted flashlights.

"I got movement!" Pik called out. "It's Isthaelia!"

"She's over here, too!" Numigh warned.

I shined my light down each hall as I rotated. Isthaelia clones were in all of the halls, and their numbers were growing rapidly.

"Steady," I said. "They aren't armed."

"That doesn't matter," Tinear pointed out. "They still far outnumber us and could smother us to death. They may be undying."

We jumped at the sound of an earsplitting shriek that dragged on and echoed through the rotunda. One of the clones was the source of the noise, and the others joined in. The reverberating shrieks tore through the rotunda until it reached a deafening pitch. Then they charged, stampeding down the halls from all directions.

"Split into pairs, take a hall, and shoot them down! Alternate reloading and cover each other!" I ordered.

We divided and took up our positions at the hall entrances.

"This is worse than our first attack on Death's Grave," Ron said.

"Think of them as zombies," I suggested.

"That doesn't help!" Ron cried out in dismay. "I don't like the idea of shooting anyone, but shooting a lady?"

"Not all women are ladies," I said with a spark of resentment, "and not all females are worthy of being called 'women'."

"Something like that could be said of men, too," Ron argued.

"I assumed that was a given. Now shut up and shoot," I ordered.

We opened fire and mowed down wave after wave of clones. The shots echoed and re-echoed throughout the rotunda. The bodies began piling up in the halls, forcing the new waves to climb over the old.

"How many of these did she need?" Ron asked in disbelief when yet another wave rushed down the hall.

"Enough to rule the world," I answered. "Status report!" I called over my shoulder.

"Never better!" Tinear shouted back over the sound of incessant gunfire. "I never dreamed I would have the chance to shoot down this witch again and again! This is *fantastic*!"

Then I heard the sound of Saeui's large caliber gun join its barks of fire with our smaller weapons. I looked over at the tunnel next to us and saw Saeui behind the large gun he had mounted on a tripod. His teeth were clenched in a vicious smile, his nose wrinkled in a snarl, and his face strobed with the fiery glow of the barrel flashes.

"What about that compassion thing?" Ron asked in disgust.

"This will have to do for now," I said as I shot another Isthaelia that was trying to squirm through a small gap between the pile of cloned corpses and the ceiling of the hall.

All at once, the gunfire stopped, and we looked around at each other.

"The hall is blocked," Tinear reported.

"Same here," Colem added.

Saeui leaned on the tripod-mounted gun and viewed the clogged hall the way a connoisseur would view fine art. "Do you think Isthaelia can feel their pain?" he asked.

"That is a beautiful thought," Numigh said dreamily. "I hope so."

"Now we have time to figure out where she is hiding," I said.

Murlem pulled out his portable Dalmour scanner and made adjustments to see the underground bunker.

"Why didn't we see this before?" I asked, pointing to a room on the map that appeared.

"Now that we are inside the radiation shielding, I can get a cleaner image from the scan," Murlem explained. He studied the scan. "She is right beneath us."

"Of course she is," I said in frustration. "I don't think there is a depth she would not stoop to. How do we get there?"

"Wait a minute," Ron mumbled. He shined his flashlight around the rotunda. "Do you see these vertical, geared tracks between the halls?" he asked, "and these strange gaps around the edges of the floor? I think this is an elevator."

"Really?" I asked as I looked around. "What do you think they needed this one for?"

"I think it went up to the surface, before we destroyed the surface structures," Ron speculated while he shined his light up into the space above us. There was only blackness beyond the light. "We're lucky the clones didn't drop down on top of us. That really would be like a zombie attack."

"Sshhh!" Colem hissed. "She may be listening. Don't give her any ideas."

"Can we take this elevator down to Isthaelia?" I asked.

Murlem studied the map and Ron looked around the rotunda as he walked toward one of the walls. Then they answered in unison, "Yes."

Ron pulled a lever on the wall, and the floor began to sink amidst the rumbles and clicks of the machinery that drove it. The halls and their collections of dead Isthaelia clones rose above us, and bare walls took their place.

Darkness still prevailed, and the sound of the large elevator's mechanisms filled the air.

"How far down does this go?" I asked after we had been descending long enough for the bare walls to get boring.

The elevator stopped.

"Never mind," I said. I shined my light down the only hall available to us.

The hall was lined with dull, steel, riveted plates. At the end of the hall, we could see large, glowing, red pods, similar to the ones we had encountered before, when the undying AI had chased us out of Death's Grave. The hall ended in a large room, filled with rows and rows of glowing, red pods.

"There are people in them. They're wrapped in some kind of cocoon and suspended in a fluid," Ron pointed out as he drew nearer to one of the pods. "They look like Isthaelia."

"I think we've found the nest," Murlem said.

Colem looked around in horror at the many columns of pods, all bearing the same face of their life-long enemy. "They all look the same, yet they are all different, stored and waiting to be removed, like books on a shelf. It's like being in a maniac's library of weirdness," he said.

I glanced at him curiously.

"Over here!" Tinear shouted from somewhere further away.

We hurried over to where he stood, in front of a slightly larger, green-glowing pod with tangles of tubes running from it and stretching across the room.

"I think I've found the queen hornet," Tinear said.

"Behold," Saeui said in his baritone voice, "the monster from within reveals its true nature."

I looked through the glass at the figure suspended in the fluid of the pod. Her body was cocooned like the others, but she had a device covering the cranium, with bundles of wires attached all around it. A mask similar to the AI soldiers we had encountered covered her face. Aged wrinkles creased around her eyes, suggesting she was very old, and her eyes were closed, as though she was sleeping.

"Is this Isthaelia, then?" I asked sternly.

"It is," I heard Isthaelia's voice reply.

We spun around and saw another one of Isthaelia's clones, standing all alone, illuminated by the glowing red light emanating from the surrounding pods.

"She is our creator and our master, even our mother" the clone of Isthaelia explained. "She sends her blood and her DNA to all of us to create us. Her thoughts are transmitted to us while we grow and

321

develop, so we think and do what she would think and do, and someday," she said with a smile, "she will be able to communicate directly with all of us."

"Not if she's dead," I said boldly. I turned toward the green pod Isthaelia was in and raised my gun.

Isthaelia's eyes snapped open and stared right at me from the capsule. Her eyes were cloudy with age, but there was still a fierce force of will and determination in them.

"Don't bother," I heard Isthaelia's voice say. I looked back at the clone of Isthaelia. "The pod is bullet proof," she said.

I turned my gun on the clone and shot her. Then I turned and fired three or four rounds at Isthaelia's pod, and the rounds ricocheted off the glass.

"You see?" I heard Isthaelia's voice say. "Besides, you are too late."

I turned around and faced yet another one of Isthaelia's clones. "What do you mean?" I demanded.

"I have mastered mind-control over all my clones and every recycled soldier with the implant," she said.

I looked at the real Isthaelia floating in the green pod, and I could see the taunting grin of victory in her eyes as she stared at me over the mechanical mask. I heard footsteps, a lot of them. From the shadows, more clones stepped into the eerie red light and surrounded us.

"I can control…" began one clone, as she emerged from the darkness.

"One…," said another clone, also emerging.

"At…," said yet another.

"A…," and another.

"Time…," and another.

"Or all together," all the clones said in unison.

Colem shivered. "Okay, that was creepy," he said.

"So I can kill you…," one clone said, continuing the monologue.

"…One at a time," said another.

"Or all at the same time," they said in unison.

"Enough talking!" Saeui roared as he dropped the tripod for his large gun and opened fire, sweeping back and forth.

The Isthaelia's rushed towards us, all at once. We fired everything we had. I pulled out my sidearm and fired it alongside my rifle. It was awkward and inaccurate, but accuracy was not an issue. Isthaelia's clones were all around. We continued firing, and the clones kept coming. There seemed to be no end to them.

Saeui swung the large gun around from one wave to another and back again, shooting down the nearest threats first. He didn't bother letting go of the trigger as he changed targets, sending stray bullets into the pods of growing clones and spilling the contents onto the floor.

Tinear grabbed the large gun from Saeui. "Cover me!" he shouted.

Tinear raised the barrel toward the real Isthaelia in the capsule. Isthaelia's eyes widened. Tinear fired. The chain of bullets spooled into the gun and shells littered the floor around his feet as the weapon hurled round after round at Isthaelia's pod. The glass began to chip, then to crack. I saw fear in Isthaelia's eyes, just before the pod shattered and burst. But Tinear did not stop shooting. I shielded my eyes from the blast of liquid, glass, and electrical sparks splattering and spraying from the pod. Then I remembered the attacking clones. I turned and raised my guns, but all the clones had collapsed to the floor.

Tinear stopped firing, and I looked back at the pod where Isthaelia had been, only to see the shredded remains of the devices that had held her in the pod.

"Edengone bullets beat Advansynergist glass, every time," Tinear said with a snarl.

"She said it was bulletproof," I said, confused.

"And you believed her?" Tinear countered.

"Where is she?" I asked.

"Over there," Tinear pointed. "And over there. And some of her is over there. She's dead this time. I'm sure of it," he said confidently.

Pik looked around at the fallen clones of Isthaelia. "All of these clones under Isthaelia's mind control are dead. They died when she did. Didn't Isthaelia also say that the undying were under her control?"

John's eyebrows rose slightly. It was the most expressive I had ever seen him. "Then they may have died also. Most of the Advansynergist's army would be dead if that is true. We may soon see the end of the war," he said, marveling.

Colem laughed. Then he almost cried. "What will it be like?"

"It will be glorious," Tinear said dreamily.

A distant look entered all of the Edengone soldiers' eyes, and a peaceful smile grew on their faces. It was apparent that whatever daydream had captured them was so vivid as to block the current gruesome scene of destruction and death around them. I then realized how accustomed Edengone had become to constant warring. Peace had only been a distant hope, but now it was within sight.

"Is that it, then?" Ron asked, looking surprised.

"What? Were you just beginning to enjoy this?" Saeui asked with a cheeky smile.

"There is one more thing," Murlem said slowly. "I found indications of a Dathfron-bomb in this facility."

"A bomb named after Dathfron?" I asked. "That can't be good."

Tinear's mouth was thin and his eyes stern as he replied, "It isn't."

"Is it like a nuclear bomb?" Ron asked.

"I'm not sure what you mean, but a Dathfron-bomb is a weapon of last resort, it is so terrible and complete in its destructive power."

"I think you could have made that sound a little more dramatic," I said.

"And it would have deserved it, every bit," Murlem said, without a hint of a smirk.

"We can't leave it here," Tinear said.

"And we can't take it with us," Murlem added.

"So we'll dismantle it," said Saeui.

"No one knows how they are built, and no one has ever successfully disarmed one," Murlem explained grimly. "Some have speculated that once the bomb is made, it cannot be unmade."

"Then let's detonate it, here," I suggested. "We can use it to bury this place for good."

"We are deep enough that the blast will be mostly contained," Murlem reasoned. "It will still leave a mess, but it won't reach its full potential."

Tinear returned the large gun to Saeui and picked up his own. "Let's get it done," he said. "Lead the way, Murlem."

We followed Murlem into a hall opposite from where we had entered, and we went deeper into Death's Grave.

"Have you noticed we haven't come across any guards?" Ron asked me.

"What did you say?" Tinear stopped abruptly and asked, almost angrily.

"There were guards down here when Mike and I escaped, but we haven't found any since we came down here," Ron explained nervously.

Murlem and Tinear looked at each other, stunned.

"They are preparing the bomb for launch!" Murlem said in a moment of horrible realization. Half of what he had said was over his shoulder as he started to run towards the bomb.

"Go! Go! Go!" Tinear barked as he spurred us on into a dead run.

The walls were a blur as we raced through the facility. Our footsteps echoed through the steel hall. The sound of our running must have been heard further down the hall because a few guards appeared around a corner. We promptly gunned them down without stopping, and we continued our charge.

"I see the silo!" Murlem shouted and put on an extra burst of speed.

Suddenly, a siren began to wail, and red lights flashed all around us. I looked ahead, and I saw the light from the silo slowly fade.

"They are closing the doors!" Tinear shouted.

We ran as fast as we could, but it was no use. The door had slid shut, and we were locked out.

"We have to get in there!" Tinear shouted in frustration. "Crews three and four, return to the surface and see if you can repel into the silo when they open the surface doors," he ordered.

Half of the squad turned and ran back the way we had come, returning to the surface.

"Are there any door-breach charges left over?" Colem asked desperately, though we all knew there were not.

"Stand back!" Saeui said as he set up the large gun. We stood well behind him, and he fired a few test rounds at the door. The shots rang through the hall and pinged off the door. "Ow!" Saeui flinched. "I caught a ricochet in my shoulder!" he said as he pressed a hand over the bleeding wound.

"What else have we got?" Tinear asked.

"Ron!" I shouted.

Ron looked at me.

"Do it!" I ordered.

"This is just like when I got caught behind the door at Death's Grave," he protested. "I could injure all of you."

"Ron!" I shouted again. My neck muscles strained with the urgency I felt. "This isn't about me or you or anyone else here. This is about the countless lives that bomb will destroy if we don't stop it," I said sternly. "Now do it!" I ordered again.

Ron nodded, stepped out in front of Saeui, and looked at the door. Then he took a deep breath, settled an intense glare on the door, and focused. A couple of moments passed that felt like they dragged on, stretching their miserable time for as long as possible, eking out as much life as they could.

The metal door abruptly rang, as though it had been struck with a battering ram. Then it rang again, but with a duller tone. The middle of the door buckled. Then again, it rang, duller still. Again, a shock wave struck the door. The door crunched, and we could see a sliver of light from the silo through a broken corner. Then the door caved in, shot out of the door frame, and flew into the silo.

We rushed out onto the platform that overlooked the silo's interior, and we stopped.

"It's empty," Numigh said. His voice echoed through the vast chamber.

I looked up. "I'm not so sure this is a missile silo," I said. "How would it get out? There aren't any doors."

"Hey! Where is everyone?" Ron's voice called from behind us. He staggered through the doorway, holding his head.

"That's exactly what I would like to know," Tinear said, as he looked around at the still and quiet walkways.

"What I would like to know is how Ron – " Colem started.

"Not now," Tinear interrupted curtly. "We'll figure that out later. We have more pressing matters." He glanced back at Ron, who was still holding his head.

"That looks like a control room," Murlem said. He pointed to a window further along the walk.

We entered the room with our weapons raised, ready to fight, but the room was empty. Murlem consulted the Dalmour scanner again and looked confused.

"The readings are gone," he said.

"Are you sure you read them correctly in the first place," John asked.

"Yes. See? Here's a record of the most recent scans. And there's the bomb."

John examined the scanner data. Then he looked at Tinear and shrugged.

"Wait a minute," Ron mumbled. He looked across the controls and calculations on one of the computer screens. "I know what this is." He studied the controls and data a moment longer while we waited. Then he faced us and, with a look of bewilderment, he said, "This is a matter-energy frequency tuner. This is similar to what Mike and I used to get to your planet, except this is meant for something much, much bigger than a couple of men and a cat."

"What's a cat?" Colem asked.

"It's a creator we tried to bring with us. He didn't make it," I answered.

"I'm sorry to hear that," Colem said somberly. "I'm sure he was courageous and honorable in his service."

I bobbed my head side to side as I considered Colem's suggestion. "More or less," I shrugged.

Ron navigated through the computer's databanks. "It looks like they've been using it for a while. They have several entries of past matter-altering jumps."

"Any idea what they sent, or where they sent it?" Tinear asked.

Ron shook his head.

John looked over Ron's shoulder. Then John also shook his head. "The important stuff seems to be in code."

"Ron," Tinear said, "we still need to destroy this place. Can you get the system to overload and self-destruct after we've copied the data to a hard drive?"

"Yes," Ron said confidently. "And I can assure you, it will be almost as good as a Dathfron-bomb."

Tinear raised an eyebrow.

"You know what I mean," Ron said, turning his attention back to the machine.

A few minutes later, Tinear was roaring through the halls as we ran ahead of him. "GO! GO! GO!" Tinear roared as we raced to the elevators that would raise us from the depths of Death's Grave. "Crews three and four," Tinear said over the radio, "Ready the vehicles for immediate departure. Repeat, get ready to haul the halibut out of here!"

John had copied the information from the computer, and Ron had rigged the device to explode, giving us a narrow window to escape to the surface. We all squeezed into the elevator. Numigh pressed the button to go up. The doors slowly creeped closed, seemingly unaware of our sense of urgency. Soothing

331

music played while the elevator began its ascension. Our eyes roved about while we waited, as though we were looking for the first sign of a cataclysmic explosion…in an elevator. Murlem shifted nervously from one foot to the other and back again. Ron cleared his throat with a gentle cough, which startled Saeui, who then nearly knocked over Colem. The elevator doors slowly slid open, and we resumed the race for our lives. We thundered down the hall and burst through the doors where the blinding sunlight hailed us.

"Colossal two, go!" Tinear ordered over the radio as he waved an arm at the driver.

The light propulsion engines around the colossal half-track lit up with a brilliant flare, and the vehicle rose into the air and vanished in a surge of speed.

We boarded our half-track. The rear hatch was still closing when Numigh fired up the engines. I fumbled with my seatbelt as Numigh reached for the lever and pressed it forward. The trees lowered beneath us as we rose into the sky. Then we launched forward. The trees were gone, and the horizon sped towards us. I groaned under the strain of the acceleration. Then Numigh backed off the throttle, and I leaned forward with a big exhale.

"Now, let's watch the fireworks," Numigh said. He turned the vehicle around in the air to face the distant facility of Death's Grave.

We leaned forward to get a better view through the windshield. Then all at once, we saw the ground heave upward, followed by a ballooning inferno, then a blinding light. We held up our hands against the light but still strained to see the blast. The light dimmed to a bearable intensity, and the fireball dissipated among static-like lightning bolts randomly arcing through the air. The sound of the blast finally reached us and rumbled through the iron hull of the vehicle. The explosion first snarled like a lion, then belted like an elephant, and then it purred like an idling muscle-car until it slowly faded away. We chuckled, delighted by that infernal symphony. It was a strangely satisfying sound.

Tinear smiled with approval. "At least no one can say we weren't thorough." Then he looked curiously at Ron. "Now you two have got some explaining to do," he said in a serious tone. "Can all people from Earth kick in a door with their mind?"

"No," I said timidly. Then I had a second thought. "Actually, I can think of a few action movie-stars that could."

Ron was more reasonable and forthcoming with his approach. "There was a, uh, an accident with Dalmour's machine, and I came out like this."

"And he stilled cleared you for duty?" Tinear asked, surprised.

"We would have told you," I explained, "But we were still unsure of your people's beliefs or ideals. We weren't sure how you would respond."

"You didn't answer my question," Tinear stated. "Did Dalmour clear you for duty?"

"Yes," Ron answered. "In fact, he recommended to the general that I join."

A knowing smile slowly formed on Tinear's face, and he began to chuckle. I looked around, and the others were also beginning to laugh.

"What's so funny?" I asked hesitantly.

"Dalmour has done this before," Tinear said, laughing. "He uses us for his experiments, with our knowing about it, of course. He's too humane and too excited about his projects to not tell us about what he is doing. I'm just glad this one worked out."

"Tell me about it," Saeui said with a smile. "He had me drinking some kind of nutrient supplement he made. It stuck to my larynx, and I sounded like a six-year-old girl for a couple of weeks."

"This is fine and all," John said soberly amidst our laughter, and to our surprise, "but is there any other reason we need to be here?"

"He's right," Tinear said, as he picked up the radio. "All units," he said into the handset, "Death's Grave has been destroyed. Let's go home."

Chapter 21 – Going Home

We flew back over Advansynergist territory. We passed over the jungle, the grasslands, and the shrub-patched, low dunes until we entered the Demog desert.

Day after day, with short stops to let the half-tracks refuel, we drove back through the unceasing sandstorm and the barrage of sand-hail. Then we entered the strange and forlorn land of red stones laced with unworldly rivers of rushing sand carried by raging winds. We flew past the Bull's Eye and the solitary mountain with its twisting funnel of sand and its dark secrets buried beneath it. Then we re-entered the sandstorm and emerged again under the light of a never-setting sun. We flew across the Demog desert, dune by dune, until Murlem announced the greatly anticipated news.

"There it is!" he shouted. "Home again!"

We looked out through the windshield into the distance and could see the little buildings we had left so many weeks ago.

Tinear picked up the radio handset and dialed in the frequency. "Colossal to HQ, come in HQ." he waited a moment.

Then we heard the glorious response. "This is HQ. We read you colossal."

Tinear smiled. "HQ, inform General Kulek that Death's End has arrived, mission accomplished."

"Copy, colossal. Will do."

A minute or two passed before we heard a familiar voice crackle across the radio. "Death's End, congratulations and welcome home. What's your ETA?" General Kulek asked.

Tinear looked at Murlem, who held up five fingers.

"ETA is four minutes, sir," Tinear said with a grin.

Murlem and Numigh looked mortified. "We'll be late!" I saw Murlem silently mouth the words.

"Then I'll see you in the carpool," General Kulek said.

"Actually, sir," Tinear said, with an even bigger smile, "we'll be coming in on the airfield."

Numigh's and Murlem's faces instantly relaxed and grew smiles of their own. An awkward silence occupied the radio. Finally, General Kulek responded. "Very well. HQ out."

"You want the general to see us *fly* in," Murlem stated.

"He won't even remember we were late after he sees this," Tinear said as he sat down.

We sped over the glistening spires of sapphire skyscrapers and white sidewalks speckled with people dressed in their plain and clean attire.

We were soon flying over headquarters, and we hovered onto the airfield, where General Kulek and a few of his staff shielded their eyes from the blinding beams of the light propulsion engines. The half-tracks rested on the ground, covered in desert dust and gundon shells, sporting strange, light-emitting spheres at their corners, and bearing a few scars from enemy fire, not to mention the one-of-a-kind hood ornament on one of them.

The rear hatch opened with a gentle but tired hiss, and we marched out onto the pavement, two by two, turned toward the general, and stood at attention.

"At ease," General Kulek said. "Tinear, you and your squad will debrief with my staff. Mike and Ron will follow me. Professor Litona has been eager to be reunited with you."

I raised my eyebrows. Ron looked at me and bounced his.

"Now will be the time to say goodbye, if you wish," the general said, almost caringly. "You've kept your end of the deal. It's time we kept ours."

I looked at the squad, particularly the crew with whom I had been through the adventure of my life. Each face had become familiar. Each one had become a friend.

"It has been an honor to serve with you," Tinear said with a salute.

I shook my head and grinned kindly. "Let's not say goodbye as soldiers," I said, "but as friends. Friendship goes far beyond the call of duty."

I stretched out my hand, and Tinear took it.

"Maybe we'll cross paths again," Tinear suggested.

"Not likely," I replied, "but it would be nice." I said my goodbyes to the rest of the crew.

Ron was also speaking with some of the friends he had made, particularly Pik and John. When he saw that I was ready to follow General Kulek, he waved to those he was speaking with and trotted up alongside me.

"What's wrong with you?" I asked.

"What do you mean?" Ron responded, puzzled.

"You're usually bawling like a baby when you say goodbye."

"Hm," he shrugged, and he walked a little quicker.

We followed General Kulek into the headquarters building we had been taken to when we first arrived on Edengone. We took a few elevators down into the depths of the facility and navigated through a labyrinth of halls. It was reminiscent of the deeper chambers at Death's Grave, but there was more light and less of a foreboding feeling of doom.

We entered a room filled with odd machinery, bizarre contraptions, contorted structures, and the hum of high voltage. Doctor Dalmour smiled warmly at us and nodded a greeting. He rocked forward onto his toes, then back to his heels, and then planted his feet back on the ground again, plainly pleased to see us. And there was Litona, looking beautifully annoyed about something.

She walked up to us. "I've been waiting for this moment for a long time," she said.

"Your waiting has paid off. I am here," I replied, throwing my arms wide.

338

She stood stiff and rigid, with her arms at her side and looking confused.

I decided to make my move, and I hugged her.

"This is very unprofessional," she said, surprised and sounding uncomfortable.

"Right," I said, letting her go. "We can talk and catch up later."

"Actually," Litona said, smoothing out her lab coat, "I was hoping you were ready to go home. I have finished the device to send you back to Earth, and I am eager to test it on my first victim."

Ron folded his arms and covered his face with a hand. His shoulders shook with a hint of silent laughter.

"Oh," I said, pulling my mouth to one side in bewilderment.

"And this!" she said excitedly, in a sudden change of mood, "this is the culmination of my life's work, to date! I have a few more crazy ideas," she said offhandedly, "which haven't been too promising, but I have high hopes. But this!" she began anew. "This is the doorway to the cosmos, the telescope that will peer into the infinite, and the microscope that will reveal the most finite! THIS," she struck out a hand toward the machine, "is the Oracle!"

The tangle of devices that made the Oracle uttered a rattle and a clunk.

"Impressive," I said apprehensively. "How does it work?"

"This will quicken your matter to the very limits of energy activation," she said. "You will not leave this energy frequency; you will add onto it. Once full energy levels have been realized, you should be able to see the entire electromagnetic spectrum! You will see colors no one has ever imagined before!" she said in an awe-inspired voice while she swept a hand before her imagined paint-chip fan book. "From there you will be able to see Earth and travel back under your own power, nearly instantaneously."

"Wow," I said, not fully understanding what she was explaining. "Can I have Ron double check your equations, before we, um, test it?" I asked. "It's not that I don't trust you. It's just that... just... Well, it couldn't hurt."

"No!" she shouted in a sudden rage. "Why do people always want an equation to be associated with *everything*?!"

I was mesmerized by her beautiful fury.

"Numbers, numbers, numbers!" she continued, to my delight. "Fools always want to see the numbers, as though math held the answer to everything, as though math contained all truth and everything could be explained mathematically." She pressed her fingertips to her thumb and waved them in front of my face emphatically. "Math is merely a fancy way of counting; nothing more! I occasionally use my fingers to count, yet I do not say that my finger can explain everything, or anything for that matter. Nor do I rely upon my finger to hypothesize, except to place it upon my chin while I think! Mathematics is nothing more than a crystal ball for the modern soothsayers, who are dubbed 'theoretical scientists'!"

"Please, forgive Litona," Doctor Dalmour said kindly. "She rarely works mathematically. Most of her work and results are founded upon intuition."

"That seems a little uncertain, don't you think?" Ron asked skeptically.

"Only if you lack the skill of intuition yourself." Doctor Dalmour stated. "Many people in many other professions rely solely upon intuition to perform their work without ever consulting a calculator beforehand. Athletes can throw a ball and have it land exactly where they want it, without calculating forces or trajectories. Surgeons make careful and precise incisions without premeasuring and often without guiding mechanisms. Mothers perceive the needs of their children, often without understanding the most basic principles of human psychology or knowing the ratios of a body's chemical balance. Lesser scientists use numbers and mathematics as a crutch because they lack the insight and foresight of intuition. However, a talented scientist, such as Professor Litona, will use both the logic of mathematics *and* the unmeasurable, unquantifiable gift of intuition. In this way, she knows she is reasoning and understanding to the fullest of her potential. However, with this pioneered work she has done, there are no equations that yet explain the principles she has used to develop this devise."

Ron nodded his head understandingly. "I can accept that. Isaac Newton had to invent a new field of math to further his studies. I suppose it's not so unusual. But could you at least clue me in on the principles you have applied and how they are related?"

Litona looked at Ron in disbelief before she said, "I have spent a lifetime studying this, and you want me to explain how it works in a few moments? Even if we had time, there would still not be enough time. Some things cannot function without time. Learning is one of them."

Doctor Dalmour placed a gentle hand on Litona's shoulder and softly said, "Professor, please, indulge them. Give them the short, simplified version."

Litona looked Dalmour in the eye, appearing very annoyed, and I thought very beautiful, and Doctor Dalmour smiled kindly back.

Litona rolled her eyes. "Fine," she said. "But listen closely!" she shouted with wide, dazzling eyes and a beautiful, angry finger pointed toward Ron and me. "I won't repeat myself and there will not be a Q&A session afterwards." She took a deep breath and then exhaled. "To state the simple point: there is no time."

"You already told us th – " Ron started to say before I elbowed him in the stomach.

Litona continued as though nothing had happened. "Time does not exist beyond here. In fact, time does not exist anywhere. There is only eternity. Time is merely a tool. Time is a means of measuring progress and puts milestones in the infinite expanse of eternity. Picture yourself in a rowboat in the middle of a vast ocean that reaches to the horizon on all sides. There are no landmarks, no clouds, and the sun is directly above you. You could start rowing, but you would have no idea whether or not you were making any progress. A buoy placed every mile or so would be helpful. In fact, the distance between buoys doesn't even need to be consistent, so long as you can see you are making progress. Time is a buoy in eternity, a mile marker in the infinite. Time is simply the counting of a reoccurring event; the rising and setting of the moon, the movement of the hands around a clock, the swing of a pendulum, the pulsing current through a crystal. Time is a concept. Beyond this, time does not exist. It is not self-existing. Therefore, events dictate time, and there is no leaving time or traveling through time. Time does not halt, accelerate, or reverse the passing of events because time *is* the event. So, applying these introductory concepts to your predicament, to circumvent the supplies, fuel, and many other resources required for space travel and altering your matter-energy frequency, we will remove time from the equation. If you remove time from the equation, then travel becomes instantaneous. How long does it take to travel thirty-six miles without time? It takes thirty-six miles. But how much time? We can't seem to talk about traveling without talking about time.

Even speed is stated as an equation of time. Speed is actually not a thing. It's just time and distance. Remove time and you are left with only the distance to cover. How do you remove time? It already is. Time is imaginary. It's a unique concept given to mortals. But what *is* time? Time is the passing of life. It is the distance between birth and death. Beyond that, there is no time." Litona stretched out an arm and pointed to some unseen, distant point. "Out there, out in reality, in outer space, in eternity and infinity, time does not exist. It does not exist."

She stopped talking. Ron and I stood dumbfounded. Doctor Dalmour clapped enthusiastically. "Wonderful!" he exclaimed.

Litona didn't look any more satisfied or pleased than she did before the explanation.

I leaned toward Ron and whispered. "What is she talking about?"

"I don't know," Ron whispered back. "Just go with it."

"So," I said slowly, thoroughly entranced, "I suppose I will just need to trust you know what you are talking about."

Litona didn't say anything. She just pierced my skull with those dazzling eyes.

"Just to make sure I understand," I said, "let me go through this once more. We can't use light propulsion engines to get back to Earth because we still need to change our matter-energy frequency. And we can't use the matter-energy frequency altering suits because we still have all that distance to cover. And we can't use both because…" My eyes roved around looking at the ceiling while I tried to come up with the answer.

"Because this is safer," Litona said. "Trust me."

I stared at her, not being entirely convinced. "Okay, so what if it doesn't work? What happens?"

She quickly smiled, like a child in a candy store. "We will see a pop and a fizzle here, but where you are, there will be a cataclysmic explosion as all your atoms split in something like an uncontrolled nuclear reaction," Litona replied with almost a cheerful ring to her voice and her hands together with her fingers curled up in glee; except for when she said "explosion", then her fingers sprung from their hiding places to wiggle around for a moment, illustrating what that might look like. "You will basically burn, very fast," she said, as her head bobbed side to side enthusiastically. I decided she was creepy when she was cheerful.

Again, I stared at her, but more in horror this time. "Really, you don't need to sugar-coat it for me. I can handle the truth," I said sarcastically.

"You will die, in tremendous fashion," Litona reiterated with a big, fine-toothed smile and excited eyes. She reminded me of how my kindergarten teacher looked when she would tell us the class was going on a fieldtrip.

"Yeah! I got that!" I covered my eyes and groaned.

"There is another hazard I should mention," Litona added casually, returning to her serious self.

"Really? In addition to death?"

"Since you will be removed from time, or in other words, events we associate with the passing of time," she explained, "you will have no perception of time. If you do not find a way back to your Earth quickly, you will age and die in that energy frequency without realizing it, and you will never get home."

"Great!" I said enthusiastically. "I'm glad there are options available for how I could *die*!"

"Life is fatal," Doctor Dalmour said, unamused by my hysteria. "It's something you need to learn to live with."

"I may not have long to live to learn if Litona keeps thinking of ways to kill me."

"Then learn quickly," Dalmour suggested.

"Wait," I said, as I came to a realization of what I would be doing. "I will be traveling through space and altering my matter's energy frequency at the same time… I'll be in space. What about air? What will I breathe until I get back to Earth?"

"You won't need to breathe," Litona said. "And you won't freeze." Then she thought. "At least, that's what the theory is. You shouldn't need to breathe. But we don't know. Your atoms will be pushed to such an energy frequency that you will be teaming with energy that will keep you from freezing and negate the need for oxygen for your body to stay vital."

"Huh?" I uttered.

Ron simplified the explanation for me. "You'll be fine."

"Oh. Okay," I said. "So I get into the machine, and then what? Do I click my heels, or does it automatically send me on the express back to Earth?"

"The theory is that you will be inundated with so much energy that mere thought will cause an action. You will only need to think about going to Earth," Litona explained.

"Just think, eh?"

"The truth is," Dalmour said gravely, "we don't know. You will need to figure that out when you get there."

I turned to Ron. "You've been awfully quiet. What are your thoughts?"

Ron glanced at the floor and hesitated.

"Ron, what's wrong with the machine?"

"Oh, nothing is wrong with the machine," he quickly clarified.

"So it will get us home in one piece, right?" I asked, looking for reassurance.

"Well," he hesitated again. "It will get *you* home in one piece."

My heart stopped, my breath stilled, and my body froze. "Ron?"

"You will get home just fine," he said, with his eyes getting moist around the lids. "You will be fine," he sniffed. "I won't be returning to Earth."

I stared at him. "Why?"

"I suppose I would rather be stuck here exploring some unknown world for the rest of my life," he said with a smile. "Earth has taught me all it has to offer. There's more for me to do here."

I thought. I thought long and hard. I had lost friends before, but I had lost them to tragedy. I had never lost a friend by choice.

"No," I said. "I'm not leaving you here, Ron. I won't leave you behind. If you are staying, then so am I. I also think Edengone has more for me than Earth," I said as I looked around at the other people in the room, particularly Litona.

Just then, John entered the room. "Litona!" he bellowed. "You have been the conqueror of my thoughts over these last difficult weeks! Were the weeks difficult because of the task at hand? No. They were difficult because I was not with you. But thinking of you saved me from destruction. The memory of you vanquished all feelings of despair, suffering, and grief. You are the photonic beam in my life!" Then he threw his arms wide.

Litona dropped her clipboard, ran to him, and threw her arms around him.

"Really?" I asked, with annoyed disbelief.

General Kulek smiled and said, "John doesn't say much, but when he does speak, it's because he knows what he's talking about."

"So I've heard," I said, as the hugging continued.

Ron leaned closer and asked in a hushed tone, "Do you remember that conversation we had with the crew while we were crossing the Demog Desert, the one about girls?"

"Yes," I replied. "This just got awkward."

"And do you remember that speech you gave about fighting for a reason, and John mentioned a fiancé?"

I slapped a hand over my eyes to hide from the shame, with the same effectiveness as an ostrich burying its head in the sand to hide from danger. "This just got really, really awkward." Then I noted, quietly, "They can't really be engaged. They aren't kissing."

"Kissing? In public?" General Kulek questioned, utterly repulsed "You Earth-people are truly uncouth barbarians."

"Do you still feel like Edengone has something to offer?" Ron asked me. "You know, you still have a family on Earth; a mother, a father, and a few annoying siblings whom you care about very much. They are probably wondering where you are. I'm sure you didn't tell them you were going to a different planet when you left for New York, and I'm sure you didn't tell them you would be staying. You should go home and let them know you are alright."

"You're right," I sighed as I thought about my family. It would trouble them to not know what had happened to me, even if they were accustomed to my long, unexplained absences. "I think I'm ready to go home now," I said, suddenly feeling depressed, and even a little homesick.

General Kulek coughed. "Ahem, hm, hem! I believe we are ready to test the machine, Professor Litona."

"Oh. Right. I'll be right back. Oops!" she whispered to John as she turned away and nearly tripped over her own foot. She walked behind the control board.

"This is goodbye, then," Ron said to me.

"Nonsense," I replied. "If this machine works, you can always come home."

He stretched out his hand. I took it, and then pulled him in and hugged him.

"Be sure to get into some trouble once in a while," I said as I let him go.

"You know I will," he replied with a grin.

Then a thought crossed my mind. "Oh! You can't stay. What will the university say? I can't tell them I left you on another planet. They would say I was on drugs."

Ron laughed. "Who cares? Tell them I joined a monastery in India or some other crazy thing a college professor might do."

"Seeking enlightenment?"

"Sure. That's close enough to the truth."

"What will you do here?"

"Pik and John have a lot of work to do analyzing our discoveries. There are new fields of science to study, inventions to be made, lands to explore, and a planet to get revolving again. I'll find something to do. What about you?"

I thought for a moment. "You know, I'm not sure. I've seen so much. I often think life couldn't have any more to offer, and yet it keeps giving me more. We'll see what happens," I said with a shrug. I turned to the others. "I'm ready. What do I do?"

"Finally." Litona rolled her eyes. "Step into the chamber."

I looked around at the tangled mess of gizmos. "What chamber?" I asked.

Litona looked up from the control board and pointed with a pronounced finger. "*That* chamber. The big ring," she said distinctly.

There was a big ring, standing about seven feet tall. There were footpads within the ring that forced me to stand with my feet far apart.

"This feels like a good opening for a rock concert," I said. "Now what?"

"Put your arms straight out to either side, like you're reaching for the ring."

"Wait a minute," I said, putting my arms out to either side.

"What's wrong?"

"I've seen this before, in one of Da Vinci's drawings."

Everyone looked confused, except for Ron.

"Back on Earth," I added.

This time, General Kulek rolled his eyes and let out a long sigh. "Stop talking about Earth! You will be there soon enough!"

"Powering up," Litona announced. "You may feel a strange burning sensation, Mike, but it is *imperative* that you do not move! The success of the test depends upon it! Oh, and so does your life. Engaging!"

I heard the moan of bearings beginning to turn and the hum of the high voltage grew louder. Then the room began to spin – at least I think it was the room because I did not feel any sensation of spinning myself. I looked one last time at Ron as his face strobed in the fierce spin. Then there was a bright flash. And then –

Peace.

Such an unworldly sense of peace. All fear was banished. Doubt felt like a bygone memory. Anger withered and altogether faded from view or recollection. Instead, a reassuring and familiar feeling crept in through my mind and worked itself into my heart and throughout my being. I felt like I had arrived. I felt as though this was the culmination of life. I felt… Home. This was where I belonged. I thought this would be it, that this was how it would be forever. But then a thought, almost like a voice, spoke to me. It said this was not my time.

Time. If time does not exist, then what was this? Then I remembered how Litona explained that time is measured by re-occurring events. Could time be marked by a single event? Perhaps there were still events for me to experience before my "time", before my last event of mortality.

I realized my eyes were closed. I opened them. And with my eyes opened my mind also became opened, and I saw all the wonder and glory of the universe before me! I saw all the stars and *all* the worlds that circled them, as well as the life that dwelt upon those worlds. I saw greater spheres that the stars themselves orbited, greater sources of light. I saw the light itself, teeming with life and pulsating throughout the infinite realms. I looked into infinity and peered through eternity. I very nearly lost myself, but my all-searching gaze had glanced upon Earth. Earth had captured my gaze, and I longed to be there more than anywhere else. I still had events to carry out, lessons to learn, and adventures to have back on Earth. I still had time to live. There was still time.

And so I returned.

There was a blinding light. I perceived that I was still in the same position as when I had entered the giant ring on Edengone. I opened my eyes and found myself in a bathroom stall. My hands were on the tops of the stall walls, and the toilet was between my knees. I recognized this stall. It was in the men's room on campus. I was back on Earth. Of all the places on Earth I could have returned to… But I didn't care.

"I'm back!" I said with joyous wonder. "I AM BACK!!" I threw open the stall door and ran to the mirror. "Yahahaa!" I yelled at myself in the mirror. Then I turned and saw the worried faces of some students at the sinks. They didn't move. They just stared at me. One still had his hands under the running water.

"It's good to be back!" I said enthusiastically and pointed at them with both hands. Then, realizing I needed to regain some dignity, I added, "It's going to be a great semester." I paused as I looked back at the mirror. There was something different about the face staring back at me. I leaned on the counter and looked closer. My eyes had changed. They looked alive again, with a spark of light in them. "How about that?" I chuckled. "That's better," I said approvingly. Then I left the men's room and returned to Earth.

Chapter 22 – Another Matter

Months had passed since I had returned to Earth, but not a day had passed that I had not thought about Edengone. I had settled back into my old life, but with new eyes. My lectures seemed to be more full, or maybe more fulfilling. There was a void where Ron had once been, and, like all true friends who come and go, there isn't anything that can fill that void. But what is to be done, other than to press on?

I attended an awards ceremony for a competition put on by the university that had students, professors, and alumni all competing for the most prestigious award the university had to offer. The competition was based around a topic upon which competitors were to write a paper. The topic was "World Changing Influence". It was a vague topic, but such leaves it opened to interpretation and creative responses.

The submitted papers were compiled, copied, and given to the attendees to review and ponder over before the award ceremony began. I found a seat in the crowded basketball stadium, the only place on campus large enough to hold all the attendees, and I skimmed through the papers. They covered diverse and varying topics, from natural phenomena to economics, and from culture to government.

But the one paper that caught my attention focused on morals. A few lines, in particular, drew my interest. I will quote them here. "Some claim knowledge is power. Well enough. But it is also said that power corrupts. In this, we find a dilemma. Has so much corruption crept into our world because we have gained so much knowledge? The author cannot conclude in the affirmative. Instead, let it be proposed that knowledge does *not* corrupt, nor does power, but rather they *magnify* a person's abilities and desires. Therefore, a good person will be able to do greater good with knowledge and power, and they can be expected to do greater good. Their goodness would become more evident. In contrast, an evil person endowed with power and knowledge will be able to do and *will* do greater evil than they would have otherwise. There is nothing intrinsically wrong with power or even wanting power. The problem does not lie in the tool. The problem lies in the craftsman. It is the author's position that, rather than try to control power and people, it would be better to teach people to control themselves. A good and morally good people can be entrusted with all the knowledge and power there is to offer, and the world would be all the better for it. In contrast, if we allow evil to become engendered within ourselves or the rising generation, and if we allow such evil to get hold of a simple match, then we can expect the world to burn."

I reflected upon the history of two worlds, and I saw the truth in these words. Prevention is always better than correction. I hoped that paper would win the prize.

I looked at my watch. The words "Time is an event" embossed on the face peered up at me as the hands ticked along their rounds.

The awards presentation was about to begin. The presenter carried on with formalities; lecturing about how the topic was chosen, the overwhelming response of all, the difficulty the judges had in selecting a winner, and so on.

My attention wandered to a little child, a wobbly, towheaded toddler. He stood in front of his chair and faced the seat. His shoulders were barely higher than the seat of the chair. He was counting how many pieces of cereal he had scattered across the seat.

He counted carefully and thoughtfully, even systematically so he wouldn't miss any.

"…sixteen, seventeen, eight - um - eighteen, nineteen… TWENTY!" he announced, just a little too loudly. His mother hushed him. Then he began to silently count his fingers.

The presenter finally began talking about the winning paper. It was not the one I had hoped for, but, instead, one that had covered an exhaustive and vast compilation of data, undergone extensive analysis, and had produced an equation that could… I can't even remember what exactly the whole point was; tracking the population of poppies and other indigenous life-forms, or something to that effect.

At the expense of greater things, this numbers game had taken the prize. But so it is with this scientific age. An equation must be associated with everything because we are so proud of how well we can count.

A woman sat down next to me. I looked over at her, and she looked at me. Her hair was blonde and short, hanging just below her earlobes. High cheekbones perched beneath her blue eyes. A slender nose – the kind people aren't born with – sat above bright red lips and a small, round chin. She smiled. It made me shiver. Where had I seen that lurking evil hidden within such glamour before?

I smiled and extended my hand. "Hi. My name is Mike. I feel like we have met before – maybe on another world, far away?" We both laughed awkwardly. "What is your name, if I may ask?"

She shook my hand. "My name is Izzy. They'll ya…um," she said, looking slightly flustered. "What did I miss?" she asked coyly.

I had heard that voice before, a thousand times from a thousand mouths. But it couldn't be.

"Izzy," I repeated. "Is that short for something?" She just smiled.

The End of Book One